Jesus
at
Walmart

... a reed shaking in the wind

rickleland.com

Jesus at Walmart...a reed shaking in the wind

Published by:
Freedom Shores Media
South Haven, MI

Scripture references are from the HOLY BIBLE, as follows:
KING JAMES VERSION.

THE NEW KING JAMES, Copyright©1982 by Thomas Nelson, Inc. Used by permission.

NEW INTERNATIONAL VERSION. Copyright © 1984 by the International Bible Society. Used by permission of Zondervan Publishing. All rights reserved.

THE MESSAGE © 1993. Used by permission of NavPress Publishing Group.

GOOD NEWS TRANSLATION©1976 by the American Bible Society. Used by permission. All rights reserved.

NEW AMERICAN STANDARD BIBLE © Copyright 1960, 1962, 1963, 1971, 1973, 1975, 1977, 1995 by the Lockman Foundation. Used by permission.

Manufactured in the United States of America

Library of Congress Control Number: 2011924736

ISBN 978-0-9833624-0-1

rickleland.com

Contents

1. The Call   1

2. Dear Wife, "Help Me"   9

3. Nights Are Dark   17

4. A Day of Death and Life   21

5. God I Wish I Was Dead   27

6. God Just Kill Me   31

7. E-mauled   33

8. Day of Destiny   37

9. In Love with Annie Again   41

10. Black Whole   45

11. The Show at St. Amos   49

12. Who's My Darling   55

13. On Hurt Heart Road   59

14. Hello Manistee   65

15. Out in the Dark   73

16. Malachi's New Life   77

17. Hello Walmart   85

18. Uncle Dale the Liar?   89

19. Malachi Shops for a New Home   93

20. Sunday without God   99

21. Walmart—Here Comes Malachi   107

22. Malachi at Walmart—the First Night   115

Contents

23. Three More Days of... 127

24. The Most Welcomed Weekend 135

25. Tougher 141

26. The Sweetness of Payday 145

27. Helpless Help, Hopeless Hope 149

28. Where Are We Going Carl? 157

29. Become 161

30. The Fire 167

31. A New Day 171

32. The Way of Love 175

33. The Greatest of These is Love...at Walmart 181

34. Wired 185

35. Unwired. Undone 193

36. Another Jesus Freak at Walmart 195

37. We're Family 205

38. Malachi Becomes 211

39. Mandy—Do You Want Some Good News? 215

40. Can Jesus Come to Walmart? 221

41. Preparing for Jesus 227

42. Yes to Jesus 233

43. Jesus at Walmart 239

Author's Note 247

To: Nancy
From: Nancy's Husband

The Call

Chapter 1

When Mattie Carson heard the words, "This is Sergeant Mike Combee from the Branch County Sherriff's Department," her Monday morning spiked to full alert.

During her eighteen years as receptionist at St. Amos Community Church, she had never received a phone call with the intensity of the Sergeant's charged request.

"I need to make immediate contact with someone in a position of authority at St. Amos Community Church."

"Pastor Neil Renner won't be in today. It's his day off," Mattie said.

"I need to talk to someone besides Pastor Neil Renner. My information shows Stephen Johnson as the church's head elder and Pastor Malachi Marble as associate pastor. Can you help me contact either of these gentlemen—right away?"

"What's this regarding?"

"Ma'am, I need to contact Stephen Johnson or Pastor Malachi

Marble immediately."

"Malachi is here today. Please hold."

Malachi was drifting through a short list of e-mails. Lethargic, his hazy-minded clicking saved him from the sin of sloth—by a nick.

Mondays were challenging. He never achieved much. Especially in the mornings. Monday equaled residual fatigue from Sunday.

No day of rest for Malachi. His morning church service duties were numerous. Followed by children's Sunday school, which consumed an hour and a half more of his time. His day finished late into the evening, when he arrived home after youth-group activities.

As typical, he assumed he could float through the day. Mondays were senior Pastor Neil's day off, and St. Amos Community Church's one-hundred and fifty members needed little attention early in the week. And he always counted on Mattie to have coffee brewing.

Well into his third cup, he heard, "Malachi, you have a call on line one."

"Thanks Mattie."

"Good morning," Malachi said. "How can I help you?"

"Is this Pastor Malachi Marble?"

"Yes, it is. Please call me Malachi. That's what everyone calls me around here."

"Malachi, this is Sergeant Mike Combee from the Branch County Sheriff's Department; we need someone to help us access St. Amos' parsonage immediately."

Pastor Neil's church-owned residence was less than two hundred feet from where Malachi was sitting. No windows in the office area faced the white and brick ranch house. With the mature row of pine trees and a six-foot tall privacy fence, the house was only faintly obvious from the parking lot.

"What's the problem, Officer?"

"I have two undercover officers onsite. We have a search warrant. The pastor refuses to allow them access. We need your intervention. If not, my men are prepared to use force."

"Oh crap," Malachi thought.

As Sergeant Combee's words rushed out like a river at flood stage, Malachi knew, even before he heard the word *marijuana*, where the torrent was rushing. Malachi's mind riveted on a six-week old experience. Even as the Sergeant's words continued to pelt him.

After a Friday night basketball game, he drove over to the church. He needed to grab some Sunday school material to work on at home the next day. He would be passing near the church on his return from the away game.

Around ten-thirty, he pulled into the parking spot nearest the entrance. He unlocked the door, entering the lobby.

Nine steps ahead on the right, a door led to the church's basement. One of three stairwells.

Malachi descended the steps and then crossed through the fellowship hall to the main lower level corridor. Accessed from the corridor were Sunday school rooms, the youth area, a conference room, and the utility and storage areas. At the far end, a door to the left opened to a set of stairs leading to an exterior exit.

As he opened the door to the hallway, the light was already on. Then, instantaneously, it was off. In the darkness, he noticed a glint of light from under the utility room door. He fumbled for the light switch for a couple of seconds.

He thought to himself, "Someone was down here." He concluded this *someone* had turned off the other light switch at the far end of the hall the moment he had opened the door. Likely exiting to the outside via the stairs.

"It must have been Pastor Neil," he determined.

He located the Sunday school material and retraced his steps.

As he passed, he opened the door to the utility room to turn off the light he had spotted earlier.

A smell rushed to his nose. One word engulfed his thoughts—*marijuana.*

He looked around as surreal feelings numbed the obvious. Malachi started rubbing above his right eye with his right hand. His face became warm on his right side. Between his ear and eye—above his cheekbone. He gazed down at the floor, drawing a slow breath though his nose.

He pondered, as the middle joint of his index finger stroked against his sealed lips, "Pastor Neil was smoking pot."

Malachi had sealed away the experience. And now, his mind was racing faster than Sergeant Combee's words.

Malachi said to himself, "Why didn't I tell anyone?"

"Pastor Renner refuses to let my men into the house," the Sergeant said. "The canine squad is on the way. If the dogs detect marijuana, my men are going in. By force. We have a search warrant."

Mattie was a blur as Malachi rushed past.

"What's wrong?" Mattie said.

Malachi stopped, turned around, and said, "Stay here! Everything will be fine."

And off he darted toward the door.

Approaching the house, he saw two unmarked cars and one marked squad car. The three officers were huddled in a conference. When they saw Malachi, they broke rank.

He reached out his hand. "I'm Malachi Marble, associate pastor here at St. Amos Community Church."

"Yes. Sergeant Combee told us you were on the way. He's filled you in; is that correct?"

"Pretty much."

"Here's the scoop—the dogs are going to be here in..." He darted a look at the other plain-clothes officer.

"Eight minutes."

"Eight minutes. If the dogs detect marijuana, we're going in. We've been talking to your guy through the door. He refuses to allow us access to the house. Pastor Malachi, that locked door is not going to stop us. You need to talk to him."

He heard one of the other officers say, "Some church you got here."

Strength sapped from Malachi's legs as if he had just run a marathon.

His feet plodded the fourteen steps to the door of the parsonage. Swinging the storm door open, he propped it against his butt.

Malachi smacked his fist repeatedly on the door and shouted, "Pastor Neil, you need to open up."

He waited for a few seconds. "Pastor, let us in," he yelled.

And then he detected a voice from the other side. "I'm not letting them in. I'm legal."

"What?" Malachi said.

"I'm legal," Pastor Neil said.

"Legal?"

Malachi moved his ear even closer to the door.

"I'm a legal medical marijuana caregiver in full compliance with the State of Michigan's Medical Marijuana Law," Pastor Neil said.

Malachi seethed, like he had the day in eighth grade when he turned on class bully, Timmy Gruber. Punching him in the stomach so hard he started to cry. Malachi surprised himself that day. And delighted his classmates.

Intense anger. Malachi still had the finger memory to roll a joint. Even though he had fought himself free of the substance well over a decade ago. The anger? He knew too many people whose long strange trip had begun with one toke of marijuana. He still could see the faces of Earl, Ken, and Rhonda, whose lives had spun out of control—never to recover.

He was mad at the destruction. He was mad at the devil. He was mad at weed.

"Go over to the window," Pastor Neil said. "I have documentation."

The window, six feet to the right of the door, opened a crack. A piece of paper and a hand poked out below the curtain-covered glass.

He snatched the paper. And delivered it to the officer, who appeared to be in charge. "He says he's legal."

Malachi was excluded as the policemen re-formed into a circle. Quickly, one of the men was on the radio. The only word Malachi heard with distinction was *dogs*. The marked car sped away in less than two minutes as the other two conversed. They examined the paperwork—talking repeatedly into their two-way radio.

Malachi rested against the security fence. The coldness of the early April day started to chill him. He thought about his coat back at his office. He thought about praying. But all his batteries were nearly drained.

"Sorry I didn't introduce myself," he heard. Malachi looked up to see a hand extended toward him. "I'm Officer Ryan Osberry."

They shook hands, "The Pastor's legal…well, he has enough to keep us out of the house."

Officer Ryan's hand felt cold. He returned the document to Malachi as his eyes scanned him for several seconds.

An abrupt turn, a couple of slammed car doors, a duty-called gunning of engines, and Malachi stood all alone.

Malachi glared at the house and then glanced back at the church; he didn't move, letting the fence comfort his weak bones.

A few decibels over a whisper, Malachi said, "I wish I was...God what are you doing to me?"

Perplexity obstructed all his momentum. Unable to formulate a more manageable option, he marched back to the church.

Stopping in the restroom outside of the offices, Malachi took a wet paper towel and washed it over his face. He looked in the mirror.

And smiled, as he proceeded to the reception area.

The instant Mattie saw him, she blurted, "Is everything alright?"

"We're good to go," Malachi said, "This is the day the Lord has made, let us..."

"Why were those cars over at Pastor's?"

"Just a little mix up."

"Are you..."

"Mattie, don't you have work that needs your attention," Malachi said. "If this was something we wanted your help with, guess what, I would have asked you to go with me."

"I'm...I'm sorry."

He looked at her. Time froze for a moment. His smile disappeared, "I'm sorry too...ah, OK?"

He turned, "I'll be in my office."

The clock read 11:42 a.m. Malachi poured himself another cup of coffee.

Slowly sipping, he bowed his head, "God don't let me do anything stupid." He then punched in Pastor Neil's number on his desk phone. No answer. Next, he tried his cell phone. Malachi was directed to voice mail.

"Pastor Neil, this is Malachi; please call me."

Malachi looked over the papers Pastor Neil had slipped out the window. And then googled, *Michigan medical marijuana*. He made a few notes on a white legal pad. Tapping on the tablet a few times, he glanced from the computer screen to the notepad.

Shaking his head, he said to himself, "This is a bunch of crap."

After jotting seven notations, Malachi flipped to a fresh page, writing, *God's view on Marijuana*. He opened his desk drawer and retrieved a peanut butter Power Bar. He nibbled off a bite. Slowly chewing and thinking. Chewing. Thinking. Chewing. Thinking.

He returned to the pad. Beside his last scribble, he added, *Would Jesus Smoke—WWJD.*

He clicked the E-Sword icon on his computer's desktop, opening his Bible software. He spent several minutes clicking and scrolling. Writing down, *be sober, drunkenness, appearance of evil, body—temple of Holy Spirit, whatever you do—do as if unto the Lord.* He moved his hand up, rubbing the right side of his face, intently scanning the unseen world of Biblical content stored inside his brain.

Adding to his notes: *Jesus and healing, faith, by His stripes we are healed.*

The phone rang. Malachi wished he had Caller I.D.

He stared at the phone, picking it up on the third ring. "This is Malachi Marble. How can I help you?"

"Malachi, this is Pastor Neil. Thank you for doing the right thing."

"What...?"

"As you can clearly see, I *fully* comply with the law. Those cops had no business harassing me. I should sick my attorney on those bozos."

"Maybe they just wanted to see how big your stash is."

"Stash? What are you talking about?"

"I mean, checking on inventory levels at your dispensary."

"Malachi, your tone is not acceptable toward a spiritual authority in your life. I comply with all the laws. My privacy is fully protected by HIPAA—the law that protects the privacy of an individual's medical records. Most importantly, we are talking about compassion here. Compassion for suffering people. Suffering people loved by Jesus. Marijuana provides a safe, natural remedy to countless types of suffering. Are you going to hold back relief, hold back hope, and compassion from suffering victims of pain? So, would you prefer to see people suffer, Malachi; is that what you want? Answer me."

"Of course not, but..."

"But what? I will tell you but what. It is going to be your butt, Malachi. Can you afford to lose this job? Do you want to start over at age 42? What is Annie going to say? You better put an Action Plan into place before you do something stupid. I am not going to tolerate insolence. The Bible says, 'Obey your leaders and submit to them for they keep watch over your souls.' *Submit.* Do you hear that word? That same verse says, 'Let them do this with joy and not with grief for this would be unprofitable for you.' This is crystal clear. Just basic Bible, Malachi."

"You're right. I've got a lot to think about."

"Are you getting on track, Malachi?"

"Close enough."

"Are you sure?"

"I understand you Pastor Neil."

"Good. See you tomorrow brother."

"O.K."

Malachi slumped in his chair. And shook his head back and forth. After a few minutes, he shifted back to an upright position. Refocusing on his notepad, he wrote down; *compassion—the compassion of Jesus—Mark Chapter 16.*

Tapping a couple of more beats on the pad, adding, "Is it OK to smoke marijuana at church?"

Malachi gathered up his paperwork and laptop. It was 2:57. He usually left the church at five o'clock on Mondays, but today, tiredness overwhelmed him.

As he passed the receptionist's desk, he focused his eyes on the papers he was holding. And said, "Mattie I'm heading out for the day. See you tomorrow."

Dear Wife,"Help Me"

Chapter 2

The day's trials had sucked the soul out of Malachi. Even his prayer during the drive home fueled an air of abandonment. A despairing dialog with no expected answer, "God why does everything I try to do for You fail?"

Malachi's fear was forecasting the implosion of another one of his faith-journeys. His job at St. Amos Community Church was the pinnacle of a challenging trudge to stability in ministry. But now, he foresaw the wrecking ball smashing against this desire of his heart.

Dust and rubble everywhere. What was Annie going to say? What was Annie going to think? He ripped himself away from these thoughts as they edged him toward a shortness-of-breath episode.

Malachi busied himself in an effort to calm the madness. He threw himself into a house-cleaning blitz—making each task an athletic endeavor. Vacuuming. Emptying the dishwasher. Dusting. Picking up. Sweeping the garage. Straightening up his office. Emptying waste paper baskets. He enjoyed helping around the house. He even brought out his cordless drill and fixed a loose leg on the dining room table.

He knew Annie would appreciate all he was doing. Both of their work schedules had been borderline unmanageable over the last four months.

Malachi smiled as he surveyed his visually pleasing accomplishments. And his athletic intensity had acted as a tension release valve.

He sat down in the living room to await Annie. From there, the driveway was visible. If she left work at the regular time, she would arrive home around six—in about fifteen minutes.

They praised God when First Commerce Bank and Trust had hired Annie. She started a month after Malachi had begun working at St. Amos Community Church. Without her job, financial survival was unlikely. He had accepted his job at St. Amos, even as they dealt with financial uncertainty.

Malachi had convinced Annie to have faith—"Let's trust God to give you a job or open up some other way to meet our needs."

What had been called a blessing from God, Malachi was now asking himself, "Is this a curse?"

Annie often worked until seven, eight, even nine o'clock at night. Their once steady marriage was presently riding treacherous waves of uncertainty.

As his hands fingered the Bible on the end table, he admitted his own erratic, challenging schedule heaped its own consequences on the pile.

They had talked two weeks ago—a good conversation. The kind Malachi termed, "We were open." Open to hearing each other. And open to hearing God. These *open-talks* had become rare in their marriage.

Annie had summarized both their feelings during this conversation. "I'm just not as close to God as I used to be. And then, I'm not as close to you."

Her honesty rekindled the same gnawing-in-the-gut Malachi suffered in seventh grade when the first girl he ever fell in love with moved away.

Malachi and Annie both knew they were drowning. Yet, the time or energy for grabbing the Life Preserver was illusive.

Annie pulled into the driveway at 6:53.

After they greeted, Annie started preparing supper.

Malachi sat mentally rehearsing what he wanted to say at dinnertime. This churning had commenced, even before arriving home. Now he was fine-tuning his words—again and again. And inside, Malachi battled fear as it attempted to sidetrack his presentation to Annie.

Recently, Malachi had perceived that even their simple discussions frequently grew into misunderstandings. And then deteriorated from there. Still, he was determined to run his script. No matter what.

"How was work today?" Malachi asked as he took his first bite of food.

Conversation spilled out. Pleasantness ascended over the dinner table. He watched Annie, not fully hearing her words for their content—only as an access point for *the talk*.

"How was your day?" she asked slowly.

She looked tired. So tired.

Malachi shifted his eyes toward his food. He took a breath.

"Is there something wrong?" Annie said, "You look like you're…"

"No, I'm just tired. I ah…it's nothing."

"Yeah, so am I. I'm really tired. Exhausted," Annie said. "Your day go O.K.?"

"Kind of a typical Monday…you know," Malachi said.

The ensuing conversation lobbed back and forth with the zest of pureed oatmeal. Reaching its peak, when Malachi said, "Let me help you clear the table."

Malachi rebuked himself for being a coward as the evening meandered toward bedtime.

When Malachi closed his eyes for the night, he relived the day in the darkness of their bedroom. Annie fell quickly asleep as Malachi tried desperately to settle his running thoughts.

He was praying silently with fresh desperation, "God help me. God help me."

Finally, he fell asleep.

He entered a vivid dream.

And woke up at 3:44 a.m.

It wasn't just a dream. It was one of *those dreams*. Malachi had his first one shortly after becoming a Christian at age thirty-one.

He crawled out of bed, heading down to the basement to his office. Tucked away near the furnace—Malachi's private retreat. Painted concrete blocks formed two of the walls. Drywall boxed in the other corner. Two fluorescent lights hung from the open rafters of the house's sub-floor. And thin cheap carpet covered the concrete.

He searched his bookshelf. His hand reached for a dark green three-tab binder. Labeled: *Dreams, Visions, Impressions, Inklings*. He opened the binder to a fresh page and began writing:

April 27, 2010

1. A dream. While asleep.

2. Pastor Neil's basement. Marijuana growing room. Healthy, green foliage. Three dozen plants—plus or minus. Pastor Neil is skillfully tending his plants. Very engaged in his work. Joyful—in high spirits.

3. Pastor Neil and Martha Renner having a focused discussion. I don't hear any words. Martha is continually shaking her head in agreement. I have a strong sense that Pastor Neil is convincing his wife of the merits of medical marijuana.

4. Pastor Neil opens the door to the parsonage. His facial expression shows he recognizes the person—a male about his age—longish white hair, wearing a baseball cap. Pastor Neil welcomes him. They go downstairs to examine Pastor's marijuana crop. They're celebrative in their enthusiasm. The scene ends with Pastor Neil rolling a joint. They smoke it together in a basement-lounge area. Reminds me of my own doper days—when I was addicted.

Malachi stood up and paced the floor. Back and forth as he rubbed his mouth with his right hand. "God, why do You give me these dreams and...I don't know...these visions and things?"

The sting of impending failure gnawed at Malachi—as if he were a farmer seeing a foreclosure notice nailed to his dream.

His eyes lifted upward. "God, why don't things ever work out for me?"

Agitation swelled into frenzied pacing. Around the room. Back and forth. And then Malachi abruptly plopped into his chair. Worn, his body became more and more devoid of motion. Until he curled into a sleep.

When he awoke, Malachi was surprised at how refreshed and confident he felt.

He traipsed upstairs when he heard Annie.

"Good morning Annie," he said. "How did you sleep?"

"Good. Really good."

"How about you?" She asked.

All the morning-cordiality drained from Malachi's face, "Annie, something happened yesterday. I need to tell you."

Her expression countered with its own swift deterioration, "What's wrong?"

Malachi ran out the narrative of the previous day. And no more. It was an eight-minute burst—whirling with emotion, fact, and conjecture.

"Why didn't you tell me this last night? You know I have to leave for work. Malachi, what's wrong with you? …sometimes."

"I just…ah…"

"I need to get going. I was planning to work late. I can see that's not going to happen."

Annie departed in a wordless-rush, so she could make it to work by nine o'clock.

Malachi was thankful when he heard her car leaving. He glanced at his watch, calculating the swift morning routine required if he wanted to get to work on time. And then his mind fastened on the image of a face to face encounter with Pastor Neil. The thought stabbed Malachi with fear.

"Crap," he said.

He sparred another round with his anxiety. Glancing again at his watch, he was sure he would be late. At least twenty minutes. Yet, no compulsion revved-up his efforts.

He gave up. And picked up the phone—dialing the number for St. Amos Community Church.

"Mattie, this is Malachi. I'm not going to be able to make it in today. I'm feeling a little under the weather."

"Sorry to hear that. Anything I can do to help?"

"No. But thanks, Mattie." He paused for a moment, "Mattie, you're the best. I really appreciate you."

He heard her laugh. "Thanks Malachi."

After a three-mile run and a shower, Malachi knew he needed to plow through a full-schedule of church duties, or he would be playing nearly impossible catch-up. First, he checked his cell phone and e-mail for messages. Even though he was proficient at technology, e-mail and cell phone communication never found a prominent place in his life. So, he moved quickly to his next task.

Lesson and program preparation for the teen-youth group and children's Sunday school took up a large slice of his time every week. This was fine with Malachi, because these two aspects of church-life brought him the most satisfaction—especially his ministry to children.

In the afternoon, he mowed the lawn. And a twenty-five-minute nap was especially invigorating.

Malachi descended back to his office, shifting his focus on the notepad from yesterday, entitled, *God's View on Marijuana*. He buried himself in searching the Scriptures for the rest of the afternoon.

He intermittently shifted his thoughts to the impending evening discussion with Annie. While his fretfulness rippled, their morning engagement and then separation buffered the dread of the upcoming conversation.

Later, Malachi sat in a chair gazing at the driveway. He reviewed in his mind what to say. Tonight, he was resolute; he was telling Annie about smelling marijuana in the church's basement.

He prayed the same words he had repeated countless times, "God, don't let me do anything stupid."

A few minutes after six, Annie's car pulled into the driveway. Earlier than the normal during the last few months. Malachi greeted her at the door. There was no question about the agenda.

"Do you want to sit down?" Malachi said as he motioned toward the living room.

"Sure." Annie said.

They both found their regular chairs—side by side. Shifted at slight angles so they faced each other—but not directly.

"Let me just go over what I told you this morning. Is that OK?"

"That'll be fine, Malachi."

"First, I want to apologize for being so insensitive in my timing and for being too emotional this morning. Can we just make a fresh run at it?"

"Yes, we can do that."

This time, Malachi calmly told what had happened as if he were reciting words from the daily newspaper. His favored lead in line defaulted to, "And next…"

Annie shifted further toward directly facing Malachi, and the subtle, yet noticeable, variation of her facial expressions coincided with the softening of Malachi's countenance. The taint of opinion and conjecture and accusations remained almost undetectable in this new account. He still hadn't spoken about the church-basement-marijuana episode. He decided, mid-discussion, to hold off until later.

When he finished, Annie calmly said, "So what are you accusing Pastor Neil of?"

"*Accusing?* I don't know if that's the right word, but I do have a concern about his use of marijuana."

"It's for medical purposes. He's not breaking any laws."

"Laws of man. Do you think it's all right to use marijuana that way? Do you think Jesus would use it that way?

"You're asking a complex question and demanding an instant simple answer. I mean, do you know positively God's against it?'

"Well, I …"

"Of course you don't. And neither do I. I'm not very fond of the concept. Especially when I know about your dope-head past. Of course, you were using it for the wrong reason. You need to consider Pastor Neil is a solid man of God. Our spiritual authority. He knows the Bible. Knows Greek and Hebrew. I trust him. You trusted him enough to go to work for him. He's the first person to give you a fulltime ministry position. How many years did you wait for it? You were sure the job was from God. Now, you're judging Pastor Neil—the one who gave you a chance. Malachi, you need to let God work this out. If you…"

"Annie, there's more…"

"You interrupted me," Annie said. "Now, what was I going to say? Please, let's use some common sense here. Let's be smart. You've followed your *inklings from God.* And where have they taken you? I'm not telling you anything you don't know. We've talked about this—many times. It seems like your *inklings* always lead you to failure or disappointing results. I mean, your big dream—Kerr Creek Guitars."

Malachi's shoulders slumped as he looked down at the carpet.

"Sure, your idea was noble," Annie said. "You love those Christian guitar makers you met in China when you were on that mission trip. And the concept of having them build some awesome guitars, you selling them in the U.S., everybody making money, and then giving piles of it to God's work—great idea. But let's be...OK.... how many guitars have you sold?"

"One," Malachi said.

"Malachi, I feel bad for you. This just seems to be the pattern your life is following. Even you told me you feel the same way. Haven't you?"

"Yeah."

"We need to get you headed toward a...ah...some victories. Even your work at St. Amos Community Church is iffy. These are things you've told me, Malachi. They brought you in to St. Amos so you could help grow the church. And this excited you. However, that hasn't exactly worked out. The only thing growing is the children's ministry. Yes, it has been enough to catch people's attention, but I remember what you told me, 'If it wasn't for the food, the hoopla, and the trinkets, half the kids wouldn't come to Sunday school.' Do you remember saying that?"

"Yeah."

"I really want to see some success in your life. I just...I..."

Annie sputtered to a halt as if she had run out of gas. They sat there. No one spoke for several minutes.

Finally, Annie said, "Malachi, I've probably talked too much. I really am on your side. I want to see you succeed." She paused for a few seconds, "Did you say there was something more you wanted to tell me? I kind of cut you off. Was there more to the story?"

Malachi took a deep breath and exhaled though his nose; he raised his head, looking at Annie, "It was nothing." He remained silent regarding smelling marijuana in the church's basement and his dream from the other night about Pastor Neil.

"Are you sure?" Annie said.

"Yeah. I'm sure."

"So, what's the Action Plan?" Annie said, imitating a man's voice.

Pastor Neil's favorite pet phrase, *Action Plan*, sliced through the tension. They both laughed.

"I guess the Action Plan is to let God work it out," Malachi said. "Are you in?"

"I'm in," Annie said.

Nights Are Dark

Chapter 3

Malachi opened the mirrored medicine cabinet. With his right hand, he clutched the plastic ibuprofen bottle. He coaxed two tablets into his left hand. He usually reserved their usage for sore muscles, but recently, he had discovered their effectiveness as a sleep aid.

There was no dream tonight. Sudden sound sleep shrouded his emotional fatigue.

At around four o'clock, he woke up—fully alert.

He gazed over at Annie as the light from the alarm clock shed illumination on her form. He stared at her face as his mind traveled back a couple of years. He remembered mornings when he would do the same thing—watching Annie as she slept. He smiled as he let his brain interact with the memory. The tingle from back then resurfaced.

Still, as the reality of the moment returned, his smile relented. No matter how much he pretended, the tingle was gone.

Malachi retreated to his office.

He approached the guitar hanging on the wall.

Malachi attached life, passion, and sentiment to every element of the instrument. The opaque-black Manchurian ash face projected a stately demeanor. The African rosewood neck promised lithe acoustic tones. The ebony tuners—a delicate artistic statement. He reflected on the hours he spent designing the logo and the headstock. And he would never forget the delight of Liu and Deng when he agreed to work with them on developing the Kerr Creek Guitar. That sweet moment now carried a cursed imprint—*Failure*.

Malachi hesitated. Then gently, he lifted the guitar from the wall bracket. The day the first Kerr Creek guitar arrived beamed into his mind. He grinned.

Strumming the guitar, he merely listened.

"A quality guitar is all about the sound," he said to himself.

And Malachi was jubilant over the *Kerr Creek Sound*—mellow intonations, rich harmony with a spritz of sparkle, unwavering sound declaration, combined with pure playability.

He played a few chords. Fumbling—his short, too-thick fingers constantly struggled. Then eased into a harmonic E-chord, D-chord pattern—a simple song he had written for the Sunday school children.

Quietly he sang, "Every good girl needs Jesus. Every good boy needs Jesus, too. For all have sinned and fall short of the glory of God. And every good girl needs Jesus. Every good boy needs Jesus, too."

His playing continued long enough to ease him over the border to the mystical place guitar playing often carried him. A place he loved to visit.

And then Malachi retreated—back over the border. To reality.

He nestled the guitar back on the wall, where it now hung more and more. As his eyes again examined his Kerr Creek Guitar, no matter how much he pretended, all he saw was a dead dream.

He opened the dark green three-tab binder—*Dreams, Visions, Impressions, Inklings*. And read what he had written the morning before.

Malachi knelt and prayed: "God, I have sinned. I fall short of Your glory. You know how dark this night is for me. God, I feel like dying. Every way I turn, an enemy of my soul is striking at me. Confusion, fear, and failure follow me. Your Holy Spirit eludes me. Dear God, I am

Your sheep; I need to hear Your voice."

Malachi remained on his knees. Quiet. Listening. A distinct impression entered his mind, "Read James 5:19-20."

Malachi whispered, "Thank you, Father."

He was familiar with the Bible passage, but not enough to quote it. So, he looked it up. "My brothers, if one of you should wander from the truth and someone should bring him back, remember this: whoever turns a sinner from the error of his way will save him from death and cover over a multitude of sins."

The scriptures aroused a zest in Malachi, as he confidently settled on his next step. Clarity displaced doubt and fear.

Malachi was certain of what he needed to do. A confrontation with Pastor Neil—gentle and loving.

Malachi sensed jubilation as his mind pictured Pastor Neil confessing his marijuana smoking habit and ungodly behavior. His imagination began to run. This private encounter, he envisioned, would strengthen their relationship. He was anticipating Pastor Neil's appreciation for the Godly intervention. Malachi could almost see them hugging, with tears streaming down their faces.

Malachi said out loud, "Yes Lord. Yes Lord."

A verse in Matthew 18 popped into his head, "Go and show him his fault just between the two of you."

Now, Malachi's resolve was absolute.

But he decided, "Annie doesn't need to know."

A Day of Death and Life

Chapter 4

"**G**ood morning, Mattie," Malachi said, "How are you doing, today?"

"I'm doing well. How about you?"

"Pretty good…Pastor Neil, he's not here yet, is he?"

"Probably around ten. An hour or so."

"Let me know when he gets in. I need to talk to him."

From his office, Malachi could see the parking lot. Most days, Pastor Neil entered the church via a rear entrance facing the parsonage. Malachi thought to himself, "Even when he comes over to the church to smoke weed at night."

He tried reconciling that memory with the dream from the other night. In the thought process, he drew upon his own experiences as a pothead. Fitting the pieces together was easier than working a child's Sponge Bob puzzle. Pastor Neil needed a smoking sanctuary away from home. Malachi surmised Pastor Neil had convinced Martha, his wife, to accept the merits of Medical Marijuana; however, she wasn't going to fall in step with his personal non-medical usage.

Malachi bowed his head, "Dear Father God, help me to be compassionate, considerate, and courageous. Dear God, help me to have clean hands and a pure heart. God, I believe I have sensed Your leading. Help me to do Your will. Prepare Pastor Neil's heart. Create in him a pure heart, O God, and renew a right spirit within him. Lead and guide both of us, for Your Namesake. In the name of Jesus. Amen."

Malachi found it increasingly difficult to focus on any work as the clock edged past ten-thirty.

He got up from his desk and walked toward the reception area. When he saw Mattie, he said, "Pastor Neil's still not in?"

"He arrived a couple of minutes ago. I was going to call you. He said he won't be able to meet with you, today."

Malachi drummed his fingers on Mattie's desk. Glancing down the hall toward Pastor Neil's office, he then returned his focus to Mattie.

"Mattie *please* tell Pastor Neil that it's very important we talk—as soon as possible. Please."

Mattie called Pastor Neil's office. In a couple of moments, with the phone still in her hand, she said, "It's not going to work out."

"Tell him this is a very important matter. It needs his immediate attention."

She relayed the message.

"He says he's sorry."

"We need to talk. Now."

Mattie shook her head with the phone still pressed to her ear.

"Let me have the phone."

Malachi grabbed it. "Listen, Pastor Neil, we need to talk. This is an important matter. If you don't have time to talk, I'll just have to call Stephen Johnson—our head elder. He'll listen to me."

"Are you still there?" Malachi asked as the silence on the other end stretched out.

"Malachi, you don't need to bother Stephen at work. Tell you what, I am going to put everything else on hold. You are sounding confused and upset. Come on down to my office, Malachi. I am here to serve your needs."

By the time Malachi walked the twelve steps to Pastor Neil's office, he had the door open. With a big smile on his face, he thrust his hand towards Malachi. "Come on in, brother."

"Sit down, Malachi. Are you feeling better? I was wondering if you would make it in today."

"I'm feeling a lot better. Thank you."

"We need an Action Plan, so we can get you back on track, Malachi. My spiritual discernment is telling me that we are going to revisit what happened on Monday. This brings a Scripture to mind. 'Forgetting what lies behind and reaching forward to what lies ahead, I press on toward the goal for the prize of the upward call of God in Christ Jesus.' Malachi, are you pressing on in life? Do you have a prize in your sights? An Action Plan in place? Or is failure lurking around the corner for you? I make it a priority to press on in my Christian walk. One of the goals, one of my prizes I am aiming for is to become a more compassionate person. To be a caregiver to people who are suffering. Is this what you want to talk about today, Malachi?"

"We'll ah...yeah. But ah..."

"That is what I thought. You seem like you have something against me. If that is the case, according to Matthew 18, you are to come to me in private so we can work things out. As you can see, I have made myself available. I am going by the *Book*. Are you?"

"What are you asking exactly?"

"Are you doing what the Bible says to do? Have you told anyone about our misunderstanding? Or have you kept it private as the Bible commands?"

"Well, I told Annie, but that's it."

"Malachi, I forgive you. I am willing to put it behind me and press on. Let us focus on resolving your turmoil and bring some clarity into your confusion. I love the way 1 John 1:7 puts it: 'If we walk in the light as Jesus is in the light, we have fellowship with one another.' Malachi, walking in the light is the key to restoring our relationship."

Malachi turned his head slightly to the left and shifted his focus to the floor. His brain replayed the scene from his basement-office earlier in the day. The determination he experienced five hours ago reignited.

"Malachi, are you listening to me?"

He heard Pastor Neil, but it took a few moments to reconnect.

He looked up, "No, I'm not. But...ah...let...Pastor Neil, this is one of the hardest moments of my life. Just let me talk. The verse before the one you just quoted, says, 'If we claim to have fellowship with Jesus yet walk in darkness, we lie and do not live by the truth.'"

"Are you calling me a liar? Saying I am walking in darkness? You're..."

"Slow down. Please. Let me finish. I have several pages in my office filled with Bible verses that I could use to make a valid case against medical marijuana. From God's perspective."

Malachi raised his hand, "Let me finish. However, that's not where I'm headed. I'm just going to say it: you're going beyond medical marijuana; you're smoking it; your hiding your habit. You have even smoked marijuana at the church. We both know that's ungodly behavior. Pastor Neil, all I want is to see you restored back to a right standing with God."

"You don't know what you're talking about. I comply with all the laws. I could cite my own list of Bible passages, easily refuting your incorrect position on Medical Marijuana. And smoking in this building? You are acting crazy. And you think I need to be restored to God? Malachi, I am not going to let you jeopardize my career with your false allegations. You are heading down a treacherous path. Your whole career could go down the tubes. If you continue, you are going to end up as a greeter at Walmart. You will never get another job in ministry—the rest of your life. You need to re-think what you are doing. And saying."

Pastor Neil laughed, "And smoking marijuana at church, you will look like a fool if you start spreading that kind of nonsense."

He paused for a moment, "Malachi, we both love Jesus. Is that right?"

"Yes. Of course."

"I have set an Action Plan in motion to show the love of Jesus through a natural, effective use of a plant God created to alleviate pain and suffering. If you love Jesus, you will do what is right."

Pastor Neil leaned back in his chair, peering intensely at Malachi. And then leaned forward. "I am going to bring some enlightenment into your spiritual life, Malachi. I am going to speculate that your prayer life and Bible reading have been lacking recently. Is that true?"

"Yes. Definitely. But you know the demands the church puts on my time. And my energy. It's difficult to find the time. It's not that I ..."

"Malachi, you're using the classic excuse. We find time for what is important in our lives. Who can deny that? When you do not read the Bible or pray, it is like holding your breath. You will get dizzy and confused and eventually die spiritually. Like it says in the Book of Revelation, you need to return to your first love. You are getting off track. Return to your first love—Jesus. Before it is too late. Malachi, I love you. Please get back to reading the Bible and praying. You are starting to slip. Praise God; it is not too late."

Pastor Neil glanced at his watch. "I really need to get going."

He stood up, offering his hand to Malachi. "I will be praying for you."

God I Wish I Was Dead

Chapter 5

Malachi forced himself to finish out the workday—like a man slogging uphill in fourteen inches of wet snow. What he needed to achieve loomed beyond the horizon of possible.

Five o'clock arrived achingly slow.

It was like a dark force greeted Malachi at the door when he arrived home. Or was it that his forced-labor resolve at work had masked his feelings. Despondency held him captive as he sat in the living room. He could see the driveway. It would be a while before Annie arrived home.

Thoughts of how twisted the chaos had become punched him in the stomach. How was he going to tell Annie the situation at work had turned worse? How would he explain that he had confronted Pastor Neil? Especially when he and Annie had agreed to let God take care of it. He shook his head repeatedly as his mind fixed on seeing her impending aggravation.

Eleven miles away and two hours earlier, the phone rang at First

Commerce Bank and Trust. The receptionist transferred the call to the office midway down the hall on the right side.

"This is Annie Marble. How can I help you?"

"Annie, this is Pastor Neil. How are you doing this lovely day?"

"Pastor...ah Neil, I don't think you've ever called me at work. Is everything O.K.?"

"Annie, this is the day the Lord has made. Everything is not ideal, but we can trust God; can't we?"

"Sure."

"Do you have a few minutes to talk?" Pastor Neil said.

"Yes, I have some time right now."

"Annie, it is my understanding that Malachi talked to you about a situation that should have been held in confidentiality between Malachi and me until we had a chance to sensibly discuss it. It is obvious that he has violated a Biblical principle set forth by Our Lord and Savior. And just to let you know, I have forgiven Malachi of this grievous trespass. Are you tracking with me so far, Annie?"

"I guess so."

"Let me just distill this down to a few points. Number one, and before I continue, let me ask a simple question—Annie, do you trust me?"

"Of course I do."

"I've earned that trust through solid leadership, consistency, and compassion for the people God has put under my care. Would you agree?"

"Well, yes."

"Annie, I have set an Action Plan in motion to demonstrate the compassion of Jesus to people who are hurting—in so many ways, so many ways. There are hurting people everywhere, Annie. Does it make sense to hold back from helping? I cannot. I love Jesus, and I love people. Are you following me?"

"Sure. I think so."

"Second, your husband is showing a rebellious spirit in his misunderstanding. The way he confronted me today was shocking. Annie, the devil goes around like a roaring lion seeing whom he can devour. Malachi is opening himself up to the devil's influence through his rebellion. If he does not turn around, his career and so much more will be over. Gone just like that. Devoured. I think you can see this. Annie, you have responsibility here also. I am your spiritual authority, too. And I must say, you are a delight. You really are."

"Thank you, Pastor Neil."

"So, here is our Action Plan. First, this is a private matter. Do you agree?"

"Well, of course."

"Annie, I'm asking you…well let me think how to say this. This may sound a little crude, but…Malachi needs a spiritual kick in the butt. A jolt back to his senses. I think you understand me. Can I count on you?"

She drew in a breath, slowly exhaling.

"Annie, can I count on you?"

"Of course you can."

"Thank you, Annie. I will be praying for you. May the Lord bless you and keep you and make His face shine upon you."

Annie sat staring down at her desk. And then looked up when she heard someone at her open door.

"You working late, Annie?"

"Hey Tim," she said. "I'm not sure."

Walking toward her, he said, "You look tense. Is there anything I can do?"

He reached toward her as he gently rubbed her shoulder. She pushed his hand away as her eyes darted toward the open door.

"Tim!"

"Well…maybe later, Annie."

She smiled as her fingers brushed her auburn hair over her ear.

Malachi's body felt arc welded to the chair in the living room. His arm protruded enough to pull the Bible from the end table.

Leafing his way to the center, he shuffled pages right, then left. The Psalms had touched Malachi often when hopelessness hit the hardest. So, he returned again—in need.

And read Psalms 116:

I love the LORD, because He hears my voice and my supplications. Because He has inclined His ear to me.

Therefore, I shall call upon Him as long as I live. The cords of death encompassed me. And the anguish of the grave came upon me. I found distress and sorrow. Then I called upon the name of the LORD: "O LORD, save me." You saved my life!

Gracious is the LORD and righteous. Yes, our God is compassionate. The LORD preserves the simplehearted.

I was brought low and He saved me.

Return to your rest, O my soul. For the LORD has dealt bountifully with you. For You have rescued my soul from death. My eyes from tears. My feet from stumbling. I shall walk before the LORD in the land of the living.

I believed when I said, "I am greatly afflicted." I said in my alarm, "All men are liars."

What shall I render to the LORD for all His benefits toward me? I shall lift up the cup of salvation and call upon the name of the LORD. I shall pay my vows to the LORD. Oh may it be in the presence of all His people.

Precious in the sight of the LORD is the death of His godly ones.

Malachi gazed at the ceiling, "God, sometimes I wish I was dead." He attempted to stifle this impression. The inkling had repeatedly crept into his mind recently—attempting to inflict its imprisonment on him—again and again.

His rambling thoughts ceased when he heard Annie's car pulling into the driveway. It was after seven o'clock.

He greeted her at the door.

The expression on her face startled Malachi.

"Why are you trying to destroy our lives?" She burst into tears. Trembling, she pushed past Malachi as she rushed to her office—slamming the door.

God Just Kill Me

Chapter 6

It was as if two giant hands had encased Malachi, crushing his frailty like a crumpled piece of paper.

He slumped toward the floor, steadying himself on a dining room chair.

"God kill me," he said a few decibels above a whisper. "Just kill me."

"Annie's the only one I can count on. I thought she would understand."

Malachi couldn't explain it. But now, anger began seeping in. The same way cold wind-driven rain finds any vulnerable crack. His fury whirled around many targets, lodging most forcefully in the disgust of his own failure.

He spared Annie from most of his barrage, even though her *secret life* was devastating him. Malachi forced his mind away from those repugnant thoughts.

Malachi had been to the edge of giving up before—repeatedly. But not this far.

His anger—or an unjustifiable rationale, a peculiar nudge, rallied his fortitude to claw back from the brink. Still, he had to face the unfaceable—this time, Annie was no longer by his side.

Then a measure of fortitude resurfaced, a warming sensation, as he inventoried all the times Annie had stood with him. Prayed for him. Sacrificed financially. Sacrificed physically. Sacrificed emotionally.

And she had agreed with his decision to pursue ministry at age thirty-five. He thought of the times she would say goodbye for two, three, four weeks at a time, as he embarked on mission trips—China, Mozambique, Nicaragua, Dominican Republic.

He almost forgot the time, not long after they became Christians, when she allowed Robby to live with them, so he could get free from drugs—with dreadful results.

And Kerr Creek Guitars—the big dream. Several thousands of dollars...gone...forever.

For some unexplainable reason, Annie had stuck by him through an amazing amount of uncertainty and turmoil.

"Maybe, just maybe—she'll come around again," Malachi thought, "Why not one more time?"

Malachi sensed a hint of hope in his misery.

Smiling faintly, he descended the steps to his basement retreat.

E-mauled

Chapter 7

As Malachi was about to open the door to his office, he stopped and retraced his steps back upstairs to the kitchen. And peered into the refrigerator. The leftover pizza stirred his appetite. A zap in the microwave, a handful of baby carrots, ranch dressing, and a Pepsi—Malachi had dinner.

Back in the basement, he placed the plate on his desk and booted up his computer. Never one to drift long in cyber space, Malachi briefly perused Facebook. Made a brief stop at his blog—which, like a weedy garden, hadn't received much attention in a while. Next, he clicked his e-mail program to life, expecting his usual thin selection of correspondences.

When he saw the subject line, "Malachi, you're an idiot!!!—from: Annie," three-quarters of his already-scant hope…vanished.

"What an insane use of technology," he thought.

He was sure if he yelled, "Annie," she would be able to hear his voice in her office. Adding to the craziness was the fact that this was not the first time they had turned to cyber-bickering. He despised it. And never initiated it. Tonight, he was thankful, realizing he was too battle worn for hand-to-hand combat.

The white flag went up after he read the message's first four words: "Pastor Neil called me..." At that moment, Malachi intuitively grasped why a person facing captivity would choose death instead.

> ...we had a good talk. He told me you confronted him. You told me you weren't going to confront him. And then you did! I don't understand why you couldn't tell me the truth.
>
> Why do you seem bent on destroying our lives? Destroying your career. You always think you hear from God, or you're believing some dream you had at night. Where has all this taken you? I know you're dissatisfied with so many things in your life. Do I need to list all your fiascos and the letdowns you've experienced?
>
> I don't know what to say...so much of the time. I keep trying to have faith and trust in God. But sometimes...
>
> You must have questions too—with no answers. We have to look somewhere for answers.
>
> Pastor Neil is a good man. I trust him. He's a Godly man. His heart is in the right place.
>
> Are you going to make a stand against his compassion?
>
> I don't know how much more I can take. Please, Malachi, get your head on straight and quit acting like an idiot.

He didn't know how to respond to Annie's e-mail. She only knew part of the truth. And it was unlikely she was in the mood for the rest of his story.

"Shouldn't truth prevail?" Malachi thought.

When he attempted to devise his next step, he visualized a church-war. With Pastor Neil rallying his troops as Malachi put on camouflage, recruiting a much smaller guerilla group. Pastor Neil had already recruited Annie. A nasty fight would ensue. Casualties on both sides would be enormous.

Would there be a winner?

Malachi opted to retreat. But even a retreat strategy eluded him.

Or maybe, "I should go undercover right in the enemy's camp?"

At 7:37 p.m., the phone rang. The sound interrupted his mulling. As usual, Malachi checked the Caller I.D. —*Stephen Johnson.*

Malachi steeled himself, sure of an uncomfortable encounter with the head elder of St. Amos Community Church. It was not that there were any difficulties in their relationship—actually the opposite.

Of all the adults in the church, Stephen's friendship was the most meaningful. A growing friendship. The first time they had coffee, not long after his arrival at St. Amos, Stephen was prodding around. He was digging deeper into Malachi's life—in a way not possible during the job interview process.

Stephen was fair. And he had become a needed and appreciated encourager. Yet, he never backed away from what he thought was right. It was best to avoid Stephen's stubbornness.

One of the main fibers of their friendship was Stephen's ten-year old daughter, Sarah. She was hands-down every Sunday school teacher's dream student. Malachi realized Sarah was a reflection of Stephen in so many ways.

One question pricked his thoughts as the phone rang for the third time, "What will Stephen think is right regarding Medical Marijuana?"

"Hello."

"Malachi, this is Gracie Johnson."

"Oh…hi, Gracie. How can I help you?"

"First of all, I want to thank you for being such a special person in Sarah's life. She talks about all the things you do in Sunday school. And for some reason, God knows why, she wanted to call you tonight. I'll just let her talk. Here she is."

"Hi, Pastor Malachi. This is Sarah."

"How are you doing tonight, Sarah?"

"Good."

"Do you know Jesus loves you, and so do I?" Malachi said.

Malachi heard her laugh.

"Pastor Malachi, I've learned two more Bible verses. Do you want to hear them?"

"Absolutely."

"This is how we know who the children of God are and who the children of the devil are; anyone who does not do what is right is not a child of God. Nor is anyone who does not love his brother. 1 John 3:10."

"Outstanding, Sarah. You said you have one more."

"So, my dear Christian friends who share in the heavenly calling—fix your thoughts on Jesus. Hebrews 3:1"

"Sarah, you're amazing."

"Thank you, Pastor Malachi."

"So, how's school going this week?"

"It's going really good," Sarah said. "Pastor Malachi, Mommy says I have to go now."

"Bye, Sarah. Call anytime."

Malachi sat nearly motionless—soaking in the pleasantness of Gracie and Sarah's words. They were more soothing than any hot tub could ever be.

But after several minutes, he knew he had to crawl out.

He looked at his e-mail again. There was another e-mail from Annie. The subject line said: "This is it!"

The message was very condensed. "Malachi, if you don't apologize to Pastor Neil and stop what you're doing, we're through!!! Let me know your decision tomorrow. P.S. I called your Dad. He agrees with me!!!!"

All his energy drained away. He couldn't even fathom a response.

To Malachi, sleeping in the basement, allowing the morning to bring a fresh perspective, emerged as the wisest choice.

Day of Destiny

Chapter 8

Even with sleeping on the thinly carpeted concrete, Malachi felt reasonably rested.

He shifted through his options—things must be resolved today.

His first decision was to stay down the basement until Annie had left, reasoning, "She would prefer not to see me."

Malachi calculated her departure would be in about an hour. With his work starting at ten o'clock today, he had some extra time.

Malachi decided he needed to do devotions this morning. For years, it was his daily routine—he rarely failed to spend time with God in the morning. While Malachi didn't appreciate what he perceived as a twisted agenda, he knew Pastor Neil's admonition to read the Bible and to pray was right. So right.

Especially for Malachi.

An absence of prayer and Bible reading had triggered unwanted results in Malachi's life. He resolved that, today, he was going to set a fresh priority in his life.

He removed his guitar from the wall. Strumming it, he began singing.

This was the key reason he played—to connect with God.

Malachi softly sang, "In You I trust. For You are the God of my salvation. In You I trust. For You are the God of my salvation."

He smiled, "I can trust God."

For another twenty minutes, he played. Afterwards, he picked up his Bible. For a few moments, he leafed through its pages, landing on the essential verse: "And we know that God causes all things to work together for good to those who love God, to those who are called according to His purpose."

His eyes traced over the words three more times. He sensed the same delight a springtime mushroom-hunter encounters when they spy their quest hidden in the leafy carpet of the forest.

He said softly, "Yes, Lord."

Shuffling from verse to verse, Malachi found other morsels, which began replenishing his running-on-empty soul. Time slipped away as the verses drew Malachi into a realm where God seemed more trustworthy, more tangible than He had in quite some time.

Focused resolve and clarity returned.

He retrieved a notepad. Malachi began writing down his thoughts. He realized this would help him to stay on track—even as emotions and turmoil continued to swirl.

He checked his watch, feeling an urgency to finish before heading to work. His thought flow produced an Action Plan in a few minutes.

With only one adjustment. He changed the Pastor Neil inspired heading, *Action Plan to God's Action Plan.*

God's Action Plan

1. Trust God.

2. I don't agree with Pastor Neil. I believe he is in sin. We all sin. Be loving and sensitive in my disagreement.

3. Focus on being a godly influence. I cannot be a godly influencer if I don't have the love of Jesus or if I lose my job.

4. Trust God through the Holy Spirit to change the situation—pray for this!

5. Work as if I'm working for God.

6. Keeping my job equals keeping my marriage.

7. Keeping my job equals keeping my sanity.

Malachi reviewed the list—satisfied with the results. He reflected on the Old Testament prophet Daniel and how he had lived and thrived as a captive among the Babylonians. In a small measure, he saw himself fulfilling a God-mission like the revered prophet. The phone rang, interrupting his thoughts.

It was St. Amos Community Church.

"Malachi, how are you doing this morning?" Mattie asked.

"I'm fine, thanks."

"Pastor Neil says you don't need to…I mean, ah…shouldn't come to work today."

"Why's that?"

"All I know is what he told me to tell you."

"Can I talk to him?"

"He's not available."

"But I need to talk to him."

"Malachi, I said he's not available. Don't get started."

"O.K. I'm sorry, Mattie. Can you give me his voice mail?"

"Pastor Neil, this is Malachi. Please give me a call when you get a chance. Thanks."

Malachi tilted his head to the left, peering at the floor. "Now what's going on? He's never told me to stay home from work before."

A few possibilities flashed through his mind. The most obvious one tried to dig in.

Malachi said to himself, "Trust God."

Pondering the situation, Malachi built a satisfying case against the possibility of losing his job. St. Amos Community Church had a written policy and procedure for terminating employees. He was clean. He also knew Pastor Neil would open himself up to scrutiny if he made a push for termination. And the evidence could land against him. The possibility of his own termination certainly would be a major deterrent. Plus, the procedure could extend to several weeks or longer—almost guaranteeing a mess.

Malachi's tension eased.

He headed upstairs to the kitchen.

Hungrier than he had been in a few days, he rummaged through the fridge, grabbing eggs, cheese, and salsa. He turned on the stovetop, placed two slices of bread in the toaster, and in less than ten minutes, he was eating what he called, *Camp Eggs Malachi*. A simple breakfast he cooked over the campfire when he and Annie went camping. Four scrambled eggs, salsa, and a heap of cheese—always enjoyable.

The question about the unexpected day-off bubbled back to the surface as he set off to the living room.

Sitting in his favorite chair, eating a food linked to good memories, Malachi's mind withdrew from the unpredictable unfurling of events.

He reflected on how much he loved where they lived. A small ranch house—simple, efficient, affordable. Quiet neighbors. Idyllic. He gazed out the window. Rains from a few days ago had renewed the vigor to their patch of green. The late morning sun cast a peaceful glow on the living room's west wall.

Malachi was making a stoic stand against thinking about work. This became easier as a good portion of his energy shifted toward digesting his breakfast. Soon, he was dozing off.

At eight minutes to eleven, Malachi shook and whimpered like a person waking from a nightmare. He stirred himself fully awake. Then, rising from his chair, Malachi said in a quiet measured tone, "They're going to burn me." He repeated it several times. Each repetition growing louder.

Finally, he was shaking his fists over his head, bellowing, "They're going to burn me! They're going to burn me!"

Falling into the chair, his body slumped over its arm. He sputtered for several more minutes. Then sunk into silence. After numerous shifts, twists, and twitches, Malachi retreated into an intense sleep.

In Love with Annie Again

That afternoon, at three forty-four, Malachi awoke. He clenched his teeth, folded his arms, and sat up straight. Staring straight ahead, his chin jutted slightly upward.

For the next dozen minutes, Malachi remained still—but only on the outside.

And then he made his way to the fridge, grabbed a Coke, and proceeded to his office.

He turned on his desktop computer and set up his laptop beside it. On a white legal pad, he began making a list. Back at the computers he initiated the transferring of files from the main computer to his laptop—documents, pictures, songs, video, etc.

He went to the storage room and brought back two large duffle bags. Malachi moved quickly—placing books, paperwork, and office supplies into the duffle as he intermittently attended to the computers.

He then headed upstairs to the bedroom with one of the duffle bags.

From the closet and dresser he systematically packed the duffle with clothes. He pulled a sleeping bag, three blankets, a pillow, and a suitcase from the guest room closet. Returning to the master bedroom, he filled the suitcase. And retrieved a pair of shoes from the closet.

He took everything he had gathered out to the garage, stuffing everything into the back of his Silver-Gray and Blue 1992 Suburban. He then draped blankets over all the items.

Malachi rushed back to the basement. He went over to his four-drawer filing cabinet in the corner of the room, pulling the bottom drawer open. On his knees, he reached past the back of the drawer to the cabinet's floor.

In his hand was a compact lock-box, which he placed on his desk. Inside were stacks of money—around five-thousand dollars. He had tucked the money away, ten, twenty, maybe fifty dollars at a time. He began amassing the money eight years ago.

He picked up three stacks. In bank wrappers—ten one-hundred dollar bills in each pile. This was the only exception to Malachi's usual small-quantity accruing.

An executive had given him the money. He had confided in Malachi regarding unresolved financial problems his company was experiencing. Unable to identify the cause, the man was overwrought with distress.

"Let me pray for you," Malachi had suggested.

As they bowed their heads, Malachi started rubbing above his right eye with his right hand. His face became warm on his right side. Between his ear and eye—above his cheekbone.

Distinct pictures and impressions entered Malachi's brain.

After the prayer, he said, "One of your employees is embezzling money from you." Malachi then went on to describe the man and the details of the situation.

Three weeks later the businessman handed Malachi an envelope, "Thank you. You were right." Malachi had kept this incident a secret from everyone.

He never had a specific plan for the money. Every time he put money in the box, he thought, "I'm really going to surprise Annie someday—big time."

He removed the money from the box. Sorting it into two piles. He shuffled back and forth with the bills. Both stacks went through several shifts in size. He counted the smaller pile—two: fifties, ten: twenties, six: tens. He put that money in his wallet. The remainder of the money he placed back inside of the lock box.

Malachi returned to the computers, determining which files were essential to download.

At four-twenty the phone rang—it was St. Amos Community Church. He answered. Mattie informed Malachi that Pastor Neil wanted to meet with him at ten o'clock tomorrow morning.

Adding, "Please be prompt."

"I'll be up early," Malachi said. "Hey...Mattie I sure like working with you."

"Well thank you Malachi."

Malachi disconnected the laptop from his desktop computer. Closing the laptop, he secured it in its travel case. It went up to the Suburban with the duffle bags along with several additional handfuls of his belongings.

Malachi walked over to his guitar hanging on the wall. He studied every line, curve, and contour. From the glossy surface, his distorted reflection stared back at him. He seemed hypnotized—his gaze locked on his own image.

He shook his head.

Turned. And bolted upstairs.

Malachi went for a quick run, showered, and then sat in the living room reading—glancing out the window occasionally.

The moment he heard Annie's car, he popped out of the chair. When she arrived at the door he opened it, greeting her in a sing-songy cadence, "Annie, Annie, Annie."

The sternness on Annie's face started to break.

Malachi blurted, "I'm so sorry. I've been so stupid."

With nearly the same speed, Annie's countenance lifted.

A bemused look set in as Malachi peppered her with his Action Plan: "I'm going to apologize to Pastor Neil. He wasn't at church today. First thing tomorrow morning I'm going to straighten everything out. I've thought about it. Maybe he's right. I need to re-think everything. He is my boss."

Then like someone pumping the breaks three times, his cadence dipped, "Keeping my job equals keeping my sanity."

Annie couldn't help laughing. They embraced. Still holding her, he said, "Hey, let's go out to eat."

"That would be nice."

Annie laughed a lot even as they were driving to the restaurant. She hadn't seen Malachi this silly in...so long. Even the waitress caught their contagious jubilation.

"Let's rent a movie," he said, "Let's make an evening of it."

"I have to work tomorrow," Annie said, "And so do you."

Touching her hand, he said, "We'll get to bed plenty early."

"So what do you want to watch?" Annie said.

"*School of Rock.*"

Annie wrinkled her forehead, "*School of Rock?*"

Malachi's exuberance won out.

The silliness of the movie matched Malachi's demeanor. Both he and Annie let the movie carry them away.

Malachi moved closer to Annie, rubbing her shoulder. She softly deflected his hand.

He tilted his head, grinning "Maybe later."

"Maybe."

But...Malachi knew the answer.

Black Whole

Chapter 10

Malachi rolled over. He saw the glow—4:28 a.m. Any hint of sleepiness dissolved as his brain spiked to attention. He made no attempt to stifle the cascade of thoughts rifling through his brain.

His mind had traveled a million miles by the time his bare feet touched the carpeted floor.

The moon illuminated the dining room through the patio door. Malachi's eyes adjusted to varying light levels as he wandered from room to room in the unlit house.

Making his way out to the garage, he turned on the light and inventoried the contents of the Suburban. Also checking to ensure the cargo was covered by the blankets.

His restlessness carried him to the basement. Drawn to the guitar on the wall, he removed it from the bracket. Sitting down in his lounge chair, Malachi strummed the guitar a few times. This aroused a long-ago memory, which Malachi sipped on like a $5.00 mug of mocha.

Recalling the sessions when his friend, John Peters, taught him to play the guitar delighted Malachi's senses. So patient, even though Malachi was wanting for skills and natural ability. John's guitar playing passion spilled over into Malachi's life. Infusing him with a zeal for playing, even to this day.

At that moment, a desire to talk with John overwhelmed Malachi. He attributed their losing touch to his shortfall in maintaining the friendship.

Malachi shook his head, feeling the sting of that relational failure. A life-pattern he had developed—almost unknowingly.

Malachi mulled it over, "Why did I lose touch with John?"

John was also the one who kept witnessing to Malachi about Jesus. He was there at the revival meeting when Malachi made the decision to become a follower of Jesus Christ. He had encouraged, nearly insisted, Malachi attend the meeting.

The guitar thing? Malachi couldn't pinpoint when it happened. Around a year after he became a Christian. One day, he decided he wanted to play guitar. It was Christmastime, because Malachi had used Christmas-money to purchase the $120.00 dark-red Spencer acoustic guitar.

John was his only teacher. They plodded through eight-months of informal lessons. Learning chords and songs—always Christian songs. For Malachi and John, as well, they had no desire to play any other type of music. The guitar was more than a musical instrument; it was an integral part of Malachi's faith-life.

He played a soothing melodic chord progression.

Then abruptly, his body quivered and his facial muscles contorted as his strumming became progressively louder. A jangly power chord riff unleashed from his guitar.

From re-fired neural paths formed in his brain two-decades earlier, the tune and lyrics from the heavy metal power anthem *Black Whole* poured out.

He stood up, becoming aggressive in his playing. And then he started singing—right in tune:

Black Whole. Fall in love

Never to return

Fall in love. And burn

Burn, burn, burn
Is love…this way
Or am I free?
A slave to you. A slave to me

Black whole. Fall in love
Never to return
Fall in love. And burn
Burn, burn, burn

With a grunting laugh, he tossed the guitar onto the chair.

He pulled a black stocking cap over his ears, put on his gray hoody, and stepped out into the early-morning world.

He figured it was two miles to Marilyn's Homecookin' Cafe. You have to know where the place is to find it. Located on a residential side street, it's the type of restaurant franchises kill.

The cool-aired trek was better than any prescription.

Marilyn's—a white building that looks like a single-story home with too many additions. Its appearance lacked even a hint of ambience— no enticement to *Eat Here*. Nevertheless, a cheap, hearty breakfast awaited. On arrival, Malachi ordered his favorite, a Mexican omelet, hash browns, wheat toast, and coffee. And more coffee.

The only part of the spread receiving due attention was the coffee. Much of the rest, tasty as ever, was pushed to the edge of the plate, like roadkill on the shoulder of the highway.

As he was traipsing back home, Annie was zipping through her morning routine.

When Annie smiled, her attractiveness elevated considerably. At forty-one, with a trim frame, bouncy auburn hair, and legs that must have come out of a very delectable gene pool, Annie looked much younger than her age. Malachi had furrowed his brow on several occasions when he thought the skirt she was wearing to work appeared too sensual.

Her soft-voiced rebuttal was always, "I need to look professional."

Annie wanted to say goodbye to Malachi and thank him for the wonderful evening. She hadn't heard him all morning. In addition, she didn't recall Malachi mentioning anything about leaving early. She went to his office and knocked on the door—which was ajar.

She knocked again. "Malachi." And then pushed the door open. His office appeared messier than usual.

When she spotted Malachi's guitar slouched in the chair, a wave of anxiety rippled through her body. "Malachi would never leave his guitar that way." Confused, she impulsively rushed out to the garage. Seeing the Suburban, her concerns escalated.

Back in the house, she called Malachi's cell phone. She knew the futility of this, since Malachi only sporadically turned on his phone.

Nothing. Like she expected.

She needed to leave to make it to work on time. As Annie pondered the situation, she lived with the conclusion that she was not actually worried.

It was odd—yes. Annie laughed to herself, "That's Malachi—odd."

She snatched her purse and keys and was out the door.

Malachi had been calculating what time Annie would leave the house, pacing his return journey accordingly. As he neared the house, he could see that his timing was flawless—Annie had departed.

He had less than an hour before his own planned departure. So, once he arrived home, he surged into his normal pre-work routine.

Once dressed, he hurried to his office. He opened the lock-box, eyeing the money. He then closed it, removed the box's key from his key ring, and placed it inside. On a blank sheet of paper, he scribbled a note. And shoved it into the box.

He rotated toward his lounge chair; his eyes fixed on his guitar. His attention was keenly on the guitar's headstock. He touched the cross logo he had designed.

And then, measuring out his words, he said, "Kerr Creek Guitars."

He wagged his head and started singing, "Black Whole. Fall in Love. Never to return..."

He snatched the moneybox. Rushing to Annie's office, he set it on her desk.

Looking around the room, he sucked in a deep breath. And then, he went into the kitchen to get a Walmart grocery bag, walked to the bathroom, and gathered up his toothbrush, razor, shaving cream, and hairbrush. Opening the vanity's lower drawer, he retrieved several more items.

Everything disappeared into the Walmart sack.

The Show at St. Amos

Cars started pulling into the parking lot at St. Amos Community Church twenty minutes before eight that morning. Pastor Neil had walked over from his house more than an hour ago. He had asked Mattie to arrive early also. The elders, Ed Spencer, Alan Gibby, Stephen Johnson, Ben Sterling, and Junior McSchmitt, made their way to the church's conference room.

Words were few. Coffee was poured. Significant eye contact was avoided. Notepads, day planners, cell phones, and file folders served as convenient distractions.

Pastor Neil entered the conference room. He sat down and immediately started, "I have called this emergency meeting of the church-elders to stave off an attack on St. Amos Community Church. Thank you for sacrificing your time. Thank you for your Godly leadership of this church. In the Bible, it talks about a wolf in sheep's clothing. We know this to mean an evil person appearing to be a good person. They look and act as if they are one of us. The devil works this way—so often. This morning, with a heavy heart on one hand, yet praising God with my lips, I encourage this group to step into their God-given leadership as we work through a difficult Action Plan. I praise God, because He has revealed this atrocity to me. Yet, my heart aches knowing someone I dearly love has...has fallen deeply into...sin and deception from the devil. The wretched soul the devil has ensnared is...Malachi Marble."

Junior McSchmitt's forehead wrinkled, "Malachi...Malachi Marble? Hasn't he been one of the best things to happen at St. Amos in years? I mean, isn't the children's ministry the only thing growing around here?"

"Exactly, Junior. We know the devil can appear as an angel of light. His deception is uncanny. That is why we must quickly thwart this evil I have uncovered—by the grace of God. Junior, do you trust me? My leadership? My spiritual authority? My discernment?"

He paused slightly, "Well yes..."

"Let me get right to the point. Here is my Action Plan for this morning. We need to complete this morning's agenda promptly. I am proposing a vote to have Malachi Marble terminated immediately."

"Malachi? Terminated?" Ed Spencer said. He looked around at everyone. "We just gave him a raise less than two months ago because of his exemplary performance."

"I agree Ed; it is very disturbing how fast he has changed."

"That's not what...."

"I have the floor," Pastor Neil said. "Let me show you the evidence. You will quickly agree with me. And the Lord. First, Mattie has a few things for you."

"I do?"

"Mattie, please answer a few questions for me. To help us all keep our focus, let us do as the Bible instructs us, 'Let your *yes* be a *yes* and your, *no*, a *no*, or you will be condemned.' James 5:12. On Wednesday morning, was Malachi pushy, obnoxious, and forceful toward me—his spiritual authority. Yes or no?"

"Well..."

"Yes or no, Mattie?"

"Yes."

Pastor Neil said, "The Bible says in Hebrews 13:17, 'Obey your leaders and submit to their authority.' Malachi has fallen into a destructive pattern, which goes one-hundred percent against this Scripture—and countless others. This is one of the most effective evils used in destroying a church. Are we going to allow this to happen here?"

Pastor Neil eyed each person sitting at the round walnut-colored conference table. "Of course not," he said. "We are not going to allow the devil to destroy St. Amos Community Church."

"Mattie, how many days of work has Malachi missed this week. Just give me a number."

"Two, but…"

"And he went home early on another day. Is that right, Mattie?"

"Yes, he did."

"Alan, you're a business man," Pastor Neil said. "Can you run a business, with excellence, carrying out your daily Action Plan, if your people miss two days a week, leave early, come in late—how would that work for you?"

"It wouldn't work."

"Have you ever terminated an employee at Miracle Molding as a result of this kind of behavior?"

"Well, ah…yes, but…"

"I have the floor, Alan," Pastor Neil said. "So, we see Malachi's work attendance is severely lacking. So, let us move on, gentleman. We have many other pieces of firm evidence against Malachi. Because of time constraints, I want to discuss the most significant grievance. I could spend a long time talking about things like tithing and…"

"What about Malachi's tithing?" Ben Sterling said. "Well, everyone here knows I'm the church treasurer. I know about this stuff. I've rarely known anyone who's so sacrificial in giving. I know Annie complains about it, sometimes."

"So, as the treasurer, Ben, what is Malachi's tithing percentage?" Pastor Neil said.

"I don't have that number in front of me. He's a generous, giving person."

"Mattie, I asked you to bring the paperwork regarding Malachi's tithing." Pastor Neil said. "Do you have it?"

"Yes, I do."

"Can I see it?"

Pastor Neil then reviewed the sheet of paper.

"This clearly shows that Malachi is nearly five percent short of his tithe. Again, Alan, as a businessperson, would it be tolerable if an employee skimmed five percent off the top at Miracle Molding."

"Well, that happened to me, and Malachi caught the guy who was doing it."

"That is not the point. *Yes* or *no*. To steal or not to steal?"

"Well, *no*, of course."

"But what about all the other money he gives, which isn't noted on his tithe record?" Ben said.

"That doesn't count. That giving falls under the category of an offering—a totally different category. A tithe is a tithe. An offering is an offering. You all know your Bible well enough to know this. Don't you? Bottom line—Malachi is flat-out robbing God from His tithe. Is there anyone here who thinks it is acceptable to rob God?"

Pastor Neil peered around the table and then said, "Let me discuss the next an area, which is difficult for me to even talk about."

His eyes circled the table again, "Gentleman...Malachi Marble is involved in pornography. Right here at church."

His eyes fixed on Stephen Johnson. "Let me ask you something, Stephen. More than once you have mentioned to me how loving Malachi is toward the Sunday school students. Seems harmless. Seems caring and loving. But what is really going on? Stephen, do you want someone addicted to pornography cuddling up to your ten-year old daughter, Sarah. It is heart rending to think about it. The anger I feel..."

Stephen Johnson said, "I'm shocked...I have to say I was fairly opposed to hiring Malachi in the first place. I don't know—I just thought he was too ah...flaky. But Sarah? She's such a different little girl. She loves Malachi. He's just so..."

"Perverted," Pastor Neil injected. "Do you want a sexual pervert around your precious daughter?"

"So, what's the evidence?" Stephen said.

"As you know, we have Brother's Keeper Software installed on the computers here at the church. It monitors all computer activity. Especially internet search categories. Mattie and I perused Malachi's computer together—yesterday. And we found many searches related to pornography.

Stephen turned to Mattie, "How many were there, Mattie?"

"I don't know. You know I really don't know computers very well. I did see it on the screen. Pastor Neil made sure I saw it. Computers are confusing. I don't really know."

"But you did see the word *pornography* repeatedly?" Pastor Neil said. "Yes or no, Mattie?"

"Yes."

"Mattie, thank you. And praise God for the strength He gave you as you had to encounter this wretched soul trapped in pornography almost daily."

Pastor Neil stood up, hugged Mattie around her shoulder, and then returned to his seat. "Let us continue with our Action…"

"Can we see the evidence on Malachi's computer?" Stephen said.

"I had our computer tech come in and scrub Malachi's computer, eradicating the infectious plague of pornography from within the holy walls of St. Amos Community Church. Stephen, would you want this plague of the devil to fester?"

Stephen looked away.

"I make a motion that we immediately terminate Malachi Marble," Pastor Neil said. "Let us get our Action Plan completed. Do I have a second?"

Ed Spencer said, "I second."

"Now, we all know Mattie doesn't vote," Pastor Neil said. "You know my vote. I vote: yes."

"Ed?"

"Yes."

"Stephen."

"Abstain."

Pastor Neil glared at him. Stephen immediately shifted his eyes toward the floor.

Gazing around the table, his silence triggered a ripple of uneasiness. Pastor Neil eyed each man, like a poker hero reading his adversaries. He looked at Alan. And then at Ben. And shifted back, "Alan."

"Yes."

"Ben?"

"Abstain."

Pastor Neil took a deep breath. And exhaled. "Junior?"

"Abstain."

"That is three: *yes* and three: *abstain*," Pastor Neil said. "In accordance with the bylaws of St. Amos Community Church, the motion is carried. I have a ten o'clock meeting with Malachi. He will be terminated immediately. In addition, after he gathers his personal items, he will be barred from the church."

He glanced around the room, "Thank you, gentlemen. You are Godly men; it is an honor to serve the Lord Jesus Christ with you here at St. Amos Community Church. Let me pray as we close this meeting. Father God, thank You for surrounding me with men of destiny and courage with hearts dedicated to doing Your will. God, we know we will not always fully agree. But help us to honor Your authority and the authorities You have placed here on earth for our benefit. Help us not to be deceived, like Malachi, in the area of spiritual authority. Let us now move on to new opportunities to serve You in our community. Let us have compassionate hearts like Jesus. Help empower St. Amos Community Church to serve You and those who are in pain. Those who needlessly suffer. Dear Lord, instill us with a fresh vision. Jesus grant us Your eyes of compassion. We ask in the name of our Lord and Savior, Jesus Christ. Amen."

Pastor Neil stood up, shaking each of the elders' hands, like a politician working a crowd. And then hurried toward the door.

He turned around when he reached it and said, "Mattie, make sure everyone takes one of those large envelopes on the table." These words were followed by his prompt exit.

In the conference room, it was like witnessing the white sheets draped at a roadside accident. No one spoke. Everyone turned away. And left.

Stephen closed his car door. He unfolded the envelope's flat silver-toned clasp, pulling out the papers halfway. And glared at the heading of Pastor Neil's multi-page document for a second. Or two.

He hurled the envelope; it hit the passenger-side window.

And fell to the floor.

Who's My Darling

Chapter 12

It was well before ten o'clock, not even nine-thirty, as Malachi approached St. Amos Community Church. He felt relaxed. Smiling. Happy. Invigorated. Not even a hint of nervousness.

He could see the church from nearly a block away.

When the parking lot came into view, Malachi thought to himself, "There are never this many cars at the church this time of day, unless they're preparing for a funeral."

He laughed out loud. "Something did die, but I'm not going to the funeral."

Malachi then fixed his eyes straight ahead. Punched the gas pedal. And honked three times as he passed St. Amos Community Church.

He turned on the radio. WGOD sprang to life. Malachi instantly hit the seek button. He hit it again. And pressed seek again, asking himself, "So what am I seeking…what am I seeking?"

When his finger pushed *seek* for the eighth time, Malachi was lured in by mesmerizing guitar licks emanating from the radio. And then the alluring lyrics blew over him like a warm wind—hooking his soul. He struggled to get free—and then went along for the ride:

Kissed you goodbye my darling
I still love you. I do

Your love was always so tender
Our friends all thought it was true

I'm turning off the light. The door beckons me
Oh now, if I turn the knob, will I be free?

Kissed you goodbye my darling
I still love you. I do

Church pews and songs of grace
God's forgiveness took its mere place

Right or wrong. How would I know?
I'm closing the door
Darling—
I must go

Kissed you goodbye my darling
I still love you. I do

Keys in my hand
The choice in my heart

I'm running a new race
Looking away
...I must depart

Kissed you goodbye my darling
I still love you

I do.

For Malachi, no tears fell like rain.

At times…even the darkest cloud clings to its weighty load.

The city limit sign was beyond the reach of the Suburban's rearview mirror by the time the song ended. And fifty-nine had been locked in on the cruise control. Malachi disengaged from the sound of the radio—its sway, no more effective than tires rolling on asphalt.

Suddenly, Malachi smacked the steering wheel, "No!"

Brakes were hit. Fifty-nine was sliced to a roll. And at the cross street, he turned right. Whipped around and started retracing his tracks. Now, he was driving even faster.

He passed St. Amos. All the cars were gone—except Mattie's.

Twelve minutes later, Malachi pulled into his driveway.

Nearly running, he unlocked the door, without breaking stride; he galloped down the basement steps.

He walked into his office, looked to the right. And picked up his Kerr Creek Guitar. He located the case, securing the guitar in its cradle-like nest.

Back up the stairs. And out the door. The guitar case was gently stowed behind the front seat.

And off he drove, saying to himself, "Who's my darling?"

On Hurt Heart Road

Chapter 13

Malachi lost his mind on Half Way Rd. The radio, the rumble of tires, and his vaporous thoughts blended into a vat of numbness.

Half Way Rd.—flat, curve-less, and no stop signs for eleven miles. Here, the road gave way to U.S. 12. The name Half Way always struck Malachi as odd. He once joked, "Half Way Rd. is halfway between nothing and nothing."

The farmers had plowed and planted. No green had appeared—at least not visible from a Suburban cruising along at sixty-one.

Malachi's arrival at U.S. 12 shifted his mind out of cruise control. He glanced at the clock—10:10. At that moment, he experienced the same jubilation he had in fifth grade when he saw Ted Bixby drink milk he had spit into while he wasn't looking. A mental picture of Pastor Neil's frustration when Malachi failed to show up triggered the same pleasant sensation. And like the fifth-grade incident with Ted Bixby, Malachi was free from even a tinge of guilt.

Now, westward bound. He was following a familiar route, yet the majority of Malachi's past travels on these roads were logged nearly a decade ago. Sunny, the intermittent clouds shielded much of the eye-level glare. He battled against the memory of what he always considered the best trip Annie and he ever went on.

The journey took place shortly after they had become Christians. Malachi, in his quirkiness and because of new-Christian sensations, kept claiming during the trip, "I'm high on Jesus." And Annie was catching a contact buzz, herself.

Malachi attempted to rid the memories from his conscience. He was fighting—but it was as if a tangible being was trying to hitch a ride. Silent...using its telepathy to alter Malachi's mental track. Malachi wanted to dislodge the past from his brain—rather than tolerate another groove being set in his hard drive.

He gave in. "Crap. I could use a companion to ride along anyway. There are a lot of miles ahead of me. We can separate up the road."

"O.K., you can ride along," Malachi said. "But when I say out, you're out."

After being on the road for less than two hours, the 1992 Suburban, with a muffler rumble signaling a future repair, glided into White Pigeon, Michigan. The bottoms of its doors were fighting the upward creeping of rust, but Malachi's focus was on the gas gauge as it danced a tick right of E.

"I'm stopping for gas and some coffee, do you want anything?"

Malachi pulled into a gas station, which included an adjoining restaurant. "Annie and I ate there. Man, their pancakes were the best. And the waitress, I had her cracking up. Then when I told her, 'Jesus loves you,' her eyes said, 'Thank you,' more than her words. You know what, though, when I did something like that, it always seemed to bug Annie. I made sure she didn't see when I left a ten-dollar tip."

Malachi reached into his wallet for the only credit card he had. He activated the gas pump, pushing the nozzle into the Suburban's fill opening. With gas pouring into the tank, he knelt with one knee on the ground. Forcefully, he sanded the credit card on the concrete. He flipped it over, repeating the process on the other side. And then bent the card in two. Pressing hard on the stiff plastic. Malachi tossed the disfigured card into the trashcan, covering it with rubbish.

West a few blocks, he spotted U.S. 131. A major north-south highway—running the entire length of Michigan's Lower Peninsula. Eight
miles south, it commences at the Indiana border and ends at the Straits
of Mackinaw three hundred and eighteen miles north.

Eleven minutes later, Malachi turned right as he merged onto U.S.
131.

His head immediately motioned to the left. "See the big rock over
there in that tiny park? Annie and I stopped. When I saw it, I said,
'Annie, look there's a rock. We need to stop.' I couldn't help myself—so
silly and childish—but so in love with Jesus. And serious, all at the
same time. Annie tried to hold back. I said, 'Jesus is our Rock. Maybe
that's a Jesus rock.' She melted."

"That rock commemorates Chief White Pigeon. It's amazing; the
guy heard about a secret plan to attack the white settlers who were his
friends, while at a meeting near Detroit. The other Indians tried to convince him to betray them. Chief White Pigeon said, 'To betray my vil-
lage of the white people is to betray myself.' He then took off, running
a hundred and fifty miles to warn the settlers. Shortly after, he died
of heart failure from exhaustion. Chief White Pigeon's story impacted
Annie more than me. I still remember her words, 'I hope we can run
our race for Jesus with that kind of determination.'"

As the Suburban set its bead north, Malachi worked his way along
in the morning traffic on the two-lane portion of the highway. When
he sighted the city limit sign of Constantine, his unseen companion
prodded his memory.

"When I saw that sign—back then—I started preaching," Malachi
said. "Did you see what it said on the city limits sign, Annie? *Constantine:
Seed Corn Capital of the World.*' Annie said, 'Wow that's so exciting I
could scream.' Her yuck, yucks didn't even slow me down. I didn't care.
The thought of all that seed got me bouncing. I expounded on Jesus'
parable on the Seed and the Sower. I remember hollering at the end, 'I
want to be in the Jesus-seed capital of the world. We'll be planting so
much Jesus-seed; we'll be strained to harvest all that God is doing.'"

"You know what? When I finished, Annie was excited too. But not
as much as me? But who cares? That was a long time ago. We're both
different people, now."

Malachi clenched his jaw as he entered the city of Three Rivers.

He was pressing hard to get away from his past thoughts. He knew he would be passing near Kerr Creek soon.

He and Annie stumbled upon this insignificant creek. Malachi spotted a two-track running along the water's edge and said to Annie, "We're in no hurry; let's take a short hike." Less than a half-mile in, they saw a deer drinking water. Malachi had an epiphany moment.

A Bible verse flashed into his brain. "A white-tailed deer drinks from the creek; I want to drink God, deep draughts of God."

Four years later, the experience inspired the name for Malachi's guitar enterprise—Kerr Creek Guitars. But this day, Malachi shook his head when he passed near the creek and said, "God, I don't need to drink any more of You."

Malachi wasn't car sick, but he felt the same way. Disappointments, failure, and misplaced trust in God nauseated him. He weakened, as energy sapped from his body.

The radio had been *on*. It had been *off*. *Seek* had been pushed. And re-pushed.

Up until the moment of this uncomfortable wave, it had been miles and miles of background noise. But now, some unknown song clutched him. Had his unseen passenger turned up the volume on the radio?

It's been known to touch me
From time to time
I've felt the presence of a love so strong
There's no denying
It would lift you up
Up off of the ground
Show you how to give
Without a sound

It's been known to touch me
From time to time

And it's been known to move me
From time to time
With the strength of a mighty hand
Straight down the line
Put my fears to rest

And get out of the cold
And one by one
Watch the miracles unfold

It's been known to touch me
From time to time

Is been known to carry me along
All through the trials of time
Brought many, many comforts to my heart
When I only want to break down crying
It's been known to travel right through me
Like the lightning from the sky

It's been known to touch me
From time to time

And I know we'll find it
I really do my love
I really do my love

As the song played on, Malachi turned off the radio. Loneliness engulfed him. The stranger had departed—the one arousing memories in his brain. He left Malachi so alone.

"Now, I don't have anyone," he said to himself as he drove in the silence.

In a few miles, maybe more, dwelling on the past dissipated as Malachi's future teetered from manageable, even simplistic, to frustratingly complex. As the miles rolled by, his mental churning accelerated.

The road and the towns smeared across the landscape, like water soaked ink on paper. Schoolcraft, Kalamazoo, Otsego...Grand Rapids and north. Another one...another one. Blurred by Malachi's intense absorption, not by speed.

He pulled onto Highway 10 near Reed City—not entirely cognizant of his swing westward. And then between the almost-invisible bergs of Chase and Nirvana, the sign for a rest stop bumped his mind back to his Action Plan for the day.

He decided it was time to put some *action* into his plan. But first, he used the restroom and walked around to freshen his mind.

And then, checking his cell phone for messages, ascended to the top of the list. Like usual, his phone had been turned off all day.

There were four messages.

10:09 "This is Mattie Carson calling for Pastor Neil. He was wondering where you are."

10:45 "This is Mattie. Please call the church immediately."

11:57 "Hey Malachi...this is Mattie. Are you doing all right? You can call me."

12:05 "Malachi, this is Stephen Johnson. Please give me a call. Please. I need to talk to you. Please."

When he heard Stephen's message, the distress in his voice startled him. A fresh wave of anxiety rippled through Malachi's body.

He decided not to return any of the calls right then. Instead, he located the phone number for his Uncle Dale and Aunt Betty. And placed a call.

Their answering machine greeted him: "You have reached the home of Dale and Betty Marble and Dale Marble Construction. Please leave a message. We look forward to serving your construction needs."

Malachi hadn't seen Uncle Dale in a few years. His father's younger brother and his wife, Betty, were two of the nicest people Malachi knew. He and Annie would visit them when they were anywhere up north near Manistee.

Malachi once worked for Uncle Dale. Three weeks during a break while attending Bible College. He needed the money, and Uncle Dale needed the help. An excellent builder, who always told Malachi, "I have too much work. And it's all good work."

He kidded Malachi, "I think I could turn you into a carpenter. If you need a real job, let me know. I've got one waiting for you."

As far as Malachi knew, Uncle Dale and Aunt Betty never attended church. And whenever Malachi hedged that way in a discussion, Uncle Dale skillfully shifted the subject.

Malachi had said to Annie—more than once, "They're nicer than most Christians we know." She agreed.

Malachi didn't leave a message but decided to call later.

He reclined in the Suburban's spacious front seat and nodded off.

Hello Manistee

Chapter 14

Contacting Uncle Dale found its rightful place at the top of Malachi's agenda when he awoke from his nap. He called him again. And reached his answering machine for a second time.

So, he set off on the last leg of his pilgrimage.

It had been less than seven hours since Malachi had pulled out of his garage that morning. When he saw the Manistee city limit sign, he felt like a man who had just washed up on shore after a shipwreck. Except, the survival of the others was off his radar.

And like a shipwreck survivor, Malachi was confused, tired, and wondering—what's next? His survival instincts were kicking in. He was happy to have endured so far. Glad to be free from the crashing, danger-laden waves, which he thought might kill him.

But now, he was sniffing potential for the future, with a cautious eye on his surroundings. And he was hungry.

Malachi hadn't visited Manistee in four years. Nonetheless, the city of 6,200, on the shores of Lake Michigan, half way between Chicago and the northern tip of Michigan's Lower Peninsula, still had a familiar vibe.

From family trips decades ago, to visiting Uncle Dale with Annie, he could find his way around. He had walked the beaches west, south, and north of town. And had hiked and camped in the Manistee National Forest scattered mainly east of town.

He spotted a Walmart. It wasn't there on his last visit. He pulled into the parking lot, trying to recall what had occupied the tract of land the store and parking lot now sprawled across.

He was going to call Uncle Dale again. But hunger absorbed his motivation. He was confident he could locate the place in downtown Manistee Uncle Dale always crowned as, "The best food in town." He had taken Malachi and Annie there a few times. Being a bar, as well as a place to eat, DT's Good Time Place was not the type of establishment Annie and Malachi would choose. But Uncle Dale always picked up the bill, and the food was exceptional.

Once parked, he bought a copy of the *Manistee News Advocate*. Then, by instinct, he made his way toward the restaurant.

When he saw the large block lettering on the rust-red canopy, he knew he was on target. Large white block lettering proclaimed *FOOD* on one side of the canopy and the same style of lettering declared *DRINK* on the opposite side.

This is it—DT's Good Time Place. Malachi noticed the Cook Wanted sign in the window, studying it for a couple of seconds before going inside.

Malachi asked for a seat in the far corner. For the privacy. And he liked the view of the Manistee River from that area of the restaurant. He ordered water and a coffee and then attempted to contact Uncle Dale.

"Uncle Dale?" Malachi smiled. "Hey, you're hard to get a hold of. How have you been?"

"I'm hanging in there."

"Uncle Dale, I'm ah…I'm visiting Manistee."

"When are you coming?"

"Well…I'm already here. I'm at DT's Good Time Place."

"That's…that's great. You've never surprised me like this before. Is everything OK?"

"Great. Everything's great."

"Yeah, what a surprise, Malachi."

"I was hoping to see you and Aunt Betty…sometime…ah soon.

"How about this? I'll come into town. I love eating at DT's. Will that work?"

"Perfect."

"It'll be a half-hour, forty-five minutes. Is that OK?"

"Works for me."

"It'll be so good to see you and Annie."

"Ah…Annie's not with me."

"Everything's OK.?"

"Uncle Dale, we can talk when you get here."

"Well…I'll see you in a half hour or so."

Malachi noticed the waitress heading toward him.

"Have you decided what you want?" she asked.

"I'm waiting for someone. Thank you."

"More coffee?"

"That would be great."

As Malachi looked around, DT's décor was as he had remembered it. Copper-toned stamped metal ceiling. The green walls were the same color as a lawn enhanced by repeated doses of fertilizer. The teal green door leading into the bathroom was so narrow he wondered how some of the patrons squeezed through.

A Red Wings banner cascaded across the restaurant—up high on the riverside wall. Claiming: *The Playoffs. History Will Be Made.* Posters announcing Trilogy Beer peaked out in multiple locations. There was the standard, long wooden bar—with a mirrored backdrop. And taking center court, the focal point, was the flat screen TV. Nearly the size of a sheet of plywood, it was all about sports. And more sports.

Beside Malachi, there was a couple three tables away enjoying their food and a man in his forties, who appeared to be a regular.

The waitress was wearing a shirt the same rust-red color as DT's canopy. A DT logo was affixed over her heart. What appeared odd to Malachi was how far down the loose-fitting shirt hung on her thin frame. At least a size too large, it reminded Malachi of the way a woman would dress to hide bulges.

He thought, "Is it a new baggy-look for women I'm unfamiliar with?"

She saw Malachi looking at her and came over to the table: "Is there anything you need?"

Malachi smiled, "Yeah, just about everything."

"More coffee."

"Sure."

As she poured the coffee, he noticed her fingers. They were long. Thin. Elegant.

Malachi felt stupid the second the words left his mouth; they tumbled out without any effort. Or thinking. "You have beautiful fingers."

The waitress laughed out loud. And Malachi's face approached the same color as her shirt.

"I've never heard that pick-up line before," she said.

"I'm sorry," Malachi said, as his gaze retreated toward the coffee cup in his hand. "I meant...I mean. I...well you do have beautiful fingers. And...I was just thinking how they looked perfect for playing guitar. That's all I meant."

"You're different. Aren't you? I mean in a good way," she said.

"A lot of people think I'm different. But not always in a good way."

"I don't think I've seen you here before. You visiting or something?"

"I'm moving to Manistee. I'm going to work for my uncle. He owns a construction company—Dale Marble Construction."

"I think I've heard of him."

"So, what's your name...I mean...I'm not flirting or anything...I mean..." Malachi shifted his eyes back to his coffee cup.

When he looked up, she said with a tight-lipped grin, "Mandy."

She turned as she heard the door open, "Gotta go."

Malachi glanced at his watch, turning his attention to the newspaper. A headline pronounced lay-offs in the local school system.

He flipped back to the classified ads. Flipped through the fourteen-page edition. Looked. Scanned. And ran his finger up and down the newsprint. He was struck by the fact that there wasn't even one help wanted ad in the newspaper. Not even one.

When Uncle Dale arrived, his appearance shocked Malachi. Uncle Dale, at nearly six-foot tall, had always been on the thick side of stout, but now, Malachi calculated him to be forty pounds lighter. Loose skinned-wrinkles hung from his face.

Still, his handshake had a hearty, trustworthy feel.

"Where's Aunt Betty?" Malachi asked as they sat down.

"Oh, she thought maybe it was a guy's-night out."

Malachi started rubbing above his right eye with his right hand. His face became warm on his right side. Between his ear and eye—above his cheekbone. He took a couple of slow deep breaths as Uncle Dale spoke. Malachi wasn't fully hearing his words. He knew the gist of what he was saying—he was talking about the unseasonably warm weather with very little rain.

In a quiet tone, only audible to Uncle Dale, Malachi said, "You're really hurting for money, aren't you? You're considering bankruptcy."

Uncle Dale sat back as he squared his shoulders. "Who told you?"

"Uncle Dale, I really feel bad for you. But I have this sense, a strong inkling—things are going to work out better than you expect. And in a way you would have never imagined."

"So, who told you?"

"No one...I mean no human told me. It's hard to explain."

"You're spooking me. Are you saying God...?"

"Please, Uncle Dale, I don't want to talk about it. I had to say what I said. Things just come to me, and I don't understand either. Can you just take the words and be encouraged? As I said before, 'things are going to work out better than you expected and in a way that will surprise you.' I can't explain it. I mean...do the words need an explanation? There's good news in your future. Could you use some good news, Uncle Dale?"

"I sure could, Malachi. I feel better already. And coming from a man of..."

"Let's just order some food. I'm hungry. What are you going to order?"

"I'm going to have the house special. The Pork Chop Sandwich. It's the best meal in town."

"That sounds good to me."

Mandy headed on over to their table, and they both ordered a Pork Chop Sandwich Platter.

"Can I get you two anything to drink?" Mandy said.

"Give me a Trilogy Dark," Uncle Dale said.

"Trilogy Dark?" Malachi said. "That sounds pretty...ah...I'm fine."

The second Mandy left, Malachi said, "So tell me what's going on, Uncle Dale."

Malachi never remembered Uncle Dale being in such a transparent mood. Even though Malachi's reason for jumping the conversation Uncle Dale's way was to avoid revealing the calamity in his own life.

Uncle Dale hadn't seen the construction business this slow—ever. He was stretching his resources on a condo project, when the economy abruptly turned.

"I got hit bad," Uncle Dale said. "Really bad."

And then he turned confessional, "I was going to the casino too much." He then told Malachi everything.

Malachi was thinking, "This is the kind of conversation Christians are supposed to have with each other—open and honest. Does it ever happen?"

Still, like most men, Uncle Dale ended with, "I'm going to be alright."

Malachi could tell by his eyes; his words were the opposite of the way he felt.

And then in a quiet measured tone, Uncle Dale said, "So you think I'm going to make it?"

"What I said, Uncle Dale, is, 'Things are going to work out better than you expect. And in a way you would have never imagined.' And I really believe those words."

Malachi had never seen Uncle Dale cry before. It would be easy to assume he hadn't cried much in his life. But when Malachi added, "Those words also include your battle against cancer."

Uncle Dale put his hand over his face and looked down.

Malachi turned away.

Neither of them saw or heard Mandy approach, "I've...I've got your food." She stood there motionless for several seconds.

The silence echoed enough to make the moment feel sacred.

Malachi shifted his focus toward Mandy. The way he looked her in the eyes welcomed her in.

And then he said, "Thank you, Mandy."

"If you guys need anything, let me know. Anything."

Uncle Dale raised his head, "You probably want to pray before we eat."

"No. Not really."

"You always pray."

"Let's eat before our food gets cold."

"You're not going to pray?" Uncle Dale said. "Well then, I'll..."

"You never pray, Uncle Dale."

"Shut up. The food's getting cold," Uncle Dale said. "God bless this food that we are about to receive. Thank You for it. In the name of Jesus. Amen."

Malachi took a bite. "Wow, this sandwich is great."

"Told you. Best food in town," Uncle Dale said. "So, what's going on with you, Malachi? Maybe start off with the no-praying deal."

"Where did you learn to pray?" Malachi said.

"Betty and I've been going to church some. When you're down looking up, you might just as well look way up." He pointed his index finger toward the ceiling. "But it's your turn, Malachi. Don't try to get me talking again."

Malachi shook his head. "There's so much." He gazed upward, shaking his head some more. "I don't know."

"I'm not asking for the whole house. Just give me the outline."

"Well, if it was a three-point sermon, it would be. Point one: I'm through with God. Point two: I'm through with Annie. Point three: I'm through with my job at St. Amos Community Church."

Malachi ate a couple more bites of food. Uncle Dale kept looking at him. But he didn't say anything. Inside, Malachi strained to hold back the mess, the failure his life had become. He despised himself for how much of a hypocrite he was being.

Somehow, he managed to hold back the tears of a broken man. But the torrent of his words started to flow. And wouldn't stop for nearly an hour. He guarded the private issues of the marriage breakdown. And he only went so far as to say, "Very ungodly things are going on at the church."

The bulk of what he told Uncle Dale centered on not being able to trust God anymore. He listed his failures. Coupled with what he thought God should have done. He told Uncle Dale, "Almost everything I've done for God has failed or has fallen short of even minimal expectations."

Uncle Dale said very little, except when Malachi started to stall out. Just about any question offered enough fuel for another spurt.

"I hung all my trust on God. I thought He would help me keep my job. I finally had a full-time ministry job. You can't imagine what I've been through in disappointments. I'm just through with God."

And with those words, Malachi was finished spilling his load.

Uncle Dale sat there without a response. Malachi was silent and spent. Then Uncle Dale folded his arms, leaning forward, "Is God through with you?"

"Uncle Dale, don't get churchy with me. Can we change the subject, now?"

"Sure. If that's the way you feel."

"Uncle Dale, I've said enough for now...I'm sorry I dumped on you."

"Yeah, I think you needed it."

"I sure did."

"Speaking of needs, do you need a job?"

"I'm going to need something."

"Why don't you get a job at Walmart? I did a bunch of remodeling work for Sally and Max Benson; she's a manager down at Walmart. I've seen her there a few times. We have a great relationship."

"I don't know, working at Walmart? I've got some other options. I mean...I'm not desperate. Thanks for the suggestion."

Malachi checked his watch, "Hey, we better get going."

Malachi hugged Uncle Dale outside the restaurant. "We'll be in touch. OK."

When Uncle Dale was out of sight, Malachi walked back into DT's.

He caught Mandy's attention. "So what's the deal on the cook's job I see posted outside?"

"I thought you were going to be working construction."

"My plans changed."

"Do you have any experience?"

"No, I've never worked in a restaurant."

"The boss won't even let you fill out an application then. Timothy is only looking for experienced help."

"Thanks, anyway."

"I'm sorry."

"It's not your fault."

"You never did tell me your name."

"It's Malachi."

"See you around, Malachi."

"I hope so."

Out in the Dark

Chapter 15

If lonesomeness was dark, pitch black would have engulfed Malachi, once he left DT's.

The light was extinguishing from the Manistee sky toward Lake Michigan. And out of the National Forest to the east, a nearly full moon rose, orange-faced. Tourists strolling the city's downtown would have described the weather as, "A perfect night."

Malachi didn't connect *separation anxiety* with the way he felt. He was only three steps from DT's front door. Yet, an insurmountable mountain separated him from a life six and a half hours to the south.

Nowhere—that was his destination as he wandered the streets of his new hometown. While his feet carried him aimlessly, his mind worked diligently to secure a strategy. Too much of his plan had revolved around working for Uncle Dale. This obstruction was disrupting, detouring, and trying to defeat his flight to freedom.

The words, "When you've got nothing—nothing man, that's when you're really free," kept careening around inside Malachi's head. Keiv Spinks had expounded this to Malachi as his axiom for living. They were both nineteen at the time. Smoking a joint together. Keiv's words had blipped into Malachi's conscience many times over the years.

Tonight, they had the comfort of a warm blanket out in the dark. And though he had never truly grasped what Keiv meant, the wearier he became, the more profound his words grew.

Still, he didn't want to be that free. And last time he had heard, Keiv was in prison.

Malachi had noticed a Days Inn bordering the Walmart parking lot. A room would cost him $62.00. He counted his money— $263.00. He parted with $62.00 and headed to Room 17.

His lostness and anxiety slipped down a couple notches as he sat on the bed of his home for the night. He turned on the T.V., flipping around a selection of channels; he landed on the Detroit Red Wings versus San Jose Sharks hockey game. He turned down the volume.

Malachi toyed with his cell phone and then laid it on the dresser.

He pulled out a notepad and wrote across the top Action Plan. He glared at it for a few moments—tore the sheet out of the pad, wadded it up, and shot a basket from four-feet away.

Starting over on a fresh sheet, Malachi wrote, To Do List—My New Life. And then numbered each item as he compiled his list:

1. Find a job
2. Find a place to live
3. Call Stephen Johnson
4. Call Annie?
5. Call church?

He stopped writing. Doodled briefly to the right of what he had written. And then crossed off Call Church?

He continued:

5. Walmart? —Sally Benson
6. Money

He tapped a beat on the notepad and then added his last item:

7. See Mandy??

He placed the pad next to his cell phone and kicked up the volume on the T.V.

Malachi followed the Red Wings enough to care, but not enough to dance when they won or to get teary when they lost. Still, he was enough of a fan to know, most of the time they lost, it was the ref's fault. This playoff game was one of those—the refereeing resulted in a Red Wing's parade to the penalty box.

Sleep won before the Red Wings lost. Without Malachi.

Malachi's New Life

Chapter 16

Malachi awoke easily. He stared into the fog of a time-warp sensation as he considered how much had transpired in the last twenty-four hours. It was as if fifty gallons of life and emotions had been dumped into a two-gallon bucket of time.

He dressed—shorts, long sleeve t-shirt, and his running shoes. And went out into the Manistee morning to gauge the weather. A cloudless, 55-degree day welcomed Malachi. Perfect—he was off on a run.

Sketchy familiarity with the roads motivated Malachi's decision to set out on an out and back route—heading west on Merkey Rd. Located one block south of the motel parking lot. He knew, if he ran far enough west, he would end up at Lake Michigan. Malachi guessed the distance was within his range.

Never a fast runner, still his pace accelerated well beyond slogging. As he hit his relaxed stride, all the essentials of a good run came together.

In the range of two miles, Malachi arrived at the bluff overlooking Lake Michigan. The low waves shimmered, reflecting the morning sun from the east.

The steep dune-bluff was suspended four stories above the water's edge. A worn switchback path descended to the shore, skirting a sizeable outcropping of rocks and stones as it neared the beach.

Malachi scanned out to where the sky touches the water—engulfed in the grandeur of the beauty.

"Are you finding what you're looking for?"

Malachi whipped around.

A lanky man had his eyes fixed on Malachi—grinning at him. His thinning, mostly brown hair was short and windblown. Besides his cockeyed smile, Malachi noticed a dancing sparkle in his eyes.

The question passed through his mind, "Is this drug or alcohol induced?"

"Did I scare you?" the man, who appeared to be in his seventies, asked.

"Ah...you startled me. Where did you come from?"

"I asked the first question; are you finding what you're looking for? You look a little lost."

"He's dressed a notch too nice for a bum," Malachi surmised. "Still?"

"I don't know," Malachi said. "I don't even know what I'm looking for."

Turning back toward the lake, he gazed again at the far away line where dark-blue water danced with bright-blue sky.

"Do you think you can hide from God?" the man said.

Malachi spun around. "I'm through with God! ...who are you?"

"But is God through with you?"

"Who are you," Malachi asked a second time.

"Does it matter who I am?"

The old man then put on a pair of sunglasses—cheap looking, oversized, black-framed, toy-like glasses. And walked to the edge of the bluff. After taking a few steps on the switchback leading to the beach, he stopped and turned around. "Maybe you should get a job at Walmart."

Malachi scowled at him.

The man then continued his descent to the beach.

Malachi said to himself, "Bum."

He stared at the old man as he reached the shoreline. Walking southward, his head cocked back and forth and up and down. Bumping Malachi's appraisal from odd to kook.

Malachi glanced the other way for five seconds. When he turned back to the south and sighted down the shore—the man had vanished.

The vista was long and clear. Malachi rubbed his right hand on his lips as he intently scoured the beach. His eyes roamed every inch of the sand.

"That was so strange," he whispered.

Malachi carried the experience back with him on the return run. He couldn't dwell on it though; his *To Do List* began tugging on his pondering brain.

Back at the motel, he showered. Packed. And headed to the complimentary breakfast. His notepad and ink pen were his morning companions. While eating, he added *8. Call Uncle Dale* to his *To Do List—My New Life* and put a check mark next to Call Stephen Johnson.

He had yesterday's newspaper with him. Skimming through it, he saw a headline—*Take a Hike in the Manistee National Forest*. As Malachi scanned the article, he stopped and placed his finger on the fourth paragraph: "The Manistee National Forest is ideal for backpackers because camping is allowed anywhere on National Forest land unless otherwise posted." He underlined: camping is allowed anywhere.

He wrote on the pad—*9. Stop by ranger's station*. Malachi recalled running by it on Merkey Rd.

He gathered everything from the breakfast table and departed to his Suburban.

The first thing he did was call Stephen Johnson.

"Hello."

"Stephen, this is Malachi returning your call."

"Where are you? What are you doing?"

"Stephen, here's the deal. Unless you agree to keep everything confidential, I'm not ready to say much."

"I guess…I mean, what are my options? I won't tell anyone; you have my word. And Malachi, I want you to know it matters a great deal to me what happens to you."

"Ah…ah…thank you," Malachi said. "Tell me what's going on back there, first."

"We've got a big mess. It's awful. Just awful."

Malachi listened as Stephen described in detail the elder's meeting, which resulted in Malachi's termination. His voice sounded so dejected—it was like one defeated soldier burdening another defeated soldier with a bad report. While Malachi was thankful to be talking to Stephen, the pain piling on broke open a wound of despair.

"There's a bunch of gossip making the rounds. You know Mattie... she's a talker...Pastor Neil should have never let her in the meeting... Annie won't answer her phone or the door...St. Amos Community Church may not survive this blow...and nobody can figure out what happened to you."

Stephen paused for several seconds. "You need to help me put this puzzle together. Tell me what's going on, Malachi. Why didn't you go to the meeting with Pastor Neil? Who told you about it? Pastor Neil is trying to figure out who squealed."

"God showed me in a dream. I knew the day before what was going to happen."

"You're serious?"

"It's exactly as I told you. And here's pretty much the rest of the story. I'm starting over, here in Manistee. Bottom line: I'm through with St. Amos Community Church. I'm through with Annie. I'm through with God."

"What are you talking about? Sure, I understand the St. Amos part. But what about Annie? You're leaving her, just like that...I mean, how long have you been married? At least fifteen years."

"Everybody thinks we have a great marriage. This mayhem has opened a door for me to get out of a situation, which has been pounding on me for a few years."

"A marriage is not a *situation* we get out of because it's convenient or inconvenient. Almost all marriages, especially good ones, are challenging. Mine is. How many times do think I've felt like giving up?"

"Stephen, tell me; how many times has Gracie been unfaithful to you?"

"You mean sexually? Like an affair?"

"Of course, that's what I mean."

"Well...never."

"Stephen, Annie and I were just faking it. Good actors, huh? We fooled everybody. Sure, we had some good times. But she doesn't love me. I don't know why we were even together anymore. She's in love, but it's not with me."

They were both silent.

"I left her over four thousand dollars," Malachi said. "She can have the house and the car and nearly everything else. I'll send her more money when I get a chance. I'm starting over."

"At age forty-two?"

"At age forty-two."

"Sounds like you're trying to be a martyr."

"I'm not going to put her through as much pain as I've had to endure. I could tell you a lot more. There's no point to it. I've made my decision."

"What did Annie say?"

"We haven't talked. I'm sure she doesn't care. Actually, more like, she's glad I'm gone. I left her a note plus the pile of cash…. she's probably celebrating. Stephen, I'm through talking about it."

"So, you're telling me your through with God, too?" Stephen said. "That doesn't make any sense."

"I ah…I don't …I…I trusted God for my job at St. Amos Community Church. Something I had waited a long time for. I have no trust for God anymore. I can't believe Him for squat. Just about everything I've done for God has failed. And what hasn't failed has been so disappointing…I really don't want to talk about it."

"What about my daughter, Sarah, and the children's Sunday school?"

"I'm through with God. Sarah's awesome because of you. Not me."

"That's not …"

"I don't want to talk about it. You heard me."

"But what…"

"I'm through talking about it!"

"OK, OK," Stephen said. "Malachi, I don't know what to say. But still, I would like to know about the incident with the police and this medical marijuana deal—this is all tied into Pastor Neil's vendetta against you—I'm foggy on all the connections."

Malachi told Stephen about the police raid and the smelling marijuana incident in the church's furnace room. He also talked about his dream regarding Pastor Neil. And confessed his own former addiction to marijuana.

"So, you think he's a user...I mean illegally. And addicted? That's what you believe."

"Stephen, I'm sure of it."

"Do you know about Pastor Neil's: *Jesus, His Compassion, and Medical Marijuana?*"

"No, I don't. Never heard of it."

Stephen then described the twenty-eight-page document, which Pastor Neil had asked Mattie to distribute to the elders.

"So, you were unaware of what Pastor Neil had written? But you knew about all these other links to his involvement with marijuana."

"That's right," Malachi said. "So, what's the consensus among the elders?"

"Pastor Neil put a lot of work into his manifesto—*Jesus, His Compassion, and Medical Marijuana.* He didn't throw it together in a few days. His arguments are compelling. Informative. Well-researched. Very convincing. In addition, no one knows your side of the story, except Annie. Is that right?"

"Annie only knows about what happened over at Pastor Neil's house on Monday. That's it. But she's on his side anyways."

"You never told Annie any of the other stuff?"

"No...I ah," Malachi said. "It's complicated, Stephen. I mean...our... Annie and I struggle with properly communicating. We struggled a lot. So, when we needed to really talk, when the pressure was on—we failed. We both failed."

"Yeah, I can understand that. Every couple needs better communication. And the devil is adept at leveraging this vulnerability against married couples. The Bible calls *the devil the prince of the power of the air* and from what..."

"Let's get back to the elders, Stephen. What do they think?"

"Well, Pastor Neil has most of the elders in his camp already. And if not, they don't have any fight left in them."

"What about you?"

"Even before I heard your side, I was opposed to medical marijuana. And the rest of it—of course. I'm going to fight. Pastor Neil goes or he gets clean or my family and I are leaving St. Amos Community Church. I'm on a mission, Malachi. I just wish more of my motivation was fueled by something other than ungodly anger."

"What a mess, Stephen."

"Yeah."

Neither one said anything for several seconds. The silence caused Stephen to say, "Malachi, are you still there?"

"I'm still here. Stephen...do you...do you believe it? I mean...I'm involved in pornography? Would I be so stupid to do it at church?"

"It's very alluring. Happens all the time. But for some reason, my gut tells me different. But that's not my style—following my gut. I'm more fact driven in my objectivity. Mattie did say she saw *porn* searches on your computer."

For several more seconds, there was silence. Then Malachi said, "All...every one of those searches involved research. For the youth group—Pastor Neil knew what I was doing...I told him. They were all anti-porn, mainly Christian sites—only a handful of sites. You know the software we have installed doesn't even allow access to porn or other offensive sites. Don't you think, if I was smart enough to bypass the software, I would have known how to cover my tracks?"

"But you didn't. And you got caught."

"I didn't have to. I didn't have anything to hide. Go over to the church and check my computer for yourself."

"Can't. Pastor Neil had a computer tech come in and clean it all out."

"You don't see anything odd about that?"

"Malachi, we're not going to resolve this right now. We could go round and round all day. I need to check out some things for myself. I need some time...everything's spinning out of control. I ah...for now... for now, I'm going with my gut—I believe you."

"Thank you, Stephen."

"But I need to absorb all this," Stephen said. "I have a meeting; I need to get going. I wish this would all just go away...I really have to go. Malachi, promise me we can talk in a couple of days."

"Absolutely. We need to talk. I would like that. And you promised me you wouldn't tell anyone. No one."

"I'll keep my word. God bless you, Malachi."

"Sure."

Hello Walmart

Chapter 17

Malachi started the Suburban and took the twenty-five second trek from the Days Inn to the adjoining Walmart parking lot.

He checked himself in the mirror. Took a deep breath. And headed into Walmart.

Saturday morning shoppers were indomitable in their quest to— Save money. Live better. Malachi turned around near the greeter's area. He had never taken the time to view Walmart from this perspective. With the steady stream of people pouring through the doors, it looked as if Manistee was being evacuated—into Walmart.

He made his way to the service desk, where another sizeable knot of people had congregated. The line moved steadily. Considering that returns and complaints ended up here, everyone was in good spirits.

Malachi recalled Pastor Neil's ironic warning, "You are heading down a treacherous path. Your whole career could go down the tubes. If you continue, you are going to end up as a greeter at Walmart." He had portrayed the job of a Walmart greeter as meaningless—a job no one would want. Even at the time, Malachi had found Pastor Neil's comments to be arrogant, smug...snobbish.

He watched every blue and khaki clad employee from a point of view he had never imagined or considered before.

As he looked around, Malachi thought to himself, "There are a lot of hard working, salt-of-the-earth types employed here. It has to be better than working for a dope-head pastor."

And by the time he left the store and had interacted with an array of Walmart associates, Malachi realized he would fit in well.

Still, he quivered when he asked the associate at the service desk, "Can you help me? I'm trying to find Sally Benson."

"She works overnights—third shift. She's usually gone by nine in the morning. But sometimes, she stays later. I'll page her for you."

"Sal call 317. Sal call 317. Thank you," reverberated overhead.

In less than a minute, he heard the service-desk phone ring. The associate said, "There's someone here to see you, Sal."

"She's still here." She pointed. "Go to the back of the store and take the double doors to the left of the *Site to Store* sign; she'll meet you there."

"Thank you," Malachi said.

He located the double doors with two-way swinging hinges and pushed it open. Straight ahead of him were three computers and one printer perched on a utilitarian countertop. Employees were working at two of the computers. One person was sitting. The other stood as he briskly punched the keys.

As Malachi glanced around, he noticed there wasn't one sniff of fancy back in the business end of Walmart. Engrossed with all the movement of people, Malachi perceived that a purposeful tempo was a common denominator among the workers.

Soon, Malachi saw a woman approaching him—probably forty, maybe a little younger. Athletic—he noticed her bulging biceps—in a feminine way. She looked like she could have played power forward in high school. And it appeared she was still capable of taking it to the hoop. Her shortish, brown hair set off her get-the-job-done build.

He tried to stifle the thought, but it plowed its way through. "She's kind of hot."

She peered at Malachi. "Are you the person who's looking for Sally Benson?"

He nodded. "That's me."

She extended her hand. "I'm Sal."

"Malachi Marble."

"How can I help you?"

"My uncle, Dale Marble, said you might be hiring."

A big smile washed across her face, and instantly, Malachi's heart rate subsided.

"I love your uncle. You couldn't find a better builder. How's he doing?"

"He's doing good...well, works a little slow. Actually, really slow. I was working for him, and well, I'm not working now. And Uncle Dale suggested I come talk to you."

"It seems like we're always hiring. Less lately, though, with the economy. We do get hundreds and hundreds of applications. And..."

Malachi interrupted, "I'm a good, dependable worker."

Sal said, "Well, if you're anything like Dale, we..."

"I am."

Sal looked at him, "Malachi, you seem a little desperate."

"I'm ah...sorry."

"Tell you what, Malachi; fill out an application on the Job Center computer. It's right outside the double doors—to the left as you exit. Do that, and I'll pull up your application when I come back tonight. But right now, I've got to go home and get some sleep." She smiled a tired smile and shook Malachi's hand.

"Thank you so much, Ms. Benson."

"Call me Sal."

Malachi needed forty-five minutes to fill out the application. He was surprised at how much concentration was required to answer the numerous arrays of questions. Satisfied with his answers, he sensed hope and excitement about the possibilities of a job. And as he continued observing with fresh eyes, the more he could envision himself working at Walmart. And enjoying it.

Before he left the store, he needed groceries. But first, he went to the Sporting Goods Department and located the camping gear.

He compared numerous items. He strolled back and forth, reading the boxes, and checking prices. The tents received the most scrutiny.

He pulled a piece of paper and an ink pen from his pocket. And jotted down a list:

9'x8' tent—$32.88

LED rechargeable lantern—$15.88

Blue coffee pot—$11.88

Blue mug—$2.88

Folding frying pan—$6.88

7 in 1 Hobo Tool—$3.88

At the bottom, he wrote *$65.00*—underlining the total cost.

Uncle Dale the Liar?

Chapter 18

Malachi returned to the Suburban.

His To-Do List had found a home on the passenger seat. He picked it up and crossed off line seven—*Walmart*. Then he counted his money—$183.00.

He looked around the Suburban. His guitar was still safely lodged behind the passenger's seat. A smattering of items was scattered on the seat behind him. And Malachi had folded down the third seat to make the cargo space larger. His eyes scanned over his gear, with a geometric analysis of the Suburban's interior space.

Malachi determined, "I could sleep in here, but camping would be so much better. More adventurous."

He pointed the Suburban in the direction of the Manistee National Forest Ranger Station. The mellow green building with the galvanized-hue metal roofing was located a mile from Walmart. The Ranger Station, which sets down a gentle embankment off Merkey Rd., already had several cars in the parking lot.

The casual, wood-motif interior had enough maps to please the most adventurous hiker. But too many for Malachi to decipher through.

So, he patiently waited his turn to speak with the uniformed ranger on duty.

"I'm looking for information on camping. I read you can camp for free in the Manistee National Forest."

"Those are called *dispersed sites*." She shuffled through some papers. "It's free, but you need to pay a $30 yearly fee for parking. Let me see here...yes, this is a list of the camping sites in the vicinity."

She pointed toward the lobby. "There are free maps over there. They coordinate with this list." She continued—noting highlights of the Manistee National Forest and explaining the basic rules. Malachi could tell she was someone who enjoyed her job. Her attentiveness and willingness to dispense information as she answered questions made camping preferable to any of Malachi's other options.

He thought, "That's her job, to enthusiastically sell the usage of the forest."

Her devotion transformed Malachi's apprehension into anticipation. He read down the list of sites: Red Bridge, Saw Dust Hole, Turquoise Bottom Creek, Elm Flats, Bowman Farm, Hopper Junction, Jackpine, Tunk Hole, Rainbow Bend, and Hodenpyle Dam. And that was just one of the lists. His adventure radar went to full-alert as the names of the camp sites stirred his imagination.

"How many acres are there in the Manistee National Forest?" Malachi said.

The question sparked the ranger's already pleasant facial expression. She looked like a *straight-A* student being asked about her report card.

"There's a half million acres in the Manistee National Forest and another half million in the Huron National Forest," she said. "When added together, the two national forests are equal to the size of Rhode Island."

"Wow, that's amazing," Malachi said. "A person could disappear forever out there."

"People try to disappear once in a while. They think they can run from their troubles. You know, there are two things I've learned: You can't run from your troubles and you surely can't run from God."

Malachi wanted to say, "I can." Instead, he tightened his cheek muscles to form a smile. "Hey, thanks for all your help."

He walked toward the Suburban, thinking, "Thirty bucks for a parking pass? Hmm?"

Malachi turned on his cell phone and punched in Uncle Dale's number.

"Uncle Dale, how are you doing today?"

"I'm not at my peak—probably overdid it last night. I really have to watch it. Still, I sure had a good time with you at DT's."

"Same here," Malachi said. "Hey, I went to Walmart and applied for a job. I talked with Sal Benson—she sure has nice things to say about you."

"She's a nice lady. I hope things work out for you at Walmart."

"I do have a favor to ask you. I put you down as a reference and ah…"

"That's fine."

"Well, there's more. I…ah…I put down that I've been working for you for the last year and a half."

"Why in the…why did you do that? That's not the truth. That's not right."

"Uncle Dale, calm down. I didn't mean to upset you. I didn't think it was a big deal."

"Maybe you don't think so. I've spent thirty-five years building my business. Honesty has always been a hallmark of Dale Marble Construction. Sure, I'm not a church goer, but I still know how to do the right thing."

"You don't want me to get the job? Is that what you're saying?"

"You know that's…"

"If I tell them I worked at St. Amos Community Church, they'll call there. I'll get burned. I'll never get the job. Pastor Neil will tell them I'm a pervert, a lousy worker. I'll get burned…I'll, I'll…please Uncle Dale, just this once. I need your help…please."

Neither one of them said anything for several seconds.

"Malachi…I'll help you. You can trust me. Just listen though; I need to do something."

"OK. But what are you talking…"

"Quiet please," Uncle Dale said. "Dear God, help me to do the right thing. Help Malachi get this job. Thank you, God. Amen."

Malachi sat silently—shaking his head. And then he said, "Maybe He'll hear you."

"He'll hear you too."

"You don't need to preach at me. I never preached at you."

"Maybe you need it more than I did."

Malachi chuckled. "Thanks for everything, Uncle Dale. I'll see you."

Malachi Shops for a New Home

Chapter 19

Clouds from the northwest smeared their dirty gray over the pure blue sky. Malachi shuffled through the stack of maps and brochures from the Ranger Station. In an ironic way, he was having the same inner response as someone searching through enticingly designed real estate handouts.

It was time to go *house shopping*. So, Malachi pumped thirty dollars' worth of gas into the Suburban and wheeled it out beyond the city's east edge—into the vast Manistee National Forest. He had his maps, but for the first part of his excursion, they rested in the passenger seat as Malachi followed the nose of the Suburban into unknown territory.

Old Stronach Rd. to Six Mile Bridge Rd. to Nine Mile Bridge Rd. to roads south with names he didn't note. And dirt roads without names.

He simply wandered. Malachi said to himself, "I need to check out the lay of the land."

When he spotted a sign for Udell Rd., he remembered the map

indicated a lookout hill at the end of it. So, he veered onto the road, following it a couple of miles as it climbed towards the high point.

He briefly considered, with a hint of angst, the $30 parking sticker—the one his financial squeeze had forced him to put off buying for now. He thought, "They'll probably give me a warning if I get caught—I hope so."

The drive, mostly uphill, cut thru a mixture of hardwoods and pines. The leaves were at the tender phase of their spring growth. Their gentle greenish hue infused a refreshing backdrop to the darkness of the heavy woods.

He expected to have a short hike after driving most of the way to the top. When he got out of the Suburban after driving as far as he could, he was disappointed. The *lookout* shown on the map was for a hundred-foot tall fire tower that was no longer in use. Moreover, barbed wire wrapped around the steel-framed tower obstructed anyone from climbing it. The tower hadn't been used in years, but in its day, it was manned by a spotter, whose job was to prevent massive forest fire devastation through early visual detection.

Staring at the tower, pondering his mistaken perception of the lookout, Malachi heard the growl of a motorcycle. It was a black Kawasaki 250 Road and Trail bike heading toward him. The driver stopped beside Malachi.

Mr. Local Friendly Guy, who Malachi soon learned was Kenny Thigpen, was an encyclopedia of information. History, folklore, legend, and likely a few lies mixed in spilled out as Kenny chatted about the tower and the Manistee National Forest. He was especially delighted in telling the story about the time he and his buddies bypassed the barbed wire to make their way to the top of the fire tower—with some beer for partying.

"I was hoping to get a big view of the forest. I thought Lake Michigan would be visible from up here," Malachi said.

"It is from the tower," Kenny said. "And there's a place the locals call The Top of the World. From there, you can see everything."

"How do you get there?"

"I know how to get to The Top of the World, but most of the roads don't have names—others are only snowmobile trails. You just have to know how to get there, to get there. If you know what I mean."

"Maybe someday, I'll make it to The Top of the World."

"Do you want to go right now?"

"Sure, I have time."

"Hop on the back."

Off they went on Kenny's Kawasaki 250.

The wide dirt road merged onto a two-track. They stayed on the two-tracks for several miles. Kenny negotiated many road intersections without signage—merely some numbers. He didn't slow down enough to look at them though.

Kenny achieved the full-thrill from his Kawasaki 250. Malachi's adrenalin was pumping full throttle as they screamed through the majestic woods. Soon, the two-tracks narrowed into trails—confining they were nearly touching the branches as they tunneled their way through.

Malachi was lost in the first five minutes.

Even with the craziness of Kenny's maneuvering through the heavy woods, Malachi felt confident in his ability. After about forty minutes, they broke through to The Top of the World.

The lookout offered an exhilarating view of treetops, the Little Manistee River, and Malachi could even see a hint of Lake Michigan to the west.

He contemplated, "My place, my campsite, is out there somewhere."

"Kenny, this is amazing. Thanks for bringing me up here. This is so awesome."

"No problem, Malachi. Hey, would you like to go higher." Kenny said with a smile.

Malachi looked around but he couldn't see any hills elevated above The Top of the World. "What do you mean?"

Kenny's smile turned into a beaming smirk as he pulled a joint out of his pocket. "You want to smoke some weed? We'll be higher than The Top of the World."

Malachi looked up at the sky and shook his head. "No thanks, Kenny. I'll pass. It's not my thing."

"That's cool."

Kenny put the joint back in his pocket and started to point out some of the sights. He was in no hurry. Malachi considered asking him for a campsite suggestion but chose to keep the matter to himself.

"Are you ready to head back down, Kenny."

"Just say the word."

Kenny's downhill driving proved to be more thrilling than the ride to the top. It was like a race. They swept through the corners, even brushing a few feathery branches. On the two-tracks, he gunned it. Dust billowed off the rear wheel, once they reached the wide dirt road. On one straightaway, Malachi saw the speedometer tick slightly over seventy miles per hour.

When they stopped, Malachi said, "Thanks Kenny. That was a ride to remember. Makes me want to get one of these Kawasaki 250s."

"They are a blast."

Kenny extended his hand. "Malachi, maybe I'll see you around town sometime."

"I hope so. Thanks again, Kenny."

Once he returned to the Suburban, Malachi ate some of the food he had bought earlier in the day at Walmart. He pondered all the possibilities for camping spots. He needed seclusion, restrooms within a reasonable distance, and a river or pond for bathing. A water spigot would be a plus.

He looked at his watch—still plenty of time. So, Malachi opted to rove some more— "Maybe, the ideal spot will find me."

Soon, he arrived at a little berg—Wellston. A few houses, stores, a church, all adjoining Crystal Lake. The lake, three quarters of a mile around, was surrounded by Norman Township Park. Malachi liked the hometown feel of the area. The park had a swimming beach, basketball hoops, a picnic shelter, and a sign on the water's edge, decreeing *No Gas Outboards.*

The whole setting said, "Laidback and welcoming," to Malachi. He could picture himself living in one of the light gray, beige, or off-white cottages across the road from the lake.

Wellston seemed like an idyllic place to stay. Malachi knew this was only a fantasy. He needed something cost-free. And closer to Walmart.

He picked up the map, moving his head closer so the small print would be legible. His eyes studied it for quite some time. And then he tapped his finger on the map—*Turquoise Bottom Creek*—a campsite with a small creek running out of a speck of a pond. He cross-referenced the campsite to another sheet with a list of its accoutrements. Only one was listed—*toilet.*

Malachi figured this would mean fewer people in the area.

He pointed the Suburban west and then south. The roads went from paved to dirt and then joined with a two-track. Leading deeper and deeper into remoteness. Malachi checked the map frequently. Two-tracks cut in and out of the forest. As he made his final two turns, he estimated the commute back into Manistee at twenty-minutes.

A big smile came over Malachi's face when he pulled into the Turquoise Bottom Creek parking area. Inside—he just had a feeling.

A path led through a sizeable grove of oak and mixed hardwoods. It gradually inclined, rising two stories above the parking lot. A two-block hike and Malachi was at the top. Here, a medium-dense stand of pines crowned the hill. Their lower branches had minimal growth, while the tops offered a draping canopy. The hill sloped south. A bit of Turquoise Bottom Creek was visible. Which was five minutes away—via a trail zigzagging through the woods. The footpath then continued as it skirted the creek. And within half a mile, it reached the spring-fed pool. Reeds lined the pond, except for an opening fifteen feet wide where campers trekking to the water's edge had created a passageway.

Up in the cascading pines, Malachi staked his claim. A patch of ground covered in pine needles—with a view to the south.

Malachi explored the area. And checked out the toilet. It smelled bad; he thought to himself, "Don't they all?"

As nightfall approached, Malachi decided to sleep in the Suburban. He still had food left. And a blanket from the cargo area kept him warm. The temperature continued to drop as the final light melted from the west…gray clouds with stiff streaks of black took over the expiring sky.

Malachi tilted the Suburban's front seat back, wrapping himself in the blanket. The dark got darker, and soon, a demanding rain sounded against the Suburban.

The pitch-blackness became eerie. Disquieting, to the brink of scary. Malachi closed his eyes, allowing his mind to glide toward the brightness of a very satisfying day.

And soon, he drifted off to sleep.

Sunday without God

Chapter 20

Malachi's cell phone rang at 7:10 a.m., waking him up.

"Hello. This is Sal Benson. Forgive me if I'm calling too early."

"No. I was hoping you would call."

"Malachi, can you come in this morning or tonight? I've received permission to hire someone for an ISS position. With summer around the corner and all the people coming up to Manistee, we get hit hard with freight. We need more help. I reviewed your application. And Dale called me. So, do you want to come in tonight or this morning?"

"What time this morning?"

"No later than 8:30."

"Great. I'll be there as soon as I can."

"Just come through the double doors. I'll be in the office."

"Thank you, Sal."

Malachi rushed down to the creek to clean up and shave. The temperature was in the forties, but his excitement vanquished the discomfort.

Before leaving for Walmart, he checked his map, knowing he would have several forks and turns to negotiate.

Malachi slowly rumbled over the two-tracks to the dirt road and then hit the pavement. He thought to himself, "That wasn't too bad."

He gunned the engine and turned up the heater to full blast.

As he neared town, the numerous tall steeples of Manistee toggled an emotion in Malachi. Yesterday, they had blended into the sky. Today, it hit him, "It's Sunday." The practice of going to church had been a part of Malachi's fiber.

Even as he pushed away the sentiment, a sensation of missing an essential family event, gnawed at him. After a little mental exertion, he jostled the thought from his mind.

This effort centered on his locked-in resolve, "I'm through with God. I'm through with God... I'm through."

A mental picture of Sarah Johnson and Sunday School made one more valiant attempt to make inroads.

Malachi countered decisively. He invoked his crucial need for the job at Walmart. "God couldn't help me keep my job at St. Amos Community Church, so I'll have to get one without His help."

He arrived at Walmart. Parked close. And soon, Malachi was going through the double doors leading to the office. Sal saw him when he appeared in the doorway of the tiny office. Malachi later learned, the office was shared by all seven of the store's assistant managers—Sal's official title.

"Good morning, Malachi," Sal said. "This is our store manager, Burt Gunner."

Burt extended his hand. "Good to meet you."

He turned toward Sal. "I'll see you before you leave." And then exited the office.

"Close the door. Sit down, Malachi. Let me pull-up your app." She swiveled her chair to face the computer screen with her back to him.

For Malachi, it was like riding in a car sitting behind the driver. If he wanted to, he could have peeked over Sal's shoulder to view the computer screen.

As she maneuvered the mouse and tapped the keyboard, Malachi thought, "I wonder what Uncle Dale said to her?"

He studied what he could see of Sal's face. "What's taking her so long?" It felt like ten minutes.

He heard squeaks when she shifted in the chair.

Malachi's face grew warm when she turned around. There was no pretense of a smile or any other token of cordiality in her expression. A ripple of emotion seized Malachi. The image of Annie's face from a dreadful moment a few days ago flashed through his mind.

"I don't like working with liars," Sal said. "Poisons any work environment. Malachi, do you like working with people you can't trust? Dishonest people."

Nearly whispering, Malachi responded, "No...ah...no I don't."

Sal stared at him. Malachi wanted to leave.

"Your Uncle Dale called me. And he told me the truth...about you, Malachi," Sal said. "He also told me about the cancer and everything. And that he might not..."

She peered over Malachi's left shoulder. Gazing upward. She swallowed hard and turned back to Malachi. "I love Dale. He's a good man. A really good man. An honest man."

She glanced away—silent for several seconds.

"Dale's...a really good man," she murmured into the air.

She then shifted back to Malachi. "If," she said firmly, "everything else checks out—your other references, drug screen, etc., you'll have a job here at Walmart."

As if he was exhaling, Malachi said, "Thank you."

"I'm not through."

"Sorry."

"We're never going to talk about this conversation. Ever. Or with anyone else," Sal said. "Do you understand!" She paused and then continued, "Walmart is a company with a high standard of integrity and ethical standards. I could lose my job over this. And I would deserve it. Do you understand!"

"Yes, I do, ma'am."

She then gradually transformed back into the Sal he had met the day before. She handed Malachi a card with all the details regarding his drug screen on Monday.

"The plan is for you to start Friday on overnights. That's 10:00 P.M. until 7:00 A.M. Your job title is ISS—In Stock Specialist."

"That's great. I'm going to be a *specialist*. I was assuming I would be a stocker or something like that. So, what will I be doing?"

She smiled. "ISS is our fancy term for stocker. Sounds impressive. Your job will be to pull your freight to the floor, get it out of the boxes, price it, put it on the shelves, make the shelves look neat, clean up after yourself. And go home. You'll start out at $8.60 an hour."

"I can do that."

Sal continued explaining details, procedures, and policies. She informed Malachi that his days off would be Tuesday and Wednesday.

"Orientation will be on Thursday. Someone will call you."

Sal explained to him what orientation involved, along with vacation and holiday particulars, the disciplinary procedure identified as coaching, and the fact that, in most instances, an associate will be given a D-day, a Decision Day, as the final step before termination—a paid day-off in which the nearly terminated associate spends the day writing out their plan for reversing their unacceptable behavior.

"An Action Plan," Malachi said.

"Exactly."

"Do you have any questions?"

"I'm sure I will, but not right now."

"Orientation will answer most of your questions."

Sal stood up. Malachi followed suit. She looked him in the eye. "One more thing, Malachi, I work my butt off, and I expect you to do the same."

"I always give it my best, Sal."

As they shook hands, Malachi thought, "I'm going to like working for her."

His excitement was irrepressible. The moment he pushed the double doors, exiting the store's back room area, he pointed his index finger toward the ceiling, swinging his eyes upward, "Praise G...ah...a... thank goodness."

Malachi nearly danced over to the Sporting Goods Department. He pulled out his list from the other day:

9'x8' tent—$32.88

LED rechargeable lantern—$15.88

Blue coffee pot—$11.88

Blue mug—$2.88

Folding frying pan—$6.88

7 in 1 Hobo Tool—$3.88

He picked out the tent, put the lantern on top, and tried to grab the coffee pot with his other hand. A Walmart associate coming around the corner from the adjacent aisle spotted Malachi fumbling.

"Do you need a shopping cart?" the associate said.

"That would be nice."

By the time the shopping cart arrived, Malachi had his list completed. He then added matches, a hatchet, and a water jug. He looked at his wallet and re-evaluated his stockpile.

Satisfied, he headed to the checkout. As he paid for his items, he calculated how much he would have saved if he had qualified for the employee's 10% discount.

As Malachi walked toward the exit, he heard, "Congratulations!"

Startled, Malachi jolted around. It was the old man he had encountered yesterday at the Lake Michigan bluff. He was standing off to the right in the returnable-can/bottle alcove.

He was smiling. "The Lord sends rain on the righteous and the unrighteous."

"What are you talking about, old man?"

"The name's Carl. And God just gave you a job. Maybe you should thank Him."

"You're full of cr..." Malachi stopped. And turned away, staring at the shopping carts in long rows on the other side of the entryway. He took a couple of deep breaths, shifting back toward the bottle-room. "I'm...ah...sor..."

He looked intensely. Carl had disappeared. Malachi stood there staring. "What's going on?"

Malachi turned and exited the store. He then loaded his new camping gear into the back of the Suburban. And re-counted his money—$86.00.

Hungry, Malachi wanted to celebrate. DT's Good Time Place had the appropriate name, the food was the best in town, and, "They have really good help."

He took in a notepad, along with his laptop, so he could check his e-mail. He arrived just as they opened, heading for the same table in the corner. He opened his laptop, looking up when he heard, "Can I get you something to drink?"

Malachi glanced around, "Is Mandy here?"

"I'm not good enough for you?" she said. "This is her day off."

"Oh. OK."

"So what can I get you?"

"Water and a coffee and your Pork Chop Sandwich Platter. Could I have a side salad, instead of the fries?"

"You sure can. Tina's my name if you need anything."

Malachi watched her walk away. She dressed exactly the opposite of Mandy. And Tina almost had the body to optimize the tight, revealing look.

Malachi shifted his attention to his laptop screen. He scanned his e-mail messages.

From Pastor Neil: "Malachi, please contact me immediately." Malachi deleted it.

From Stephen Johnson:

Malachi, thanks for talking with me. Please stay in touch. Church-life has never been so awful. In spite of that, my faith and confidence in God remains firm. For now, I'm just trying to let some things land. If you know what I mean. Everything's up in the air—needs to settle before moving forward.

God bless, Stephen.

Malachi quickly replied:

Good talking with you. Think I've got a job. Used you as a reference. Hope that's OK. Will call soon.

Malachi.

He was surprised to have an e-mail from Junior McSchmitt—one of the elders.

Malachi, I feel terrible about what happened. We were sabotaged. That is no excuse. Please forgive me. I wish I had said some things to you when you were still here. Seeing all the new children coming to St. Amos Community Church was inspiring. I remember thinking about how much you loved the children. And how dedicated you were to Sunday School. Your efforts to bring life back to St. Amos through your work with the children surely pleased God. I will be praying for you.

Junior.

He added a Bible verse at the bottom of his e-mail: "And we know that all things work together for good to those who love God, to those who are the called according to His purpose."

Malachi sat staring at the computer so intently that Tina startled him. "You doing OK.?"

"Sure. I'm fine."

He sent Junior a reply. "Thank you. Your kind words mean a lot to me."

The absence of any e-mail from Annie didn't shock Malachi. Though he couldn't pretend it didn't matter.

He soothed his own guilt by thinking, "At least I left a note."

As he slowly ate, he gawked disconnectedly at the big screen TV on the wall. The restaurant started to fill with people and noise. Malachi noticed neither.

He composed an e-mail for Annie.

Annie, my intent was not to hurt you. Actually, the opposite. I just couldn't handle everything that hit me all at one time. Realistically, you will be happier without me. I apologize for everything. I hope you can try to understand. I will send you money when I can. I check my e-mail about once a week.

Malachi.

He hit *send* and shut down his laptop.

Once the bill was paid and the tip placed on the table, he concentrated on getting back out to Turquoise Bottom Creek to set up his campsite.

It had been years since Malachi had camped, but he remembered how to set up a tent. He carefully prepared the ground—the spot where he would erect the tent, making sure the door faced toward the optimal southerly vista. He gathered rocks to make a fire ring. And then spent nearly an hour scouring the forest for a sizeable pile of wood, covering it with pine branches to help keep it dry.

Malachi arranged the interior of the tent. He placed one of his blankets under the sleeping bag and the other two beside it, realizing there would be some cold nights ahead.

Then he built a fire and cooked his first meal. A simple supper—he heated up a 40-ounce can of Walmart chili. Once he started working, his plan was to eat most of his largest meals at work, using the microwave for cooking, and the break room refrigerator for storing select groceries.

Malachi retrieved his notepad. He wrote, *Pay $30 at ranger station* and *Get chair.* He tapped on the pad a few beats and then counted his money—$76.

He put his hand up to the side of his face, touching his finger to his lips. He glanced at his money and stared into the fire. Scanning the notepad again, he placed a question mark after the note; *Pay $30 at ranger station.*

Malachi thought about retrieving his guitar from the Suburban. Except...as the fire faded, so did he.

The guitar did not move. And either did Malachi—until he crawled into the tent for the night.

Walmart-Here Comes Malachi

Chapter 21

Malachi woke up with a fresh outlook. The swirl of life had subsided, and he was anticipating getting back into a routine. He reflected on a peculiar concept, "When you're in a routine, it seems like a rut. But when you're not in a routine, it feels chaotic."

So, after the most chaotic week of his life, Malachi longed for a rut. He sensed the week's pace would intensify as it built toward his first night at Walmart—Friday.

On Monday, Malachi went for the drug test, did his laundry, and acquired a P.O. Box. He continued exploring the Manistee area. And fine-tuned his campsite.

He sensed a bit of good fortune when he found a white plastic chair along the curb, mixed in with some other trash. One of the legs was cracked—some duct tape from the Suburban, a hearty stick, and Malachi had his fireside-throne.

On Tuesday, Malachi went to Walmart for the official you've-got-the-job paperwork. Called a *Job Offer*. This sealed the deal. It wasn't exactly like signing for the Red Wings, but Malachi could tell that he was inking a deal with a championship team—the world champion in retailing. At that time, Sal gave Malachi his official team uniform. A blue Walmart-issue, two-button, collared shirt. She also informed him, "Overnight associates are allowed to wear blue jeans."

After leaving the store, Malachi knew he should make some phone calls and check his e-mail. But he opted to slide the tasks to another day.

Wednesday was orientation—an all-dayer at the store. Malachi was celebrative knowing Walmart was paying him for this effort. And receiving his official Walmart name badge made him feel like an insider. Additionally, the badge would activate the time clock and ninety days down the road, it could be used to secure a ten-percent discount on general merchandise and select groceries.

One other new associate was also being oriented with Malachi. Her name was Molly—a first shift cashier.

Walmart's three guiding principles were the overriding theme for the orientation. Distilled to the simplest terms: be nice to the customers, be nice to each other, and do your best.

Malachi fully accepted the principles the first time around. But by the eleventh presentation, each a varying hue of the same concept, he was getting a little antsy. Unfortunately, the trainer used the same repetitiveness to ingrain numerous other Walmart tenets and essential information.

Yet, on further reflection, Malachi thought, "Walmart is the most profitable retailer on Earth; they know what they're doing."

A store tour, especially in the non-public area, fascinated Malachi— since he had no retail experience. He found out that his assumptions regarding the retail process and the actual process were a planet or two apart. The idea of learning this Walmart-style of doing business intrigued Malachi.

Serena, the trainer who guided them through orientation, knew volumes. And her humor added a pleasant zing to the day.

Once Malachi left the store, making a couple of calls became his number one priority. Procrastinating any further would have unpleasant consequences.

So, he made the call he was dreading.

"Hey Uncle Dale, this is Malachi. Thanks for your help. I got the job at Walmart."

"Good."

"How are you doing?"

"Fine."

"I hope you're not still upset with me."

"So, is there something else you're going to ask me to do? You're probably running out of friends."

"Uncle Dale, I was desperate. Come on. I know you have a reputation for being honest. But even you would be lying if you said you were one-hundred percent honest all the time. And you expect me to be perfect."

"It's that: whoever is without sin, let him cast the first stone sort of deal," Uncle Dale said. "Like it says in John 8:7. I understand—no stone throwing."

"Exactly," Malachi said. "Are you turning into a Bible thumper?"

"I don't know about that. I do have a lot of free time. Can you think of anything better to do?"

"We'll, ah…see you, Uncle Dale."

Malachi needed to call Stephen. Beyond his promise, he understood that maintaining this link was important. In addition to the fact that their friendship was growing.

"Stephen, this is Malachi. Do you have time to talk?"

"All the time you need," Stephen said. "So, you got a job?"

"Yeah, I sure did. I'm pretty excited."

"So, what are you going to be doing?"

"I'll be working at Walmart. I'm an In-Stock Specialist."

"That's impressive. It's great you didn't have to start at an entry-level position. So, what are you going to be doing?"

"Stocking—on third shift."

"Oh…ah that's great. A job's a job, especially in this economy. You've got something to praise God for there, Malachi."

"Not really," Malachi said. "So, what's going on with you?"

"Pastor Neil had the propaganda machine spewing on Sunday. You should have heard his sermon. You were in it a couple of times. Not by name. Let's see; you were a wolf in sheep's clothing, a serpent, tares among the wheat, and I thought for sure you were going to appear as the anti-Christ. In all seriousness, it was awful. I almost walked out. Gracie keeps reminding me, if I leave, I won't be able to influence the outcome. She's right. Good news for you. You're going to get three weeks' pay. Some of it's your regular pay, and the rest is stipulated in the church bylaws."

"Give it to Annie."

"Are you sure?"

"Yes. And I would appreciate if you could take care of getting it to her."

"I can do that," Stephen said. "So, you're doing OK?"

"Things are turning my way. I mean, I've only been here a few days. I think I'm going to like living up here. Manistee impresses me as a great place to live."

"Glad to hear it."

"Stephen, I have another favor to ask you. It's kind of a big one."

"What do you need?"

"Tomorrow evening at 6:15, drop in on Annie. It would be a plus if you could take your computer tech with you and check out my home computer. Give it a thorough examination. See what you find in the *pornography* search category and stuff like that. You know what I mean."

"I can do that. I'll give Annie a call right away."

"Don't do that."

"What?"

"Just go. A surprise visit at 6:15."

"Are you going to tell me what's going on?"

"I had a dream on Saturday night."

"A dream?"

"It was one of *those dreams.*"

"I thought you were through with God. And now you're telling me you've had one of *those dreams.* So, what's going on?"

"I don't know. I'm asking you for a favor. I can't explain everything. I never have understood why I get dreams and visions and inklings. I have the same questions. Can you trust me?"

"I'll do it."

"Thanks, Stephen. We'll be in touch."

On Thursday morning, Malachi was back at Walmart for a full-day of work. On the day's agenda were CBL's. Most Walmart employees learn to groan when they hear *CBL*—Computer Based Learning. "Boring," is the mantra chanted by many Walmart associates offering their opinions on CBL's.

Malachi spent hours in front of a computer screen watching a vast array of learning oriented videos. Followed by a test on the material just viewed. A failed test required re-watching the training video, followed by a re-test.

Even after today's marathon, CBL's will become an ongoing way of life for Malachi as a Walmart associate. One or two a month will become the norm. And they are not optional.

While CBL's are an excellent training tool, Malachi had to fight frequent drowsiness. The CBL's covered nearly every aspect of Walmart-life. From how to avoid selling cigarettes to minors to the proper procedure for cleaning up a bleach spill to defining behavior considered sexual harassment to how to use the motorized lift equipment. On and on…and on and on…and…

Malachi was pleased with his performance for the day. He completed and passed his required CBL's. This achievement allowed him to go home early for the day.

His mind was already out the door as he approached the Apparel Department.

Malachi turned when he heard someone say, "What do you think of these t-shirts?"

It was the old man, Carl, holding up an olive-green t-shirt. Across the top in three-inch, brown letters was the word: *WANTED*—with a picture of Jesus affixed below. And underneath the picture, in three-inch letters, it said: *JESUS CHRIST*. Followed by more text, half the size—in red: *To give His people the message of salvation through the forgiveness of their sins—approach with open arms—REWARD—ETERNAL SALVATION.*

"Malachi, do you like them?" Carl said.

"How do…you know my name?"

Carl pointed at him. "It's on your name tag."

Malachi glanced down. "Oh, yeah."

Carl held up another t-shirt. "This one's nice; isn't it?"

Behind Carl was a standard blue cardboard Walmart t-shirt display case, emblazoned with white letters touting: *Save Money. Live Better.* It held a variety of Jesus-oriented t-shirts. With a pricing placard above the merchandise, claiming: *Unbeatable Prices. $8.50.*

"What was your name again?" Malachi said.

"Carl," he said. "It sure is nice to see Jesus at Walmart."

"Hey, Carl, I'm sorry I got mad at you the other day." In Malachi's mind, he was thinking, "This guy's a nut-case, but that's no excuse for my behavior."

"I accept your apology."

As Malachi turned to leave, Carl thrust his hand toward him. In it was a sealed envelope. "This is for you."

Malachi opened the envelope while walking out the door. Inside were three ten-dollar bills and a Manistee National Forest parking decal. He said to himself, "I was wondering how I was going to eat until payday."

Malachi stuck the sticker on his windshield and drove out to his campsite. When he pulled into the parking lot, he saw a Ranger's truck.

The Ranger approached him. "So how are you doing? Looks like you've found a nice spot."

"I'm doing well. Camping's great out here."

As they talked, Malachi noticed the Ranger glancing over at his windshield.

"Just making sure you had your window sticker. The boss told us to crack down on people without parking stickers. It's irritating when people think they can get away with such inconsiderate behavior. It's only thirty bucks. And it is the law."

"I hear you. Thanks for stopping by."

"See you around."

At 8:15 that evening, Malachi called Stephen. "Stephen, this is Malachi. How did your adventure turn out?"

"Wow, you nailed it. Annie was cooking out with ah...some guy."

"Tim."

"I don't know his name. Annie was extremely flustered. It was easy to see the guilt on her face. It was so apparent; I felt awkward. Tyler, my tech guy, spotted the same thing. When I asked if we could look at the computer, Annie went spastic, telling us to just take it—get it out of here. We didn't stick around long; we grabbed the computer and left. She never even bothered to say goodbye."

"How did my computer check out?"

"Exactly as you said, Malachi. A handful of searches for anti-porn sites. I think they were all Christian ones. Tyler scoured your computer for evidence. He knows his stuff. You're clean."

"Thanks, Stephen."

"But now, I feel even worse about what happened."

"Don't. If Pastor Neil hadn't used the porn-angle, he would have figured out some other way to burn me."

"You're right."

"One more thing," Stephen said. "And I hope I didn't overstep my bounds. I dropped a note off at the bank for Annie. It was strictly about the pornography situation. The best I could, I explained everything to her. I hope ah...that's OK with you. I just thought..."

"Stephen, thank you so much...I didn't...ah...I didn't know how to deal with it. Thank you so much."

"Let's stay in touch, Malachi."

"Definitely."

Malachi at Walmart -the First Night

Chapter 22

Malachi paced around the campsite, checking and re-checking to see if he had his Walmart badge and the official company box cutter Serena had issued him at orientation—the Easy Cut.

How do I look?

Lunch?

What time should I leave for work?

He thought, "I hope I can do this." He felt like a bead of water sizzling away on a red-hot skillet. "Crap, what if I fail at this too."

The twenty-minute drive to work had more emotional jostling than the road had turns.

Maybe I could have gotten a better job...I'm fortunate to have a job...maybe I won't be able to handle the job physically ...I'm in excellent shape for forty-two—most people guess me to be a lot younger...there are probably a lot of losers working on third shift... you're not exactly a winner yourself; besides, this is Walmart; they know what they're doing...why did I even move to Manistee? What were the options...insanity? I hope I can stay awake all night...that's what coffee's for...I'm a loser...what do you have to lose?

Ah...nothing.

Malachi sat in the Suburban for a few minutes, once he had landed at Walmart. He watched, trying to speculate which people walking into the store might be his coworkers. Malachi realized he was about to face the most awkward part of the new job experience.

He gave himself one last encouragement, "I've always liked meeting new people."

A six-inch thick wall separated the break room from the massive retail area. The break room—this is the associate's home-away-from-home. The size of a two-car garage, yet elongated in its layout. Nine-foot drop ceiling, with the walls painted one tone darker than off-white.

On one end is a kitchenette. This straight run of countertop and cabinets filled one of the room's narrow-dimensioned walls. Two microwaves are suspended above the counter—one on each side of a stainless-steel sink. Two white residential-style refrigerators are perpendicular to the rest of the kitchenette.

Grayish-white vinyl tiles with dark-hued speckles cover the floor— worn, yet shiny and clean. Four white molded plastic tables sit at a right angle to the same elongated wall the refrigerators rest against. The tables skirt very close to the wall, and in some places, they touched the wall, leaving scuffs on the paint. They are the standard church-potluck size. Additionally, two more run down the middle of the room, flowing in the direction of the room's long dimension. Adjacent to these tables and on the opposite side of the room were four vending machines. Coke, Pepsi, and Sam's Club receive equal billing. The other vending machine tempts associates with candy bars, snacks, junk food, etc.

People gathered in different configurations. A few associates sat alone.

A smattering of newspapers, books, and stuff connected to food consumption lay on the tables. No one paid any attention to Malachi.

People were coming and going—through doors at opposite ends of the room. At nearly ten o'clock at night, the swirl of movement was steady.

He placed his lunch in the fridge and sat down two chairs from the edge of the table nearest the kitchenette area. The chairs were the basic-issue, brown molded plastic with chrome tubular legs. Malachi leaned forward and rested his left elbow on the table. His left hand rubbed against his chin.

Moments before ten o'clock, Sal hurried into the room with papers in hand. "How's everybody doing?"

She received a minimal response. And then said, "I want everyone to meet our new associate, Malachi." She pointed at him with the hand still holding the papers. "He's our new ISS associate. Make sure you make him feel welcome."

Sal continued, "I want to thank everyone for working so hard last night. We got hit pretty hard. And we were down a couple of stockers. I'm hoping to get one or two more ISS associates in the next week or so. Those of you who were here last summer know how intense it gets around here when the vacationers return."

Then Sal assigned the associates their stocking duties for the night. She designated either an aisle or a department.

"Malachi, you'll be working with Stu in Four and Thirteen."

One of the associates turned to look at Malachi when she said this.

"Who wants to lead stretches tonight?" Sal said as the team meeting neared its conclusion.

Malachi soon discovered that no one ever wanted to lead stretches. But they were consistently a springboard for jovial bantering.

Once the stretching routine was completed, Sal raised her voice, "One, two, three; Walmart!"

The rest of the associates, with mild enthusiasm, chimed in, "One, two, three; Walmart."

Everyone then trooped to the office, where Sal issued pricing guns. And then they were off to the warehouse area.

Malachi had never touched a pricing gun before. Upon seeing it, he did have a vague recollection of store employees using this popular model while he was shopping.

The Monarch 1131 was almost toy-like in appearance. It's brown, textured plastic surface hid an intricate mini-machine. Within this rugged fifteen-ounce tool is a sophisticated mechanism.

A small twist-knob selects the combination of numbers and symbols, which the gun inks onto the pricing tape. The ink cartridge, half the size of an AAA battery, provides black fuel for over ten thousand pricing stickers before expiring. A paper coil of pricing tape five inches across and half an inch thick works its way past the ink cartridge, rollers, and pins before exiting the top of the Monarch 1131. A squeeze of the hand-activated trigger spits a pricing sticker out of the gun. A slap on the merchandise and the adhesive backed label was affixed to the product.

Malachi grew to respect his pricing gun. He was amazed at how the seemingly flimsy tool stood up to nonstop pounding night after night or how the tool rebounded from being accidentally dropped on the concrete floor. And more than once in his stocking career, Malachi would hurl the Monarch 1131 to the floor in a burst of frustration.

He was looking at his newly issued pricing gun, when he heard, "I'm Stu. You'll be working with me tonight."

"I'm Malachi."

"First, we'll pull our freight out to the floor," Stu said as he pointed to a pallet jack.

Stu led by example. He shoved the jack's nose under a pallet, pushing it until the vertical body collided with the load. Pump, pump, pump on the handle as the load lifted off the floor. He spun around, his arms stretching backward, gripping the jack's handle. He leaned forward like a horse pulling a plow.

Stu appeared to be fifteen years younger than Malachi with a nearly identical body build—5'9", 155 pounds. Malachi noticed one thing different—Stu's arms. Taut muscles protruding from his blue t-shirt bulged with engraved definition as Stu drug the weighty merchandise to its destination out on the sales floor.

Malachi mimicked Stu's skid pulling maneuvers. And within ten minutes, fourteen skids were out on the floor adjacent to Four and Thirteen.

Department 4: *Paper Goods*—toilet paper, paper towels, paper plates, all types of bags, aluminum foil, napkins, tissue paper, etc. Department 13: *Chemicals*—bleach, laundry detergent, fabric softener sheets, liquid fabric softener, dishwasher products, sponges, brooms, mops, air fresheners, drain cleaners, bathroom cleaners, kitchen cleaners, insect and rodent control items, etc.

Within three weeks, Thirteen became, as Sal called it, "Your home." Malachi would spend the majority of his time stocking Department 13—which occupied an aisle and a half of the store's interior real estate.

Malachi sized up the skids piled high with shrink-wrapped merchandise.

"Wow...there's a lot of stuff here."

Stu laughed. "You just wait until summer—when Manistee gets crowded. We'll get killed. Some nights, we'll have twice this much. Or more."

"Are you serious?"

"Serious as sin. Yeah...ah, serious as sin. Yeah, sin."

Stu looked directly at Malachi. "Sin...what do you think of sin, Malachi?"

Malachi wrinkled his forehead, "What are you talking about?"

"Sin...ah, well what I really meant, do you know Jesus?"

"Which aisle is He working in? Is that the Hispanic guy working in Frozen Foods?"

"Do not be deceived; God cannot be mocked."

"OK, OK, Stu."

"So, are you saved, Malachi?"

Malachi grinned, "Saved from what?"

Stu started talking faster than an early-morning radio DJ fueled on three cups of coffee. "'For God so loved the world that He gave His only begotten Son that whosoever believeth in Him should not perish but have everlasting life.' John 3:16. You need to believe in Jesus, and you shall be saved."

"Is that it?" Malachi said.

Stu plowed onward, "'For whosoever shall call upon the name of the Lord shall be saved.' Romans 10:13. Malachi, do you want to hear my testimony? I should be dead. The Bible says, 'For by grace are ye saved through faith and that not of yourselves it is the gift of God.' That's Ephesians 2:8."

"So, do I call or believe, or is it grace or faith or what? Seems to me a simple call would be easiest."

"Well...it doesn't exactly work that way."

"I can't just call the Lord. And be saved?"

"Let me explain..."

"Hey Stu, you know what? I think maybe Jesus wants us to put some of this stuff on the shelves, so we don't get fired."

"Yeah, we can talk later."

"Ah...sure."

For the next twenty-five minutes, Stu showed Malachi all the basics of the job. They started unloading the freight for Chemicals by maneuvering skids into the aisle. Stu would grab a box and toss it on the floor near its destination. Stu darted up and down the aisle unloading the pallets. One skid after another were *down stacked* in this fashion.

Malachi was picking up boxes also, but Stu was doing three times more work. Malachi would determine the box's content and then scan the shelves trying to find the products' destination.

Many times, Stu would glance at the box he was holding and point, "It goes right there." Adding, "Don't worry; you'll catch on."

Soon, boxes cascaded in mini-mountains up and down the aisle—a chaotic mess from Malachi's perspective.

"Once you figure out where things go, you won't be able to down stack," Stu said. "Sal won't let you. You'll have to work off the skid or load your freight onto a rocket cart."

"Rocket cart?" Malachi said.

Stu pointed toward the grocery section of the store to a four-wheel cart, which resembled a chrome tubular shelving unit. With no top shelf.

"OK, Malachi, I need to get over to Paper Goods so I can get my freight up," Stu said. "Start getting your freight out of the boxes, price it, and put the stuff on the shelves. Be neat. Go as fast as you can. If there's no room on the shelf for a full box, leave it, and I'll show you later what to do with it. And when I get finished with Paper Goods, I'll be back to help you. If you need anything, I'll be in the next aisle."

And then, before departing, Stu taught Malachi how to work the pricing gun—in eighty seconds. He slapped the gun on a box top—bap, bap, bap—emphasizing his verbal explanation.

"If you run out of pricing tape, let me know; I'll show you how to change it." Stu snapped open the gun, "You'll probably have enough for tonight." Reclosing the Monarch 1131, he handed it back.

"Look on the pricing labels on the shelf to find the price for an item." Stu placed his finger on a shelf label as he further explained the procedure.

He then ran the short course on how to use the official Walmart box cutter—the Easy Cut.

"Tell you what, Malachi, this is what I do most of the time." Stu wedged his right hand under the sealed box's flap and yanked upward. He spun his hand around, jerking the other flap open.

"And if the box is taped closed, this works." With the heel of his hand he smacked the side of the box just below where the two top flaps were taped together. His pounding hand dented the box enough to cause a small loop of tape to project upward. He snagged the tape, ripping the box open. The whole procedure was done in a smooth, refined motion.

"Wow, that's slick."

"You need to learn every trick you can. Sal and Robert will be timing you soon. Believe me, they will let you know if you're not fast enough—it won't be pleasant," Stu said. "Nobody likes stocking Chemicals. So, you're probably going to get stuck here."

"Why don't people like Chemicals?"

"Lots of freight. Heavy lifting. It's difficult to make your times. You can, but it's demanding."

Stu then left.

Malachi *gave it his best.* And started experiencing a measure of athletic exhilaration as the minutes swiftly evaporated.

Not long after he had crossed over into *the zone*, Malachi heard, "Here are your picks."

He looked up to see a rocket cart three-quarters full of freight.

"I thought I already had all my freight," Malachi said.

"These are *picks*," the lady said. "By the way, my name's JC."

Malachi slowly repeated, "JC."

"Janet Collings. I go by JC. That's what my pappy always called me."

"I'm Malachi."

She stretched out her hand. "Well, I'm glad to meet you, Malachi."

"So, what's all this stuff?"

"These are *picks.*"

JC went on to explain an integral part of the stocking process. When freight is being stocked, if there's a box of merchandise in which all the items cannot be placed on the shelf because of lack of space, it is called *overstock*. So, the overstock ends up in the backroom warehouse area of the store.

There, an associate systematically scans the overstock with a tool similar to a cashier's handheld scanner. In addition to being scanned, the item is labeled and placed on a specific warehouse shelve. And a designated area of that shelf. The scanning and labeling allows the item to be located via the store's computer system. When it's placed on the shelf, it goes from being overstock to being designated as *backstock*.

"A day or two later, when shelf space opens up, our computerized system tells us to bring the item back to the sales floor, so you can stock it. So, these picks were picked from backstock for you to put on the shelves tonight," JC said.

"How am I going to get all this stuff up too?"

"Better kick it up a notch."

JC lowered her voice, moving closer to Malachi, "Did Stu get you *saved*?"

"Tried to."

"He does that to everybody. He can be a pain in the behind—just plain irritating. But he's the fastest stocker here. Stu's a workhorse. We call Stu, *The Finisher*. After he blitzes through his own freight, he'll jump in and help everybody else finish their freight on time. You have to love him for that...he really has a good heart. And even away from work, he'll do anything for you. A couple of weeks ago, he came over and fixed a leak in my roof. Wouldn't take any money. He's a great guy."

By break time, Malachi was already experiencing fatigue. Entering the break room, he noticed Stu was sitting by himself. Malachi opted to avoid him.

He sat down at the table where JC was, along with two other associates—Martin and Spencer. Malachi sat drinking a Coke.

He heard Spencer, who works in the backroom warehouse with JC, say to her, "When are you going partying with me?"

"I think my husband would frown on that," JC said.

"Don't tell him."

"He would find out. And then he'll come looking for you and beat you up."

"I think I can take him."

"Oh, you do, Mr. Round Guy?"

"Hey, that hurt. I'm trying to lose some weight."

JC pointed at the bag of potato chips Spencer's hand had been disappearing into. "So it looks like you're on the onion-flavored potato chip diet?"

They both laughed. So did Martin. Malachi was nearly asleep.

"We better get back to work, slacker," JC said.

JC and Spencer headed back to their warehouse responsibilities.

Ten minutes later, Malachi was back out on the floor facing down his mountain of freight plus a growing heap of empty boxes.

Stu swung by to show Malachi the solution for disposing of piles of cardboard.

They stacked the boxes on an empty skid, trying to keep them from falling over. The tipsy stack was especially vulnerable when being pulled through the swinging double doors leading to the store's backroom area.

From there, Malachi maneuvered the skid to the rear corner of the store's warehouse. Here, he fed the cardboard boxes into the baler. It was called a baler, because the machine's final product is bales of cardboard prepared for recycling.

This green hydraulic monster, ten-foot-high and nine-foot-wide, had a mouth large enough to swallow twenty boxes in one gulp. To shut its mouth, a steel gate was pulled down from the upper lip. Once secured, a bop on a marshmallow-size green button activated the machine. Hydraulics drove an inch-thick steel plate from the top as the force crushed the boxes into flatish submission.

The steel plate then returned to the roof of the monster's mouth as the steel-gated mouth automatically popped open. With an enormous appetite, the monster sometimes would eat boxes all night. When full, a heavy metal door, which extended across the entire bottom of the green monster, was released and swung open. Five wires the gauge of clothes hangers were wrapped around the bale—twisted together at the ends to keep the cardboard from exploding.

Prods in the back of the lower level of the monster's mouth ejected the bale onto an awaiting skid. Then, once the heavy door was re-secured, the monster was empty. Ready for more cardboard boxes.

Not long before lunch, Sal came by to see how Malachi was doing.

"I'm doing OK," Malachi said.

"Tomorrow, I don't want you to down stack. Tonight was OK, so you could see where things go," she said. "And you need to take care of your empty boxes as you go—no more big piles. You have to keep things neater. You'll learn. Do you have any questions?"

"I think I'm good for now."

"Looks like you need to turn the dial up a little; I know you can do it," Sal said. "Can you give me your best?"

"You got it," Malachi said. But in his mind, he was thinking, "I'm already going at full capacity."

Still he dug a little deeper. And pushed a little harder. The main stimulation came from Sal's words—which he found irritating. And a voice in his head dispensing a fear-of-failure prophecy, pressed him to his physical limit.

By lunch, Malachi felt a sweaty, numbing buzz of exhaustion. But no hunger. His fuel for the rest of the night would be a two liter of Sam's Club Cola. Craving a quiet place to rest, a picture of comfy lawn furniture popped into his head. Malachi made his way to The Lawn and Garden Center. He was pleased with Walmart's selection of lawn furniture. He sprawled out on the cushy, canopied swing—hugging his two-liter. And promptly nodded off.

Fifty minutes later, he shook himself awake and looked at his watch. Alarmed, he darted for the time clock, punching back just in time.

The last half of the day rushed by. All of Malachi's mathematical calculations signaled a sizeable short fall of time needed to complete his assignment. He had been working his full-aisle, full tilt. But his half-aisle still remained untouched—mocking his ability to finish on time.

With an hour and a half left in the day, Malachi moved to the half-aisle portion of Chemicals. He stood there for a few seconds, staring at a sizeable mound of freight waiting on skids. He thought, "This is impossible."

Still he wasn't ready to give up—with determination, he thrashed into the awaiting pile, even as his energy waned.

A few minutes later, he saw Stu on the far end of the aisle. Malachi smiled, "The Finisher has arrived!" He also thought, "Praise God." He hastily dismissed the mental slip as an old habit. A bad one.

Malachi kept his head down, determined to do his part. He looked up intermittently—astonished at the speed in which Stu attacked the freight.

His pace was well over twice, closer to three times what Malachi was achieving.

They were going down to the wire.

Stu looked at Malachi, "You take the cardboard to the baler and do a quick zone. I'll finish the freight."

"*Zone?*" Malachi said.

"Neaten up the shelves. Pull the merchandise forward...get going."

"Hey Stu, thanks a lot."

"No problem. We're a team."

"We sure are."

At 7:01, Malachi clocked out. He drove the Suburban to the far corner of the parking lot and tilted the seat back. Sleep arrived swiftly.

When he woke up, his muscles ached, and his head was foggy—slightly disoriented. It was after nine o'clock.

As his cognizance returned, he eyed the store's looming façade. "In twelve hours, I've got to go through the whole thing again."

The entire night of work bounced around inside Malachi's head as he drove out to the Manistee National Forest.

His thoughts took a common human voyage. The exhilaration of crossing the finish line erased Malachi's painful experience. Like the marathoner collapsing in agony at the end, Malachi reveled in beating the challenge more than he dreaded the suffering.

Three More Days of...

Chapter 23

Malachi had left work. But his mind was still there.

From the time he woke-up, until pulling back into the Walmart parking lot for his second night of work, he had been mulling over solutions to the physical test he was facing.

At age forty-two, he was one of the older stockers. But in looks and physical strength, he felt more like thirty-five. He decided to scratch age off his list of obstacles. Even though he had significant muscle soreness, he knew his body would adapt. He was already looking forward to his days off. Figuring he would blob-out in an effort to allow his tired muscles to recoup. And for an immediate solution, he planned on buying a bottle of ibuprofen for ache relief.

Malachi thought, "I've got to work smarter not harder." And he had three immediate ideas for this category: knee pads, work gloves, and learn from Stu.

For some reason, one thought repeatedly edged into his brain. "It's not about the work; it's about the people."

He countered with, "It is about the work; I need this job to survive."

Malachi envisioned that the next three workdays would require a survival-mode attitude. When they were over, he would be on weekend. He could regroup then.

Sal assigned Malachi to Thirteen—Department 13. He laughed to himself. "I guess I've got Thirteen locked in."

With gloves, knee pads, and a triple shot of ibuprofen, Malachi was off to the races.

After about an hour, he heard from behind, "Looks like you're getting faster." It was Stu.

"It helps when you start to know where things go."

"What time are you taking break?"

"Ah...why do you..." As he looked at Stu, he felt grateful to The Finisher's stellar performance last night. But taking a break with the store evangelist?

"I'll come by," Malachi said. "I guess we can take break together."

Stu must have read Malachi's face. "I didn't mean to get so stirred up, yesterday." He looked up toward the ceiling and then at Malachi. "Do you want to go to Hell? I don't want you to end up there."

Malachi froze for a few seconds and then said, "Have you noticed? Nobody ever wants to take a break with you. Well, maybe once...if they're new. Ah...let me think how to say this...your, ah... let me put it this way. In the Bible, Jesus always seemed to have people around Him. Lots of them. You don't."

Stu looked down at the floor.

"Stu, let me know when you're going to break. OK."

Malachi found his stocker's rhythm. He grabbed a box. Set it down in front of the same item on the shelf. Ripped the box open. He spun the knob on his Monarch 1131, setting the price to match the shelf tag. With a flicking of the wrist and a squeeze of his hand, he hammered each item in the box to affix pricing tags. Speed, rhythm, concentration, and a compact motion produced the best results.

As fast and as neatly as possible, Malachi removed the merchandise from the containers placing the contents in their assigned spots. Tonight, Malachi needed to repeat this process nearly two hundred times—his freight for the night totaled one hundred and eighty-two boxes.

"Hey Malachi, I'm going to break," Stu said.

The conversation as they walked to the break room was all work. How's your freight going? Did you get many picks? I hope someone makes a bale.

They sat at Stu's regular table. Like church, after a while, most associates gravitate to the same seat or at least the same table.

"So where do you live?" Stu said.

"I just moved to Manistee. I'm ah...camping—out in the Manistee National Forest."

"So, do you go to church?"

"Are you trying to get me saved again?"

"Always."

"Haven't you ever heard that you're not supposed to talk about religion and politics?"

"I've heard that." Stu peered over Malachi's right shoulder, blankly gazing toward the wall and then returned his eyes to Malachi. "So, what do you think everybody was talking about in here during the Presidential election?"

Malachi laughed. "Probably politics."

"So, Malachi, who did you vote for in the Presidential election?"

"Ah...probably the same person you did."

"So now, I'm just trying to find out if you voted for Jesus—in your heart."

"You are something else, Stu."

"Tell you what, I'll still help you finish you're freight tonight, even if you don't..."

Malachi interrupted, "I'll tell you what. Here's the deal. We're probably going to be working next door for a while. Maybe a long time. You're going to stay on the Jesus thing until I crack. I can respect your dedication, but it's something I do not want to talk about."

"Why's that?"

"Stu, just give it a rest!" Malachi stood up. "I'm through with God. That's why!"

He exited the break room and returned to the floor. He sized up his progress so far. Malachi estimated that his load was lighter and his stocking pace was brisker than the night before.

Three more skids remained on the edge of the main walkway adjacent to Thirteen, and he had already killed off one sizeable pallet. This visual calculation pumped up Malachi. He was ready to roar back into his work.

He looked over at the three full skids. His eyes were searching. He scanned down his full aisle. And then walked over to Department 13's half-aisle, gazing up and down the aisle. He saw Stu down at the end on his side of the split aisle.

"You looking for something?" Stu said.

"Have you seen my pallet jack?" Malachi said. "I need it to move my skids around."

"No. Check Frozen. Gary probably snagged it. That's the way he is."

"Thanks...hey, Stu, I'm sorry I got mad."

"I'm sorry you're through with God. But we're cool. OK?"

"Sure."

The Frozen Department, merely referred to as *Frozen*, is separated from Thirteen by Aisle 12—Pop, Water, and Snacks.

Frozen encompasses three and a half aisles of glass-doored freezers. Gary, Kent, and Christine were the main associates assigned to this area of the store. They received a twenty cent per hour premium for handling the ice-cold stock. While unofficial and with no financial benefit, Gary was the pack leader of Frozen.

Stu was right. At least, it appeared so. "Did you take my pallet jack?" Malachi asked Gary.

He shifted, staring at Malachi. They had never spoken to each other. Possibly a "Hey" or a head nod.

"I think Walmart owns all the jacks. Not you." Gary said.

"That's the one I was using."

"I needed it," Gary replied.

"You don't think I needed it."

"Listen slick, our freight's different. You may not know this, but ice cream melts."

Malachi pointed to the doors leading to the backroom. "There are plenty of jacks back there."

"Well, go get yourself one."

Gary turned back to his work. Malachi walked to the backroom and pulled another pallet jack to the floor.

He turned his attention to stocking his freight as he attempted to tame his anger.

Lunch-hour showed up on time. Because of Malachi's focus and a shortfall in his desired progress, it seemed to arrive too early.

With an hour, he had time to shop. Not only for his lunch but also for some groceries, which he decided to store in the break room refrigerator, since he didn't have any means of refrigeration out at his campsite. Malachi purchased milk, a plastic container of salad, salad dressing, a small bag of apples, and an eight-pack of yogurt.

When he was placing the items in the refrigerator, he heard someone behind him say, "What's wrong, slick? Don't you have a fridge at home?'

He turned around. It was Gary.

"Malachi's my name. Is there a problem?"

"OK, Malachi. You may not realize it, but some of us want to put stuff in there too. It looks like you're hogging more than your share of space."

"Listen, Gary, I don't see anything on your name badge that says you're the *Fridge Supervisor*. You can't even figure out where to find your own pallet jack. Maybe you should work on that first."

"Listen, Slick..."

Malachi closed the refrigerator door and walked away.

After lunch, Malachi remained aggravated at Gary. Even as he rushed through the rest of the day, his mind kept flashing back to his two encounters with Gary.

Still, Malachi was able to put up the majority of Thirteen's freight. Stu handled a dozen or so boxes to help him finish. And then, as promised the night before, he gave Malachi a lesson on Zoning.

Malachi found the term zoning to be odd. He wondered why the procedure wasn't called *neatening the shelves* or simply *neatening*.

Stu said, "See this number in the top corner of the pricing sticker?" He placed his finger on it. "This tells you how many facings each product should have on the shelf."

He went over to the Great Value Lavender Bleach—96-ounce size. "See, the number is three, but there are four bottles of bleach across the front of this shelf." He rearranged the bleach so it had three *facings*. "You've really got to watch it. Otherwise, the shelves get all screwed up.

All the merchandise needs to be in its properly designated *zone*. And if you don't keep the counts of the facings right, you create a big mess."

He showed Malachi how to line up the faces of all the merchandise neatly and efficiently, while pulling items forward from the back.

He went on to describe four types of zoning. A Deep Zone: There's enough time to pull everything from the very back forward as far as possible. Quick Zone: Make the front of the shelf look good. Establish the correct face count. Pull forward one item from behind the front item. End Zone: Do a quick zone only at the end of the aisles. This is done, so when the managers walk by, there's an illusion that the entire aisle has been zoned.

Stu said, "Sometimes, that's all there's time for."

No Zoning: The freight load is so large or there are several call-ins. This forces zoning off the agenda—by necessity. This is rare, but it happens.

Stu concluded, "Typically, your zoning will be a blend between a Quick Zone and a Deep Zone."

Stu then helped Malachi do a Quick Zone.

And by 7:03, Malachi was sliding his name badge through the time clock's card reader.

Tired, but not as tired as the previous day, Malachi drove back to his tent in a light rain.

Sleep quickly overtook him, once he crawled into the tent. His sleeping bag with two blankets piled on top kept him generously warm. He woke up after nearly ten hours of sleep. The rain had quit. Malachi was pleased that his tent had remained dry. The pine-tree canopy helped assure this.

Awake but moving slowly, Malachi took care of business around the campsite. Time evaporated, and soon, he was heading back to work. He soothed his achy body and hazy mind with a TGIF cheer.

The calendar indicated Monday, but being his last day before two days off, it was like a Friday. All his co-workers used this vernacular. From Malachi's first day at Walmart, he heard workers saying, "It's my Friday...It's my Wednesday...It's my Monday." He found this to be an effective way for tracking the varying schedules of the third-shifters.

It didn't take long for the work routine to become a rut. While there was variety in the overall composite of the workday, it mainly followed a set pattern:

> 10:00 team meeting...*one, two, three, Walmart.*
> Pull the freight to floor.
> Stock.
> Take boxes to baler.
> 12:00 break.
> Stock.
> Take cardboard to baler.
> 2:00 to 3:00 lunch.
> Stock.
> Take cardboard to baler.
> 5:00 break.
> Stock.
> Take cardboard to baler
> Zone.
> Go home.

Malachi relished the comfort in the rut. The stability. The routine did not bore him because of the physical challenge. And the stimulation from all the new learning—which he realized could be ongoing if he decided to shift around the numerous opportunities available to Walmart associates. This included both vertical and horizontal job movement.

"Here's your picks, hon."

Malachi looked up, holding a bottle of liquid fabric softener in both hands. It was JC—smiling.

"Is she always smiling?" he wondered to himself.

"How are you doing, tonight?" JC asked.

"I'm doing well; it's my Friday."

"Good for you...party time."

"I don't know about that."

"You mean we're not going out partying?"

He laughed, "I thought you were married."

"Don't you like surprises?" she said.

Malachi watched her walk away. Her long black hair flowed to the middle of her back—pulled into a ponytail. Square shouldered and solid, a little roundish, JC looked like a farm girl who knew how to bale hay and catch the boy's attention at the same time.

The workday rushed by. Malachi really wanted to nail it. He felt a pulse of adrenalin as he was shooting to finish his freight by himself.

He looked at his watch, realizing he had worked past the usual break time. It was not a big deal. Associates did it all the time. He headed for the break room, thinking, "Coke."

Only two people were in the break room. JC and someone he didn't know—at least by name. JC, at a table alone, appeared to be sleeping.

He walked quietly past her and inserted his money into a vending machine. Click. Clunk. And he had his Coke.

Malachi made his way toward a vacant table.

As he prepared to sit down, he heard, "Too good to sit at my table." He recognized JC's hint-of-southern voice.

So, he went over and sat across from her.

"I thought you were sleeping. I didn't want to disturb you."

"Well, maybe, I was dreaming about you." She didn't smile. She already was.

Malachi felt his heart beating faster, especially after JC's foot bumped his under the table.

"So, where do you live, Malachi?" JC asked.

"I just moved to the area. It's a long story."

"There are a lot of long stories around here."

"Yeah. I've got a long story," Malachi said.

"If you ever want to talk—after work sometime, let me know." She was still smiling.

"Maybe. Maybe sometime, JC."

She stood up. "I guess break's over."

Malachi watched her leave the break room.

In a few minutes, he returned to the floor, making the final push to the end.

There was no pretending; his load of freight was lighter than the first two nights. Nevertheless, this took zero away from the satisfaction Malachi sensed upon completing everything on his own—freight, cardboard disposal, zoning. Everything.

And when Stu flashed him a wordless two-thumbs up, Malachi felt like a conqueror, a champion, a hero.

He couldn't help it.

And he didn't even try.

The Most Welcomed Weekend

Chapter 24

Malachi stepped out of Walmart and into the sunrise. Dissipating clouds. Cool. The muted sun had already made its way out of the National Forest. He was still a little buzzed up on adrenalin, resulting from the dash to complete the night's mission.

Bouncing around in his brain was the strange notion of having a weekend on a Tuesday and Wednesday. And he had already calculated—he had enough money left to *party* at DT's Good Time Place over the weekend.

Tired, muscle throbs; Malachi figured a solid-block of sleep would launch his first Walmart weekend.

By the time Malachi awoke, Tuesday evening was approaching. He lay on his back tucked deep into the inseparable warmth of his sleeping bag. He was limp—strength only for blinking and shifting his eyes. Lying motionless, it seemed so.

He fell back asleep; he dreamed.

When he stirred next, inside the tent, only muted light remained.

As the dream resurfaced. Malachi thought to himself, "I can't even get away from Walmart when I'm sleeping and dreaming."

He laughed. "If I'm going to be dreaming about stocking, maybe Walmart should pay me for sleeping."

Like a soldier with no battle to fight, he missed the clash, yet relished the R&R. Sleep engulfed him again.

He needed his flashlight when he rolled around the next time. His muscles were stiff, but the fatigue had dissipated. His mind was clearing.

Soon, he was outside building a roaring fire. He had had little time to enjoy the camping-experience aspect of his residence.

Malachi heated a pan of canned chili and cut up smoky links to enhance his simple fare. He stared into the fire late into the night. Several times, he thought about his guitar in the Suburban—still tucked behind the front seat. The guitar, he had at one time played almost daily, remained neglected.

Malachi knew predominantly God-centered music—this thwarted his desire to play the guitar. This separation from his guitar caused Malachi an extra measure of loneliness out in the big woods.

He shifted his thoughts to Wednesday's to-do-list. And he looked forward to visiting DT's. Planning to get there around four o'clock in the afternoon, he was hoping Mandy would be working.

Soon, the sleeping bag called him back into its cocoon.

Another overtime shift of sleep left Malachi refreshed.

Now, he was anxious to get into town to take care of a few necessities before visiting DT's.

First, he went for a run. Wooden legged at first. And while he achieved no appreciable tempo, his mind and body benefited from the therapeutic effects of maneuvering the trails.

He followed the run with a screamingly brisk bath in Turquoise Bottom Pond.

With all his other duties complete, he arrived at DT's shortly before four o'clock.

He saw Mandy as soon as he walked in.

In a couple of seconds, she spotted Malachi and smiled. "Hey, where have you been? Thought maybe you left town."

"No, I've been working."

As he walked toward the table in the corner, she finished up with the only other customer.

Malachi popped open his laptop.

And Mandy came over to the table. "What can I get you to drink?"

"A water and a coffee please."

"So where are you working?"

"Walmart—third shift"

"That's great; there aren't many jobs out there," Mandy said. "So, when are we going out to celebrate?"

"I'm celebrating right now."

She frowned. "But you didn't invite me."

And laughed.

Mandy's laugh captivated Malachi. Not simply a laugh—she became the laugh. Her vocal inflection flowed out in a pleasing range of tone and volume as her face brightened like a flash bulb going off. Her body swaying gently. If *freedom* had a laugh, it would be Mandy's laugh.

"Who's buying?" Malachi said. "You know, I'm living on Walmart wages."

She replied, "And of course, I'm raking in the big bucks working here? I guess it depends on how the tips are today."

Malachi looked around; he was the only one there. "Looks like a bunch of light tippers in here."

They both laughed.

He ordered a Pork Chop Sandwich with a side salad.

And turned his attention to his laptop.

Other customers arrived, and soon, Mandy was scampering from table to table.

Malachi glanced up on occasion, watching Mandy. He was sure she was ten or more years younger than him.

He pondered, "She probably always jokes around like that. She wouldn't want to go out with me."

As Malachi sat there, he realized he was still somewhat numb from work—physically and mentally. He knew there were some e-mails he should answer. And some phone calls he should make.

He let most of them slide— "It is the weekend."

Malachi did see an e-mail with the subject line, "Malachi you're an idiot!!!" From: Annie.

It didn't take much to guess its flavor. And for the first time in years, he was in control. "She doesn't even know where I am."

This thought delighted Malachi. With a slight hook of guilt.

The hook shrunk as he read the e-mail. And his guilt had completely vanished by the time he had finished scrolling the message.

Malachi, you're some man of God. You're a coward. You have to send your spies over. I should be allowed to have my own life. You left me. You're always doing stupid things. I can understand why Pastor Neil fired you. You're not going to destroy my life—only your own.

Malachi decided to reply immediately.

He shifted through a couple of different approaches. Trying to evaluate the outcome he wanted to achieve.

And then he said in a just-audible voice, "I don't care what happens."

He clicked: New Message.

Annie, thank you for your note. I appreciate your consistency.

A coward is someone who shows fear. You're probably above this human emotion. Perfection overcomes many of the human flaws us lesser people struggle with. A coward is known to run from the battle. I've chosen a strategy to win the battle in the only way I could see to win it.

I had to face down significant fear to do this.

It seems like the words coward and idiot come easier than true conversation. You know, I suggested marriage counseling many times to help us improve our communication skills as a couple.

You refused every time. Was it fear? Are you the coward?

Stephen was only a spy because you had something to hide.

Annie, you're not hiding anything from me. I've seen Tim in person—and the two of you in other ways, also. If you would like detailed proof, let me know. Or if you prefer, I can send the information directly to your boss. I feel certain he would be interested in knowing the full details of the projects you and Tim so passionately worked on together late into the night at the bank.

Let me know what you want me to do on this one.

Maybe Pastor Neil wouldn't have fired me if some people had listened to me. Maybe even encouraged or supported the pursuit of truth. Or heaven forbid, elevated God's viewpoint over man's viewpoint.

Annie, the time in my life when I was the lowest, you abandoned me. Did you offer me even one word of encouragement? Did you hear me out—with love?

You don't need any help in destroying your life. But I'm not going down with you. And Tim.

Just to let you know, as if it would matter to you, I'm through with God. He's not a part of my new life.

And neither are you.

...Malachi

Malachi carefully studied what he had written. Slowly re-reading it. He said to himself, "She deserves this—perfect."

He scrolled to the left side of the screen and placed the arrow on *Send*. He shook his head, moved the pointer to the upper right hand corner, and clicked on the *X*.

A dialog box popped up on the computer screen, "Do you want to save changes? *Yes. No. Cancel.*"

Malachi hit *No*. Deleting the message.

He quickly composed a new one. "Annie, received your e-mail... Malachi."

And hit, *Send*.

"Are you through, Malachi," he heard Mandy ask.

"I'm all set. Thanks."

He stared at her fingers again as she cleared the table. "Perfect for playing guitar."

When he looked up, Mandy was grinning.

"You caught me," Malachi said.

She returned with his bill.

"You sure do an excellent job, Mandy."

"Thank you. That's thoughtful of you to say so. I'll see you around."

"Sure will."

Malachi returned to his Turquoise Bottom Creek campsite. He built a fire. And stared into it. Stirred it. Fed it. Stared. And stared some more.

His guitar called from the Suburban. He thought, "Why bother?"

He was tired—but not sleepy.

His mind pictured Mandy. Her laugh. Her efficient, graceful waitressing. He even imagined her fingers caressing a guitar—gliding, dancing, soaring along the fret board.

Malachi smiled.

But then the smile—he despised the smile. "This is foolish—she is pain on the way."

His guitar called.

Malachi didn't answer.

He stared into the fire.

He half-grunted and half-laughed when a thought seemed to jump out of the fire. "If I stood up on the top of this hill and screamed, would anyone hear me? Would anyone care?"

"God would care."

Malachi jerked around to see who said the words. The light was fading, but he could see adequately into the darkening woods.

"Am I hearing things?"

And then he heard an even clearer voice from inside his own head. "God wouldn't care."

Malachi cuddled up with those words as he went off to sleep.

They stayed with him when he awoke.

The words spent the day with him— "God wouldn't care."

They rode with him into Manistee.

And they sat with him in the Walmart parking lot as Malachi forced himself to make his way to the time clock.

Tougher

Chapter 25

"Is everybody doing OK, tonight?" Robert asked. Malachi knew who Robert was, though he had never met him. He was the other assistant manager on overnights. Each assistant manager worked four days, followed by four days off.

"A couple of things. We're having burgers and hot dogs on the grill. And we'll have some side dishes. Sixty days accident free—thank you, everyone, for working safe."

Robert peered down at his paperwork, making a few notes. "The bad news is we really got pounded tonight. We're going to have to pull off a mini-miracle. Store numbers have been up—off the charts. A lot more summer people are in town because of the unseasonably warm weather. So, that all adds up to a very demanding night...very demanding. It's not going to be pleasant. I need your best tonight, team."

Malachi noticed many of the associates were tensing in their chairs. Eyes were wider. Humorous banter subsided.

"One, two, three—Walmart! Let's do it!"

The skids rolled out and rolled out and rolled out some more. And rolled out. And rolled out some more.

Malachi couldn't fathom how he could be even close to stocking his assigned freight by the end of the night. And he saw Stu's skids of paper goods piled everywhere—no help from The Finisher could be expected.

Malachi eyed his seven skids of freight—four skids was a monumental struggle the other night. Now seven?

Stu saw him contemplating the situation. "What do you think?"

"Impossible. Totally impossible."

"Not really."

"What are you talking about? Look at all this stuff."

"Never tell anybody I told you any of this. OK?"

"Sure."

"Here's how you do it. Don't price anything."

"Don't price anything?"

"Just do what I tell you. Put your pricing gun away. And if you trash the aisle, Robert won't say anything. He won't care—he's stocking too. So, down stack, shove your cardboard in piles...whatever's fastest. Just clean up at the end. Forget zoning. There's so much freight, if you throw it up halfway decent, it'll look OK. And you might not like this, but you probably need to skip both of your breaks tonight."

"It seems like I'm breaking a bunch of rules."

"You are. You do what you want. I've already counted my load—twenty-two skids of freight."

With that, Stu took off.

Malachi stood still for a couple of seconds. A hum of intensity had already descended onto the work area. No one was talking—at all. He listened more intently. No pricing guns sounded.

He whipped the first skid into the aisle, heaving the boxes close to their assigned spots. He down stacked three skids this way in a whirling blitz. And then started ripping boxes open, snatching handfuls of merchandise—practically throwing the items on the shelves. He marched down the aisle, leaving a war zone of cardboard in flailing heaps.

His head was down. His focus—rigorous. Sweating; breathing hard. The exertion reminded Malachi of his high school track days.

JC walked up behind him as he was bending over a box. "Got your picks," she said.

He looked up. "I think you're trying to kill me."

She laughed. "How was your weekend?"

"Good...ah... it was good."

"If you want to make it better, let me know."

He shook his head and laughed. "You're funny, JC."

He watched her walk away. And then tore back into his freight.

At lunch, the free food was especially tasty. Complaining about the massive amount of freight dominated conversations around the long white tables.

Malachi listened. It was an odd complaining. It had all the front-end elements of any gripe session: This is terrible. Why are they doing this to us? They're trying to kill us. This isn't fair.

But there was this other ingredient. And Malachi liked being part of it. It was a shake your fist in the air, raise your head high attitude. It was defiant.

No matter what they throw at us, we're tougher.

No matter how much work they give us, we're tougher

We're tougher, just to prove we're tougher.

We're not backing down; we're tougher.

Bring on the impossible; we're tougher.

After lunch, the frenzied pace of the Walmart Overnighters collided with the reality of expiring time.

Their whipping torrent of determination surged against the improbable odds.

But...at the end of the night, all the freight was in place. It looked good on the shelves. All the cardboard had been crushed into chunky bales. The sales floor was ready for a fresh flow of consumers.

The customers started streaming in.

The Overnighters—they marched out.

The Sweetness of Payday

Chapter 26

Malachi woke up on Thursday. He smiled, "Hey, it's payday."

Walmart had electronically transferred the funds to Malachi's debit card seconds after midnight. No one in the company received paper checks anymore.

He felt a renewed sense of, "I'm going to make it."

Only mildly worried, still it was a strange experience for Malachi to be within three dollars of being flat broke. It did make him consider the fact that many people face this type of situation repeatedly—with fewer options than he had.

The freedom of not being on the edge financially elevated his mood.

Gas in the Suburban, buying groceries, and minutes on his cell phone; lined up with their hands out. And the idea of returning to DT's was enticing him.

So, he set his plan. DT's at seven o'clock that evening. Take care of some business, make a few phone calls, and then off to work.

Malachi made DT's his first stop. He was pleased to see Mandy was working. But disappointed when he noticed his table was unavailable.

"Wow, it's busy tonight."

Mandy smiled. "You're getting to be a regular. Water and coffee?"

"Perfect."

Malachi fired up his laptop. And Mandy returned with his water and coffee.

"What can I get you, Malachi?"

"So, what else is good here...besides you."

Mandy laughed out loud. And then they looked each other in the eye.

"Ah...um...a lot of people really like our Cajun Cod Basket."

"Sounds great. That's what I'll have."

Malachi checked his e-mail. There was one from Pastor Neil. He opened it, even though he would have preferred to delete it.

A scathing attack on Malachi—the words *coward, hypocrite, ungodly, uncaring, uncompassionate, fool* blazed anger into Malachi's heart. So badly that he wanted to hurt Pastor Neil. Malachi's hateful thoughts sat uncomfortably in his gut. The further he read, the more vicious his desire to inflict pain became. The words *legal action, lawsuit, ruined career* incensed Malachi.

He stared at the screen. And was oblivious to Mandy when she returned with his food. "Here you go."

He didn't look up. "Thanks."

Outwardly frozen—with only his lips moving, they tensed and then eased. Tensed and eased.

He made his decision. He hit *Delete*. And then added Pastor Neil to his Block Sender list.

Then, seeing a message from Daniel Hernandez relieved much of the angst inflicted by the previous e-mail.

Daniel was Malachi's favorite student in the youth group at St. Amos Community Church. His most endearing quality was his love for Jesus. And in a genuine, natural way, he communicated his faith—through words and, more often, by the way he lived.

Malachi especially loved the memory of seeing Daniel bringing his four younger siblings, Maria, Nohemi, Magaly, and Marcos, to Sunday School. If it wasn't for his efforts, they wouldn't have attended.

Still Daniel was far from perfect.

Malachi remembered, on one occasion, the depth of Daniel's sorrow for the wrong he had done. He marveled at his true and humble repentance. And his determination to then, "do the right thing." All encompassed in an unwavering trust in God.

In a paradoxical way, when Malachi was at St. Amos Community Church, he wanted to be more like Daniel.

> Dear Pastor Malachi,
>
> I feel a significant loss in my life because you are no longer my Pastor. I'm losing a lot more than a Pastor.
>
> No one understood me like you did. Sometimes, my words to you, about what was going on in my life, didn't really say how I felt. I just didn't know how to express what my brain was thinking. It was weird, but it was like you knew what I meant, even when I was unable to describe it myself.
>
> Your words to me have been strengthening, encouraging, and comforting in a way beyond the human realm.
>
> It's not that your words were overly profound, but they connected with me as if they were words from God. They hit the target. It's hard to explain.
>
> Your words changed my life.
>
> Pastor Malachi, God gave me this Bible verse for you. "When our days there were ended, we left and started on our journey…after kneeling down on the beach and praying, we said farewell to one another."
>
> I am kneeling and praying for you.
>
> Love,
> Daniel

Malachi closed his eyes tight. And drew a long breath in through his nose. His tears pressed hard—but none escaped.

"Daniel, if I could only be like you," he whispered. "How do I respond to your e-mail?"

He stared at the screen. "I can't do it."

Malachi turned off his laptop and folded it down.

He slowly chewed his food—unmindful when Mandy returned to his table.

"Are you OK, Malachi?" he heard Mandy say.

"Oh...just going through some stuff...I mean..."

"Maybe your luck's about to change."

"Ah...luck?"

"Luck can change. You've got to believe. We all need something to hold on to."

"Yeah, you're right," Malachi said.

He looked intently at Mandy. At that moment, he had never been more confused about what he should be holding onto.

He paid his bill. And left a twenty-dollar tip.

He drove the Suburban over to the Walmart parking lot. He had time for a few calls and some rest before work began.

"Uncle Dale, this is Malachi. How are you doing?"

They talked about Uncle Dale's health. And Malachi's job. The conversation drifted pleasantly back and forth.

"One of the main reasons I called was to set up a time to come and visit you and Aunt Betty."

"Ah...ah...when were you thinking about coming out? We've been really busy. And...well, you know how that is."

Malachi laughed. "It sounds like you don't want to see me."

"It's not...it's just...maybe next weekend."

"OK. I'll give you a call and see what we can work out."

Malachi sifted through his memory, trying to recall if he had offended Uncle Dale again. He was sure, for some reason, Uncle Dale didn't want him to visit.

"Most likely, it's because he's not feeling well."

Malachi made a couple more calls and then turned off his cell phone.

He sat, thinking, "I need to call Annie sometime."

He glanced at his watch, mentally explaining away the urge. "Not enough time. Besides, e-mail works best."

Helpless Help, Hopeless Hope

Chapter 27

Malachi sat in the break room making final preparations for work. He fiddled around with his faithful Monarch 1131—his pricing gun. He checked to make sure his Easy Cut had a sharp blade. Mainly, he was checking himself out. His body was creaky from the previous night's brutal effort.

Then he moved his awareness to his co-workers gathered in the room. His first ten days at Walmart had been a blast of gritty survival. Now that he had hit a groove, the people he worked with started to matter to him more.

He kept stifling this outlook, though. Telling himself, "I've got to take care of my own crap." He warned himself about being sucked into relationships that he would later regret. He attempted to convince himself that being a loner would work out best.

Malachi had attempted to remember everyone's name. Yet, besides casual chitchat, he had carried on only a few meaningful conversations

Leslie, Paul, and Carvin worked mainly in the Dairy Area. Gary, Kent, and Christine worked Frozen. Stu in Paper Goods. JC and Spencer staffed the back room and delivered picks. Taylor, Harmony, Dan, Jack, Rich, Cecilia, Gret, Eddie, and Janis stocked the Grocery aisles. And Martin, Ry, Mellissa, Travis, and Trisha labored in the store's General Merchandise area—all non-grocery items.

Malachi already sensed an attachment, a bonding with the other associates. He glanced around. "Sheep without a shepherd."

He tried to free himself from this type of mindset. "That God stuff doesn't matter. Take care of yourself."

"How's everybody doing tonight?" he heard Sal say.

This nudged Malachi's brain back to the night's work.

She followed the regular routine, until she addressed Malachi, "I need you to do Paper Goods and Chemicals tonight. Stu called in."

A shiver sliced through Malachi.

"One more issue we need to talk about before we head out," Sal said. "We're going to be having a pricing audit in two weeks."

She explained that a private auditing company would be coming into the store to make sure all items were being priced according to the state laws.

While she never accused anyone of not pricing, Sal was adamant, "Everything needs to be priced. Does everyone understand?"

Out on the floor, Malachi sized up his workload. Blended with the fact that the paper good aisle was unfamiliar turf, his workload seemed overwhelming. Again.

He saw Sal making her first sweep down through his work area.

"Sal," he said, "I need to talk with you."

"How can I help you?"

"I can't get all this done tonight."

"That's a negative attitude. Malachi, you have a lot of room for improvement. Maybe you should concentrate on stepping up to the challenge, rather than giving in to failure before you have even tried. Before you've given your best effort. And if you can't do the work, maybe we need to hire someone who can."

Pure anger fueled the rest of Malachi's night. Along with the suggestion that he was very dispensable—very replaceable.

By the end of the night, Malachi's attitude had changed. He was surprised, realizing Sal's kick in the behind had caused him to achieve what he had deemed impossible. He couldn't exactly figure out what had happened. Until he analyzed the situation. Still, somewhat perplexed, he asked himself, "Did my *fear of failure* chase me to victory?"

A pleasant buzz came over Malachi as he made the final inspection of his aisles. Everything was finished—with a little help from Martin, who had swung into the aisle for the final assault of the night.

As he passed the office, he saw Sal. "Malachi, you rocked tonight."

"Thanks."

And then he was surprised by her candor. "If I wasn't hardnosed, everybody would walk all over me."

Malachi thought, "She's right."

"I'm graded on a scorecard every night. On every aspect of what we get accomplished. And how well it's done. Every night."

Her tone softened. Malachi wondered why she was confiding in him. "It's really harsh, sometimes. The pressure is almost more...I ah...really need this job. I just don't know where to turn, sometimes."

"Sheep without a shepherd," drifted into Malachi's brain. He forced it out quickly.

"I'll always give you my best," Malachi said—but he wished he had words more encouraging, words to sustain Sal.

"Thanks, Malachi. I know you do."

Stu was back the next night. He looked awful—pale, slumped shoulders, disoriented.

"It looks like someone beat you up," Malachi said.

"Someone did," Stu said. "The devil. And I helped him."

Malachi didn't ask what he meant. He knew.

Stu reminded him of Mel Fendman. An *on-fire* Christian like Stu.

Mel would stumble in his Christian walk—going off on partying binges. He was constantly up and down. When he was up, he was all about Jesus. And when he was down, it was sad. Pitiful. There were even times Malachi wondered if he would ever see him alive again.

"Sheep without a shepherd."

Malachi shook his head. "Quit it."

It was heartbreaking to see Stu work. He seemed to be walking in deep mud as he dragged through his freight.

Malachi's goal for the night was to finish up early, so he could help

Stu.

He eked out an hour and a half at the end of the night. And as Stu seemed to crawl to the end, Malachi charged as hard as possible to the finish.

Inside, Malachi felt dreadful. He kept thinking of Mel Fendman—last he knew, Mel had gone off the deep end, never to return.

Malachi repeatedly asked Stu as they were leaving at the end of the shift, "Are you going to be alright?"

"Are you sure?"

"Are you sure?"

Just before they parted, Stu said, "Malachi, thanks for your help. I really appreciate what you did." Stu looked down. "Your help was great... but it's not the kind of help I really need...right now."

Malachi stared upward, "I...ah...know what you mean...ah, I'm sorry."

He wanted to hug Stu. Instead, they both stepped away from each other to face their own aloneness.

The next night, Stu appeared to be making a comeback—but maybe only a few paces from the edge of no-return.

Malachi hadn't been that happy to see someone in a long time. All day, he kept having a frightful thought of Stu going over the cliff.

"Hey Stu, you look a lot better."

"I was pretty hopeless last night. Thanks for your help."

Then he looked Malachi in the eye. "You know, there's really no hope without Jesus. If I didn't have Jesus, I'd be dead...gone. Jesus pulled me away from destruction again. There's just no hope in this world, unless you have Jesus...no hope...no hope."

Malachi spun Stu's words through his brain and it came out, "You were helpful, but you didn't offer me any hope."

Malachi put all his freight on the shelves. He finished his duties, but his heart stayed hooked on Stu's message all night long.

At the end of the shift, Malachi found himself walking out with Stu.

"Hey, Malachi, we should hang out sometime."

"I would like that, Stu."

"See you tomorrow."

The next night, Malachi made an observation; the cardboard baler was like the office water cooler for Walmart stockers.

Frequently, wait-time occurred at the baler because associates would arrive to crush cardboard at the same time. Waiting usually equaled conversation.

Gossip and gripes. Jokes and semi-nothingness. Serious life moments and tragedy. Casual and caustic. Conversation flowed.

That night, Malachi was startled while talking with Gret near the baler.

He heard an echoing bang!

Martin had slammed the sledgehammer used in the back room against the side of the baler, bellowing, "I hate Walmart."

No one argued with him.

Malachi thought for a second and then asked, "What are you talking about, Martin?"

"I hate working here. I feel trapped."

"That's not Walmart's fault."

"I know...still, that's the way I feel."

"Why don't you get another job," Malachi asked, "or get some training for the career you really want?"

"You make it sound so easy. Why don't you go get a better job if it's that easy?" Martin said. "With all the junk going on in my life, I would need a miracle to get out of this prison. I feel hopeless."

"What do you want to be?"

"I'm a musician. I play guitar. And I write songs. This work is ruining my hands. I'm too tired to practice. Or write. It's hopeless. And you know it. What's the use? I hate it here."

Malachi paused. Took a deep breath. "I don't know what to tell you."

When Martin said the word guitar, a rotten spot grew in Malachi's stomach. It stayed with him the rest of the night. And Martin's words, "What's the use?" dug it in even deeper.

Punching in on Monday night, Malachi smiled, knowing it was his Friday. His smile dissipated when he spotted JC arriving for her Monday.

There was no smile on her face.

She always smiled.

He looked away, avoiding any eye contact with JC.

She had been one of the sparks that made work more pleasant. Her smile and playfulness always lifted his spirits. Now, something had doused her spirit.

He kept thinking, "What should I do? What should I do?"

Malachi saw her bringing picks toward him. He tried to convince himself, "Don't get involved."

JC turned to leave, without even looking up.

"You're not going to say *hi* or anything?" Malachi said.

"No. Not really."

Malachi walked over to her, noticing her left arm was wrapped in a cloth bandage.

"What happened to you?"

"I fell. It's nothing."

"You sure?"

"I don't want to talk about it."

"Where's your beautiful smile."

She took a deep breath. "I don't feel like smiling."

"No smile?"

"Not tonight."

All of a sudden, Malachi's mind flashed to a scene from his youth-group-leader days at St. Amos Community Church. One of the students performing an impromptu rap song, which had incited uncontrollable hilarity among those gathered that night.

He laughed when this mental impression hit his brain. JC gave him a quizzical look. So, Malachi broke into the rap:

> Smile, smile, smile
> For a while
> While
> While
> While
>
> You've been good
> And you've bad
>
> Is a smile the best thing you've ever had?
> Had
> Had
> Had...

"What are you doing, Malachi? I hate rap music," JC said. "Why are you acting like an idiot?"

Malachi stood silent. He wrinkled his forehead. "I was…just trying to make you smile."

"Well…I'm…I didn't mean to call you an idiot." JC forced a smile on her face. "Thanks…but…thanks, Malachi."

And then, her smile quickly folded back into her bleakness as she walked away.

Malachi replayed JC's countenance plunge in his mind for the rest of the night, thinking repeatedly, "I sure blew that one."

Leaving the store at the end of the night, his mind was fixed on JC.

Gazing directly ahead, he heard a clear voice coming from the produce section of the store as he was passing by. "My sheep are scattered like sheep without a shepherd."

He jolted to the right. It was Carl, standing by a display of oranges. He kept talking, "Whom shall I send? Who will go for Me?"

"I don't think they allow sheep in the store," Malachi said.

They both smiled.

And then Malachi said, "Hey ah…thanks for the money and the parking sticker. You shocked me. How did you know?"

"The same way you know things, sometimes." He pointed toward the ceiling.

Malachi shook his head "Thanks again. If I can ever do anything for you, let me know."

"I do need a ride on Wednesday night."

"Ah…sure…if I'm not busy. What time were you thinking?"

"Six-fifteen. Here—in the parking lot."

"Well…ah sure. I can do that."

Malachi walked toward the exit. Carl returned to the oranges.

When Malachi neared the door, he spun back around. Carl was looking directly at him—with a smirk on his face.

Malachi then continued toward the exit, happy to have made it to his second Walmart weekend.

Where Are We Going Carl?

Chapter 28

By Wednesday morning, Malachi was trying to devise a way out of giving Carl a ride. However, he could imagine if he pulled a no-show, Carl might just appear at the campsite.

So, Malachi decided to give him a ride as planned—it could be fun. Or odd—like Carl.

Malachi pulled into the Walmart parking lot at 6:08 that evening. Carl arrived exactly at 6:15.

"Here's a present for you," Carl said.

Malachi reached for the traditional brown grocery sack folded tent-like.

Carl turned around, placing it on the back seat, "Open it later."

"OK. I'll do that," Malachi said. "So where are we going, Carl?"

"I'm meeting with some friends." He pointed south. "Go down to the second stoplight. Take a right."

They turned west on Red Apple Rd.

Malachi, despite his initial apprehension, was at ease with Carl. But he didn't know why.

Carl asked him many questions about himself. The basic non-threatening type—thoughtful questions. Yet, when Malachi gave any hint of reservation, Carl gently guided the conversation in another direction.

Walmart questions or comments became Carl's default bailout technique.

His queries caused Malachi to think thoughts about himself he hadn't pondered in a long time.

"Where do you see yourself in five years?"

Malachi hesitated, "I...ah...I don't know."

"Well, haven't you ever had a dream business you've wanted to start or something like that?"

Click...Malachi launched into reliving his hopes for Kerr Creek Guitars. As Carl nudged the conversation along, all the good aspects of Malachi's dream bubbled forth.

No one, not even Annie, had ever listened or seemed interested in Kerr Creek Guitars the way Carl did.

Malachi was so engrossed in the conversation, he lost track of where he was.

Furthermore, he surprised himself when he injected God and serving God and helping further God's work into the discussion.

Malachi went into detail—from guitar design, to the people he loved in China, their church, the craftsmanship.

He described the arrival of the first prototype. "I was all tingly when I saw the box. I had just got home from work. I knew what it was."

His talking pace started to race. "I think I hugged the box. I was so careful when I opened the package. When I saw the stunning beauty of the guitar's Manchurian Ash face, I almost cried. I had to sit down. The guitar was so cool—tuned almost perfectly right out of the box...I cherished the sound from the first strum. My friends, my partners in China, had built it to exceed all my expectations."

He could tell the story intrigued Carl.

As they drove along the bluff overlooking the shore, Malachi barely noticed the sun dropping low over Lake Michigan or the sparkly silver dance of the low waves.

Driving on autopilot, he heard Carl say, "Go around the curve to the left. Turn right. Turn left."

Finally, his story started to run out of momentum. And Malachi's pace slowed as he unfolded the complications that stifled him. "I couldn't get the guitars to sell. There's too much competition. And we didn't have an advertising budget or any real marketing plan."

He sputtered to a stop. "Well, that's a dream that'll never come true."

"Malachi," Carl said. "With God, all things are possible."

He contemplated Carl's words for a long moment. Glanced at him. And then stared back at the road.

Become

Chapter 29

The dashboard clock read 6:52.

"We're almost there," Carl said. "See the big sign up there on the right. That's my destination."

Malachi saw the sign.

Become Ministries—*Become Lovers of Jesus, Become God's Servant, Become Sensitive to the Holy Spirit, Become the Person God Gifted You to Be.*

The faded blue metal pole barn looked aged—but well-maintained. Four low evergreen shrubs encircled with red woodchips accentuated the entrance. A dark green canvas awning with the words, Jesus is for Everyone hung above the door. People were getting out of their cars, heading toward the entrance. Others were visiting outside in the serene spring evening. Sixty cars or so were scattered around the crushed limestone parking lot.

Malachi was thinking, "Wacko church."

And said to Carl, "You have a ride back to Manistee?"

"Yeah, I'll be fine," Carl said.

Malachi stopped the Suburban. He didn't pull into a parking space as he held his foot on the brake.

"Hey, Malachi, thanks so much for the ride. I enjoyed talking with you."

Malachi knew Carl was sincere. He relaxed and put the car in park. "I probably talked too much."

"No, you had a lot to say. You've been through a lot," Carl said. "I've got one more favor."

"What's that? Let me guess. You want me to go in with you. You set me up, old man. I'm not stupid."

Both of them were silent.

Then Malachi said, "Are you going to get out!"

Carl's face scrunched. He was near tears.

He spoke slowly, "I'm sorry; I don't want to upset you, but it matters to me what happens to you. It's hard to explain. I almost quit God once...it's a long story. I ah..."

He rubbed his right hand slowly over his lips. "Just come in for..." Carl looked straight at Malachi and sighed, "Just do what you want."

They were both silent again.

Malachi shifted into drive and parked the Suburban.

"What the crap; it's not going to kill me," Malachi said. "If there are a bunch of freaks in there, I'm leaving."

He followed Carl inside. Malachi smiled at everyone, hiding the turmoil boiling inside.

The interior looked like a warehouse. The steel I-beam structure accentuated the industrial decor. Mega-rolls of insulation with a white plastic facing filled the wall's open cavities. The ceiling and walls, with pipes, conduit, and miscellaneous mechanicals, were painted an off-white. Generous overspray indicated a paint job executed by well-meaning volunteers.

The floor, which was basic gray, had many visible cracks. Malachi could imagine lift trucks darting about as he visualized the building's former life. A raw-wood stage held a fine selection of rock-band instruments. Two hundred chairs—blue economy models with entry-level padding, were set in neat semi-circular rows. A sound booth raised three feet above the concrete was perched in a rear corner. Behind the seating area, four rectangle tables lined up parallel near a large bank of shelved books.

The inside space was open, except for one sizeable room, formed by dark-brown painted plywood and two clearly marked restrooms. A table near the entry door held a few stacks of papers and two Bibles.

Carl greeted a few friends. Malachi avoided eye contact as he made his way to a seat on the aisle—one row from the back.

Malachi's legs were crossed. He folded his arms and aimed his eyes at the floor.

Moments after Malachi had set up camp, the sound of an electric guitar captured his attention. He raised his eyes just enough to see someone on the stage playing a tomato-red Peavey electric guitar.

The guitar player's skill astonished Malachi. He delicately worked up and down the fretboard, coaxing stunning riffs from his guitar. The mellow soulfulness carried Malachi to another world.

Soon, other musicians assembled on the stage— a bass player, a keyboard player. Three singers stood together on the right side of the stage. In addition, a drummer, set back slightly, found his place in the middle of the stage. The guitar maestro faded to a background player as the drummer with a microphone hanging from his ear led the singing.

"Please stand," the drummer said. "Let's worship the Lord with our singing:"

> Oh Lord our praises rise. To You. Oh Lord
> With thankful hearts. We look. To You
> Jesus we look. To You
> Jesus we look. To You
>
> Oh Lord our praises rise. To You. Oh Lord
> With joyful hearts. We look. To You
> Jesus we look. To You
> Jesus we look. To You
>
> Oh Lord our praises rise. To You. Oh Lord
> With humble hearts. We look. To You
> Jesus we look. To You
> Jesus we look. To You

Oh Lord our praises rise. To You. Oh Lord.
With hearts flowing with praise. We look. To You.
Jesus we look. To You.
Jesus we look. To You.

The drummer led those gathered through the song several times.

Malachi was touched by an undeniable warmth. A sense of being, encircled with love, weighed pleasingly on him. Every care melted away.

The experience so enraptured Malachi that he didn't realize the band had quit playing.

The Pastor moved onto the stage. "In Psalm 121:1 the question is asked, 'Where does my help come from?'"

The sound of his voice moved Malachi from his dreamlike state, shifting his attention to the Pastor's words.

"Where does your help come from? Where are you looking? Work? Your wife? Your husband? Your big dream? Even church? Children? Sports? Addictions? If you're looking to any of these, you're vulnerable to running out of gas. Running out of spiritual gas. You'll stall on the road God has for your life."

The Pastor moved down from the stage, pacing back and forth out in front of his attentive congregation.

"Friends. Everything that can be shaken will be shaken. Hebrews 12 tells us: 'And His voice shook the earth then. But now He has promised, saying, yet once more I will shake not only the Earth but also the Heaven. This expression, *yet once more* denotes the removing of those things which can be shaken. As of created things so that those things which cannot be shaken may remain.'"

His voice intensified, "Everything that can be shaken, will be shaken. When that shaking happens, are you going to be shaken from your marriage, your job, your children? Shaken from your dream... your God given dream...shaken from God. Shaken from Jesus."

And then the Pastor lowered his voice, "Jesus, who became the likeness of man, died for your sins and faced every trial you have ever faced."

He started pacing back and forth vigorously and gazing upward as his voice notched up in volume, "And friends, aren't you glad, aren't you happy, aren't you thankful that Jesus wasn't shaken from what God had for His life…for His death?"

"That's right, let's give Jesus a cheer," the Pastor said.

"So where did Jesus' help come from? Hey Peter, you got My back. The church guys…wrong. Martha…just you and me…hey babe, take a walk on the wild side. No. He didn't turn to friends, women…wine… wacky weed from the desert. Or the big church guys. Most of the big church guys hated Jesus. They hated Him…"

He continued to stride back and forth. "Go with me to the darkest moment in Jesus' life. A moment so dark I don't see how any human could have faced any worse agony. Could anyone ever be shaken any worse? Let's read Luke 22:44, 'And being in anguish, Jesus prayed more earnestly and his sweat was like drops of blood falling on the ground.'"

"Let's get this picture, friends. Anguish so absolutely dreadful… blood…Jesus had blood dripping from his sweat. Moments before this happened, He had prayed, 'Father if You are willing take this cup from me.' He's praying what is likely the most impassioned prayer anyone has ever breathed. Jesus is pleading, 'Father take this awful shaking from Me. Take the cross I have to face…take it away. Remove it.'"

"Friends, where did Jesus get His help? Jesus ended His prayer of anguish with, 'Yet not My will, but Your will be done.' Friends, where did Jesus get His help? Jesus trusted everything to God. And trusted nothing, not one speck, to all the other possibilities…not one speck."

"Friends, everything that can be shaken will be shaken. Where will your help come from? We started in Psalm 121:1 this evening with the question, 'Where does my help come from?' And we find the answer immediately in the next verse. 'My help comes from the LORD, the Maker of Heaven and Earth.'"

The Pastor then started singing, "Oh Lord our praises rise. To You. Oh Lord. With thankful hearts. We look. To You. Jesus we look. To You…"

He nodded at the guitar player, who then came up on the stage. And played softly.

Soon, the Pastor quit singing.

Malachi bowed his head. And after many minutes, he glanced up. Most of the people had left.

He quietly sang, "Jesus we look. To You. Jesus we look. To You…"

He felt something inside—an intensity he had never experienced in his life. Warmth. Protection. Love...deep love.

But now, he had a desire to be alone.

He walked out to the Suburban. Carl was already outside. They both got in.

Besides a few directions from Carl, neither one spoke any other words on the return trip to the Walmart parking lot.

Malachi stopped the Suburban. "Thank you, Carl."

Carl nodded.

As Malachi drove out to his campsite, he sang, "Jesus we look. To You. Jesus we look. To You..."

The Fire

Chapter 30

The solitude of Malachi's pine covered nub hummed a resounding peace into his soul.

But the peace inside contrasted with his energized body. So, Malachi funneled his zest toward "getting settled in" for the night. He built a fire, grabbed his lantern from the tent, and retrieved his guitar and the bag Carl had left in the Suburban.

He said to himself, when he saw the contents of the brown sack, "Thank you, God."

Inside the bag were a Bible and a book, entitled *Preparing for Revival*.

In addition, there was a note from Carl. "This book has helped me. I know others who have grown closer in their relationship with God by reading this excellent book. It's about personal revival—changes we need in our lives. Always know this, though; it is essential to make reading the Bible your priority."

For the moment, all Malachi wanted to do was gaze into the fire as he relived the evening at Become Ministries.

His mind reconnected with the main points of the sermon when he opened his new Bible. He then turned to the verse the Pastor had launched his talk with—Psalm 121:1. And read it three times. Followed by searching for the rest of the verses the Pastor had referenced. As he leafed through the Bible, Malachi stopped to meditate on numerous passages.

They were pumping him with spiritual adrenalin. He sensed a renewed strength flowing into his soul and spirit.

Malachi was near-giddy when he *randomly* encountered a scripture, which would be the very morsel of God's Word he needed.

"Praise God," Malachi said when this happened. "Praise God."

But unexpectedly, the happy-trails-to-you Bible verses turned down another path.

One Malachi had read many times over the years drew him in:

> Do not suppose that I have come to bring peace to the earth. I did not come to bring peace but a sword. For I have come to turn a man against his father, a daughter against her mother, a daughter-in-law against her mother-in-law. A man's enemies will be the members of his own household.

Anyone who loves his father or mother more than Me is not worthy of Me. Anyone who loves his son or daughter more than Me is not worthy of Me. And anyone who does not take up his cross and follow Me is not worthy of Me. Whoever finds his life will lose it and whoever loses his life for My sake will find it.

The giddy, happy man jumping around inside Malachi found a seat.

The Bible verse was burning so deeply into Malachi's being, only God's audible voice could have been more impactful.

Malachi didn't want to think, "Crap."

But he did. "Crap. God wants me to lose my life. Can I give up everything for God? Have I ever given up everything for God?"

Malachi didn't have to think how to answer the second question. He knew he had never given up everything for God. Even at the peak of his former Jesus-experience.

He had always gone with, "I'm doing better than most of the Christians I know."

Staring into the fire didn't help.

Pacing around didn't help.

Sleeping would be impossible.

Malachi's insides were experiencing a crushing—it sure seemed so. He felt warmth on his face. And body. Not a pleasant sensation. Something was burning. But it wasn't the campfire.

And then, like a bowling ball smashing down ten pins, all of his resistance tumbled as a Bible verse blew into his spirit. "Those who know Your Name put their trust in You. For You, O LORD, have never forsaken those who seek You."

Malachi bowed his head. And folded his hands. "God I give You everything. I trust You. God help me. God I need your help. I will seek You with all my heart, with all my soul, with all my mind. Amen—let it be so."

A New Day

Malachi slept the best he had in as long as he could remember. The cloudy cool morning was a joy for him to behold as he stirred the fire back to life, brewed coffee, and ate his standard breakfast—three granola bars and an apple.

He retrieved his guitar from the tent, removing it from the case with renewed tenderness. His emotions flickered when he touched the guitar—almost as intensely as the moment long ago, when he first cradled his cherished instrument.

Strumming, he raised his eyes to the sky. "God, this guitar is Yours. Everything I have is Yours. I am Yours." And then he began to play.

Thirty-five minutes later, he returned from a spiritual expedition, which carried him a million miles away. Into the celestials, without moving even an inch further from the campfire. He sang his Jesus songs. He praised God. And played as feebly as ever. Still, he returned from his guitar-playing voyage a changed man. Closer to God…so much closer.

Malachi was in no hurry this morning. He savored the afterglow from the night before. He read the entire book of James. Passages he had read many times over the years, but today, the words lit up like fireflies.

The last verse in the third chapter especially exploded. "As the body without the spirit is dead, so faith without works is dead."

Sitting near the fire, his guitar resting nearby, thoughts of last night still bouncing around his head; his faith had never been more vibrant.

His mulling mind kept asking, "Now, what do I do? Faith needs some works. Some action. Now what? Now what?"

He picked up the book from Carl—*Preparing for Revival* and his notepad and an ink pen. At the top of the pad in bold letters, he wrote *NOW WHAT.*

He leafed through the book. The short section on page twenty-two, *THE PAST,* prodded him. And so did the Bible verse printed below the title.

"Brothers...one thing I do: forgetting what is behind and straining toward what is ahead, I press on... Philippians 3:13-14."

He underlined *I press on.*

Then, Malachi jotted down and underlined Press On at the top of the notepad.

Next, he read all of chapter entitled THE PAST. And underlined the last three lines, "Learn from the past. Pray more. Listen more. Serve more. Give more. Love more. If you will practice these things, you will be certain to overcome any obstacles from the devil or from the past."

He circled *Love More* in the book. And then wrote and underlined *Love More* on his pad.

Malachi turned in his Bible to 1 Corinthians 13 and read the entire chapter. And then reread and pondered the last verse, "And now these three remain; faith, hope, and love. But the greatest of these is love."

"The greatest of these is love. The greatest of these is love. The greatest of these is love," he murmured over and over again.

Malachi then wrote down, *The greatest of these is love...follow the way of love.*

Next, he prepared a list, which he entitled, MALACHI'S LOVE MORE LIST— *Annie, Uncle Dale and Aunt Betty, Pastor Neil, Stephen/*

elders, Sarah, Daniel, Workers at Walmart, Carl, Mandy, and Dad.
He shook his head when he digested the reality of the anemic bond between him and his father. There hadn't even been any contact since Malachi's move. Or any before his departure.

Friends I've lost touch with was also placed on the list—as he pictured in his mind several friendships he had allowed to fade, slip, and shrivel from existence.

Malachi had allowed the Sunday school children and the youth group to become his main circle of friends. And in an unhealthy manner, neglected too many vital adult connections.

Fresh spiritual eyes caused him to view life differently. His failures challenged him. But he was also encountering a surge of God's forgiveness and guidance to the path of reconciliation and change.

He pondered his list for a few more minutes. And smiled as he added Jesus to MALACHI'S LOVE MORE LIST.

The Way of Love

Malachi decided to kick his *Now What* plan into gear with a phone call to Uncle Dale. He had a God-revealed insight into Uncle Dale's reason for resisting his visit.

"Hey, Uncle Dale, this is Malachi. How are you doing?"

"Not too bad. I have my ups and downs."

"When can we get together? I want to come out and visit you and Aunt Betty."

"Sure, but… we're always so busy. We…ah, it just never seems to…"

"Uncle Dale, I love you and Aunt Betty. You two have been some of the nicest people on the planet to me. I know you've moved and ah… well shoot, I live out in a tent in the forest. I mean…I'm forty-two, and I don't even have a place to stay. Practically homeless. I kind of figured… I've been down Muskrat Rd. It's not the same as where you use to live up on Crescent Circle. I don't care if your house isn't as nice. Look at me; I'm living in a $32 Walmart tent."

Malachi laughed, "I bet your tent's bigger than mine. We're family. We need to stick together."

Uncle Dale laughed. "Yeah...things are tough...and..."

"Uncle Dale, you've got a grill?"

"Well sure."

"How about this? I'll bring steaks. You fire up the grill. Aunt Betty can make some of her world's best potato salad; I'll grab some garlic bread too. We'll pretend we're kings. Do you want to eat like kings? I'm going to bring some good steaks. I'm talking about the best I can find."

Uncle Dale laughed again, "That would be nice. Really nice. I feel better already."

They agreed upon Tuesday evening at six.

"I love you, Uncle Dale."

Malachi looked at his watch as he planned his day.

He went for a run on the trails—east along Turquoise Bottom Creek.

Afterwards, he brought water up from the creek, heated it, and washed up. On warm days, he had been bathing in the pond. Bracing, but Malachi was acclimating to the chilly water.

He considered going to DT's to eat and to check his e-mail but opted for McDonalds instead—less distractions.

He took his *Now What* list in with him.

Burger, Fries, Coke, his open laptop, and notepad—Malachi was determined to *press on* as he *followed the way of love.*

This required some e-mailing. And phone calls. He wasted no time plowing into his tasks. First, his e-mails.

Pastor Neil,

It's difficult to know where to start.

First, I would like to ask for your forgiveness. I could have handled the situation much better.

I'm not saying I agree with all that happened, but I realize I have fallen woefully short of following the way of love.

Things will not return to the way they were. I'm starting over, here in Manistee. And have found a job at Walmart. I have renewed my dedication to God and my love for Jesus. I am determined to do my best to work through the upheaval I have created.

I'm trusting God to bring out good from the bad. I hope, one day, we can agree with what I once heard a pastor preach, "The good news is, the bad news is wrong." May God grant us the grace and wisdom to turn the bad news in front of us into good news down the road.

We know God has a way of turning bad into good—when it seems impossible. I believe our part is to approach the healing process with love.

I'll be praying for you. I ask the same from you. I look forward to further communications—either via e-mail or on the phone.

Here's a Bible verse for you—for both of us. John 13:34, "A new commandment I give to you, that you love one another, even as I have loved you, that you also love one another."

Love,
Malachi
P.S. Give Mattie my love.

Malachi clicked on *Send*.

Dear Stephen,

Thank you for your friendship. I'm sorry for the stress I have caused you.

I have renewed my relationship with Jesus. And my faith is strong.

With this, I know I have many issues to work out. I have dedicated myself to following the way of love as I clean-up the junk in my life. I thank God that I have you to stand with me. Keep praying for me.

Also, to let you know, you can tell people, elders, etc. about what's going on. My life is no longer a secret.

Here's a Bible verse for you from Psalm 121. "Where does my help come from? My help comes from the LORD, the Maker of Heaven and Earth."

Stephen, God is faithful. Keep trusting in Him.

Love,
Malachi
P.S. Below is a note to Sarah. I hope you can pass it on to her.

Hey Sarah,

Hope you're doing well.

I miss you. You're the most awesome Sunday school student I've ever had! You mean so much to me. I have a new job now. I'm not sure when I can visit.

But always know this; Jesus loves you. And so do I.

Pastor Malachi

Malachi hit *Send.*

Dear Daniel,

Your e-mail went right to my heart—in a good way. I wish I could be more like you in so many ways.

I live in Manistee now. Long story.

We can see each other when I visit. We'll grab a bite to eat. It might be a while, but I won't forget.

I've been through a lot recently. It's been difficult. One thing I've learned and I am continuing to understand more clearly; God can be trusted. You can trust Him with your whole life.

I look forward to seeing what God is going to do in your life.

Daniel, you mean a lot to me. More than you can understand.

Please, let's stay in touch.

Love,

Pastor Malachi

Malachi hit *Send.*

It was 5:08. Malachi folded up his laptop and decided to go down to the beach.

Manistee has gorgeous beaches, yet Malachi had only been near the beach once. The morning he met Carl.

He returned to the same spot. But he wasn't going to the beach for the view.

Malachi was fortifying himself. A call to Annie was next on his agenda.

Wearing a jacket and a cap, he strolled on the beach, praying, "God help me."

The volume of thoughts bombing his brain made it difficult to sort things out. A barrage of emotions attempted to blast him away from his follow-the-way-of-love determination.

Malachi locked on a Bible verse, which referred to Jesus. "I have set My face like flint." Malachi stirred up his own stone-faced grit in order to remain true to his way-of-love vow.

He walked back toward the small park on the bluff overlooking Lake Michigan. And made his way up the switchback to a bench.

Malachi knew Annie's schedule. If she didn't work late, six would be a convenient time to call. He looked at his notepad, writing *love* with an arrow pointing toward *Annie*.

He prayed once more, "Dear God help me," and placed the call at 6:04.

"Hello. This is Malachi."

"I know."

Malachi heard a muffled male voice in the background, "Who is it?"

"Can you hear me?" Malachi asked, when all he heard was silence for a few seconds.

When Annie returned to the phone, she went ballistic. "You sent spies...you're a coward...you're such an idiot...an unstable idiot." On and on she ranted.

Finally, after several minutes, she sputtered to a halt. To Malachi, her words were forcing him to relive his failures—machine gun style.

He sat calmly. Making sure Annie had fired all her bullets of misery. Her tirade had siphoned off most of his inner strength.

All he wanted to do was hang up. Or even better, return fire. Crushing, damaging, hurtful fire. It seemed so appropriate. Certainly, she deserved it. Except...

"I love you, Annie. And I don't have a good argument or any excuses for what I've done. I do ask for your forgi..."

Annie cut him off, "Are...are...you telling...telling me you're coming back? I mean ah...what are you...ah saying?"

Malachi was silent for a few moments.

He could mentally visualize Tim. He had seen him at Annie's workplace. He didn't know everything about their relationship, but his stone-face resolve was all that held back a torrent of rage.

In a devious way, Malachi imagined himself saying in a soft, loving voice, "Would you like that? Would you like if I came home? Tonight. We can make a fresh start."

His mind envisioned Annie squirming in response as she glanced at Tim. The discomfort Malachi could inflict on Annie with a few choice words and voice inflections was so alluring.

So justifiable.

"Annie, could we...ah. Let me put it another way." He was silent as he gathered his thoughts.

"Just say it!" Annie said.

"Annie, I'm not planning on returning. We don't have to discuss every detail of the past. Wouldn't it be nice if we could peaceably go our separate ways? Leaving the past behind and pressing on to the future. Let's be honest; we don't want to be married. Well you...I mean; let's just move on. I'll send you $300 in a couple of days, and they're supposed to send you my last paycheck from St. Amos. Annie, I do love you, but I don't want to be married to you. And you don't want to be married to me. Can we work it out? We've been through so much together. Just one more lap around the track. We can take care of most of the details by e-mail. You can have the house and everything. Well, I might want a few more of my things. But not many. Annie you're so talented and beautiful. You'll succeed in whatever you do. I've always told you that you're a lot smarter and a lot more gifted than I am. All I want is the best for you."

Malachi slumped on the park bench. He sat there for several seconds without saying anything.

"Are you there, Annie? Annie. Are you there, Annie?"

"Malachi...I...ah. Yeah. We can do that."

"Thank you, Annie."

"You don't have to send me any more money."

"You sure?"

"Yeah," Annie said. "And I'll e-mail you when I get some information and stuff around."

"Thank you."

"No problem."

"Bye, Annie. I love you...bye."

"Malachi...I'm ah...I'm...ah...ah, goodbye, Malachi."

Malachi hung up.

And started to cry.

Abruptly, the breeze off Lake Michigan blew colder. And Malachi became limp with fatigue.

He then took a nap in the Suburban before driving the seven-minutes to work.

The Greatest of These is Love
...at Walmart

Chapter 33

"**H**ow was your weekend?" Stu asked Malachi.

"Fantastic. I'm back with God and in love with Jesus. Let me know when you go to break; I'll tell you all about it."

"Praise God," Stu said.

All the boxes were just as heavy. The skids were piled high. Bleach, eleven flavors of soap, a box of brooms, rat killer, five varieties of fabric softeners, an assortment of bathroom maintenance items, room de-stinkers, and sponges. And that was only the top half of pallet one. While Malachi had never been happier at Walmart or more satisfied with his stocking job, putting stuff on the shelves had a purposeless feel.

He understood the value of the job. What would happen if he and his co-workers did not stock in the middle of the night? Sure, nobody would die, but people would suffer. And the concept of serving human-ity in a dignified, behind the scenes manner as a stocker seemed very

Jesus-like.

Bottom line—Malachi wanted to be preaching about Jesus, not throwing freight on the shelves—like Jesus.

He pondered what would happen if he told Sal, as she was checking out progress on the floor, "I want to preach about Jesus."

She would probably respond, "Get your freight done, first."

He laughed to himself. "I better kick it into gear. Preach with my actions first. Words can come later." So, Malachi was off to the races with his Monarch 1131.

Time flew. Like usual.

"Hey Malachi, I'm going to break."

Malachi could hardly contain himself, almost exploding as he told Stu about what had happened.

He glided lightly over his leaving-God scenario. Carefully choosing his words and the amount of detail he revealed to Stu. Enough for him to understand but not enough for Stu to bend it into something weird. Stu-style weird.

"There's just so much more to it," Malachi said. "The whole deal was—God and I were through, but He wouldn't let go of me. God is so awesome."

"Yeah, Malachi, the Bible says, 'Be strong and of good courage and do it: fear not, nor be dismayed. For the LORD God, even my God, will be with thee. He will not leave thee, nor forsake thee until thou hast finished all the work for the service of the house of the LORD.' Dude, God's not through with you. He was chasing you down."

"And He caught me."

"So, what church did you go to?"

"Become Ministries. It was awesome and..."

Suddenly, Malachi noticed a radical change in Stu's facial expression. "What's wrong?"

Stu glanced around. And lowered his voice. Nearly whispering, "That's a cult."

"A cult?"

"A cult. You know, they speak in tongues."

"Maybe. I never heard any."

"They have a woman pastor."

"They do? I didn't see one."

"What version of the Bible did they use?"

"I don't know."

"See they were hiding it from you...I've heard a lot of people talk about them...I would never go there...you can't be too careful..."

Stu kept talking. But Malachi, for the most part, had disconnected from his rambling—only holding onto the thread of the context.

Malachi started rubbing the top of his right eye. His face became warm on his right side—between his ear and eye above his cheekbone.

Stu finally ended his exposition.

"Brother Stu, I love you," Malachi said. "The Bible says, 'Thanks be to God who always leads us in triumph in Christ and manifests through us the sweet aroma of the knowledge of Him in every place,' That's my goal, Stu. I want to be the sweet aroma of Jesus—every place I go. And tonight, and most nights, it's going to be here at Walmart. If I stink, let me know. Can I trust you to keep an eye on me? See if I stink or if I have the pleasing aroma of Jesus. Can you do that, Stu?"

"Well...ah sure. I can do that."

"Thanks, brother. Let's get back to work. Stu, let me know if you need any help."

Malachi stopped. His eyes met Stu's. "I mean that. Anything."

He hugged him around his shoulder.

Stu grinned. Kind of.

Malachi returned to the floor and began ripping boxes open, quickly pricing the merchandise, and properly positioning the items on the shelves. He was softly singing— "Jesus we look. To You. Jesus we look. To You."

"You sure are happy." It was JC. "What are you on, Malachi? I need to get some."

"You sure do, JC. How's your arm?"

She grew somber. "Better. Thanks."

"I need to tell you something," Malachi said.

"What's that?"

"Jesus loves you, JC."

She smiled—like she used to, "No one ever told me that before."

"It's true."

She smiled some more.

Malachi was eager to leave work. He wanted to read his Bible. Play his guitar. Run. Walk on the beach. "Maybe I'll go see Mandy."

As he was departing at the end of the shift, Malachi thought, "I wonder when I'll see Carl next..."

"Hey, Malachi."

It was Carl—standing in front of the glass-faced display cases in the bakery.

A grateful sentiment gripped Malachi when he spotted Carl. Only a couple notches beyond being a stranger, he had been instrumental in changing the course of his life. He had a significant bond with a man he knew almost nothing about. Malachi didn't even know his last name. Or where he lived. Or...

Wired

Chapter 34

"**D**o you have time for some coffee?" Carl said.

"Sure. I'm wired—couldn't sleep anyways."

"Want some donuts?"

"That sounds good. I burn a ton of calories working here at Walmart."

"Looks like you're getting in shape."

"Yeah. The other workers told me they lost weight when they started working here. Eddie said he lost twenty-five pounds in two months. It's like going to the gym, except they pay us."

"Where are we going?" Malachi said.

"My place."

Malachi headed toward the Suburban.

"No, this way. We can walk," Carl said.

"So where do you live?"

"You'll see."

They walked the width of the parking lot, east toward the main road—U.S. 31. They turned south and traveled behind the Days Inn, where Malachi had stayed when he first arrived in Manistee. When they hit Merkey Rd., they headed west toward the beach. The same way Malachi had been taking when he went to the beach.

They were talking, reliving the experience at Become Ministries. And the whole night.

"You saved my life," Malachi said.

"No...Jesus saved your life, Malachi. Not me."

"He sure did."

"Turn here."

They veered north down a dirt and sand two-track. "So where exactly are we going, Carl?"

"You'll see."

Carl's tone softened. He measured his words, "In a strange way... only God could do it...you saved my life...in a way. It's not easy to explain."

They walked silently. Following the path to the right as it inclined upward a story and a half.

A scattering of mixed hardwoods filtered the morning sun. Casting long shadows down the hill. The trail then hedged down and slightly to the left. And then back to the right, rising to the trail's highest peak—a mound capped by medium-sized pines. It resembled Malachi's camp-site.

The trail next tracked downward into a valley—the ground there was more sand than dirt. The trees thinned. Edging the trail, new growth of mixed grasses added a glint of green to the golden-brown mat from last year's growth.

"We're right behind Walmart, aren't we?" Malachi said.

Carl smiled.

The trail turned slightly left, continuing the descent. Ahead, Malachi saw a pond half the size of a football field—guarded with a thick barrier of reeds extending twenty, thirty, or more feet from the edge of the pond. There was one break in the wall of reeds. A narrow, trampled path leading to the water's edge. Skirting the reeds was a cinder block building the size of a single-car garage. Its metal roof glowed silvery-gray in the rising sun.

Nearing the building, Malachi noticed a wooden door painted

a shade darker than lime green and, to the right, a three-foot square metal framed window.

The pond sat to the southwest of the structure. To the north, the building was backdropped by a well-maintained football field. Complete with a rising configuration of bleachers. And a press box towering above.

"Here we are," Carl said. "Come on in."

The interior of the *cabin* exceeded the exterior's utilitarian appearance. Three-foot wide, floor-to-ceiling bolts of upholstery material partitioned off the north one-third, except for a two-foot-wide plank door. The fabric design was Van Gogh's *Sunflowers* encounters country décor. Twelve-inch rusty-red and pale-blue borders, framed funky-vased sunflowers. It created a patchwork quilt-like partition. Malachi could imagine Van Gogh giving the wall his approval.

The other walls were banana peel yellow—maybe a hint lighter. A countertop constructed of 2"x6" boards formed an L-shape on the south and west walls. The south portion had a window with bookshelves flanking both sides. All painted pure white—as were the open rafters and ceiling beams. The bottom side of the grayish metal roofing was exposed.

A microwave, hot plate, single bowl stainless steel sink, and a dorm-size refrigerator under the counter made up the kitchen on the west wall. Open shelving under the counter served as the storage area. The other section of counter Carl utilized as a desk. A chair nestled under this section of counter. No more than fifteen books resided on the shelf. A Bible lay open on the desk near a cell phone plugged into a charger.

An oval-shaped braided rug—mixed hues of medium to light brown covered half the floor. A deer-hide brown, aged recliner sat on the northwest edge of the rug. Two other chairs resided in the room. A basic plastic green lawn chair. And a maple-armed chair with square cushions—a hearty yellow dominated its richly toned plaid material.

Two fluorescent fixtures with four thin bulbs provided a natural-like illumination. A heat duct overhead running to the north disappeared behind the curtained wall. Malachi felt warmth flowing from a ceiling register.

On the south wall, Carl had placed a cross of reeds above the window.

"Sit down, Malachi. I'll get some coffee going."

"This is nice. It seems like we're a long distance from Walmart, but we must be less than a quarter of a mile away. We took the long route?"

"I could hike here directly from the back of the store, but I don't want people to see me coming and going. It works out better that way."

Carl went on to explain that his *home* was owned by the private school to the north. Pumps that draw water from the pond were located behind the cloth wall. The pond's water irrigates the football field.

"I help the groundskeeper. And other jobs for the school—whatever they ask me to do. I caught some would-be vandals one night. I keep an eye on things. They pay me a little. And let me stay down here. Also, there's a cemetery up the hill from the football field; I help out up there once in a while too."

"Huh, that's interesting."

"Do you take anything in your coffee?" Carl said.

"Black's fine."

"Have a donut."

"Thanks."

"Let me pray," Carl said. "Father God, we thank You for this food we are about to receive. Give us strength to honor and glorify You. In the precious Name of Jesus Christ our Savior. Amen."

They both sipped their coffee. Neither one had the urge to cover the silence with hurried words, the response of hurried thoughts.

"Malachi, I'm not going to pretend. I feel awkward, right now. I'm not surprising you by telling you that God has shown me several things about you. But probably less than you realize. I'm sure my behavior appeared strange."

Malachi laughed, "Yeah, it sure did. It was odd."

"It felt just as odd on my end. Probably odder."

Carl took a bite of his donut. Chewed slowly for several seconds. And then said, "Malachi, God has revealed to me only snippets of your life. The things I did, I did in faith, because I was certain God was directing me to do them. I didn't know why. Except by my own mental capacities. For example, when I bought you the Manistee National Forest parking pass, I didn't know why. I still don't. I could make some guesses. I simply did what God was asking me to do. I was walking in faith. Am I making sense?"

"Yes, you are. I was thinking you knew everything about me. So, except for the things I told you when we were driving to Become Ministries, we're essentially strangers."

"Exactly. I want to get to know you. I'm hoping the feeling is mutual."

"You read my mind."

They both laughed

"Instead of me trying to read your mind, tell me your story, Malachi."

"I can do that. But I want you to go first."

"Where do I start? Well I was born again in the early wave of the Jesus Movement in 1967. I was a full-blown twenty-six-year-old hippy. Drugs, the whole deal. Lived in southern California. I floated around most of the time. One day, I'm sitting in McDonalds with my best friend, Len. A Jesus freak had given him a Bible. We were into everything. So, it was like, 'Wow man. Check out this groovy book.' Honest truth, Malachi; between us we knew almost nothing about Jesus. Len started reading right there in McDonalds. And some of the passages struck him. We didn't know what was going on. He thought he was finding random Bible verses—by chance. I remember Len going, "Hey, check this out, man; it says in here, 'All have sinned and fallen short of the glory of God.'" Len couldn't stop reading the verses aloud. Verse after verse. Before we left McDonalds—just Len and me and the Bible, we found enough Bible verses to get saved. Or I should say, God led us to enough verses. We knelt down on the tile floor. The last verse Len read was, 'for whoever calls on the name of the Lord shall be saved.' We were calling out right in McDonalds, 'Lord save us. Jesus save us. We're sinners. Jesus, we need you.' We got saved and high on Jesus at the same time. We tracked down the guy who gave Len the Bible, and both of us were baptized in the ocean that evening."

"Wow. What an amazing story," Malachi said.

Malachi sipped coffee, engrossed in Carl's story.

Carl soon realized God had given him a gift to know things about people and situations. It came through dreams, while awake in dream-like experiences—visions and, many times, as an intense inner knowing. Generally, they were not spectacular revelations. Merely simple insights to strengthen, encourage, and comfort people. At times, God did give him amazing foreknowledge. In addition, there were occasions when God directed Carl to carry out an assignment—like the ones involving Malachi. The gift functioned when God decided to turn on the faucet. But other times, Carl's supernatural gift would trickle to a halt. He wondered, at times, if it had permanently departed.

Carl was experiencing a four-year drought preceding Malachi's arrival in Manistee.

"My gift was recognized early in my new Christian life," Carl said.

And soon, he was involved in ministry. He linked up with a ministry birthed out of the Jesus Movement.

This organization saw God do amazing things. Miracles, salvations, and Carl's gift was very active and accurate. They traveled all over the U.S. and into Mexico, Central and South America. He dedicated his life to serving God, never marrying.

He was with the same group for twenty years.

Well, before the end, he knew things weren't right. God's miracle machine had turned into man's moneymaking machine.

"We were raking in some big bucks. It nauseates me to think about it. We were faking, hyping, lying, and manipulating people as we carried on with our scam. I was so sick of it. Even though I was part of it. I cried out to God one night and got born again—again. That night, I had a dream. I was sure if one of the leaders would leave the ministry or repent, we would be able to return to serving God. God revealed to me how this man had deceived many of us. Setting the wrong course for a once Godly ministry. Two days later, I confronted him. The whole situation then spun out of control. And the leader turned everything against me. I was marked as a heretic, steeped in sin. Everything I was from the moment I became a Jesus follower was ripped away in a couple of days. I nearly gave up on God. I couldn't trust God any more. My life was horrible; I considered suicide."

Carl stood up and walked to the window. He stared out of it. Malachi sat as quietly as possible. He didn't know what to do or say.

"Do you have time to go for a walk, Malachi?"

"Sure."

As they stepped outside into the cool day, the sun warmed Malachi.

They headed north, up to the west edge of the football field. A steep bank on the left toward the tree-lined cemetery perched above the field. The bank also curved around on two other sides of the sports complex. The bleachers stood across from and below the cemetery.

Carl was walking toward the embankment at the far end of the football field. Past the goal post.

"Malachi, you've had some similar experiences to mine in ministry, haven't you?"

"Yes, I have. But I've never thought about suicide…I mean, not seriously. I have asked God to kill me, though."

"For the last twenty years, it was like I was on the backside of the desert," Carl said. "Waiting on God. Sort of, 'Come on, God, put me in. I want to be in the game.'"

"Twenty-years?"

"A little over twenty."

"What have you been doing?"

"Surviving."

Carl laughed. "God's been refining me. And I've been working on following James 1, 'Consider it pure joy my brothers, whenever you face various trials, knowing that the testing of your faith produces endurance. And let endurance have its perfect result so that you may be perfect and complete and mature—not lacking anything.'"

"Twenty years?"

"I guess I'm a slow learner."

They both laughed.

Malachi saw their destination.

Halfway up the hill, straight ahead was a ten-foot tall cross with a life-size figure of Jesus hanging on it. No details were missing. Nails, blood, crown of thorns. They walked right up to it.

"Whenever I'm near the edge, the edge of giving up, thinking I can't handle it anymore," Carl said, "I come up here and look at Jesus. Sure, it's manmade. I've been up here at night numerous times. The beams of light shining on Him make it look like He's being crucified right in front of me. Dying for my sins. Malachi, I decided, way back twenty years ago, when I nearly gave up on God—if Jesus died for me, I'm willing to die for Him. I think about the Apostle Peter's words to Jesus, 'Lord, to whom shall we go? You have the words of eternal life.'"

They stood there gazing at Jesus. A warmth of love washed over Malachi.

He heard Carl whispering, "Fix your thoughts on Jesus. Fix your thoughts on Jesus. Fix your thoughts on Jesus…"

"I sure love Jesus," Malachi said.

"Me too."

No words passed between them for several minutes.

Until Malachi turned toward Carl said softly, "I've got to get going so I can get some sleep."

They turned around, walking towards Carl's place.

"So, where is home, Malachi?"

He told Carl about his campsite out at Turquoise Bottom Creek. "And that's why God had you buy me a parking sticker."

"You still need to tell me your story," Carl said.

"That'll have to wait for another day."

As they walked back, Malachi had to know something about Carl. "Those two times you vanished. Ah what...exactly...how did God...or how did you do that?"

Carl burst out laughing. So hard he had to stop.

"What's so funny?"

"Remember back twenty years ago, before they booted me out of the ministry? I told you we were faking things. Well, I learned to be tricky. When I was walking down the beach, those sunglasses I was wearing had hidden mirrors on the back of the lens. So, I could see backwards. They're called *Spy Glasses*. I was watching for you to look the other way. The second you did, I dove into the dune grass. The other time? I had scoped out a hiding spot ahead of time. When you glanced away, I bolted out of sight."

Malachi punched Carl on the shoulder. "God's going to strike you dead."

When they arrived at the cottage, Carl said, "Can you find your way back?

"I'm sure I can," Malachi said. "When will I see you next?"

"We can go to Become Ministries on Wednesday. Can you drive?"

"Definitely. That would be great. You may find this interesting; some guy at work told me Become Ministries is a cult."

Carl chuckled, "Sounds like Stu...I sure love that guy."

"So, you know Stu?"

"Our paths have crossed."

"See you Wednesday."

They hugged as Malachi departed.

Unwired. Undone

Chapter 35

Malachi walked back up the valley toward the paved road leading to Walmart.

"Fix your thoughts on Jesus."

"Fix your thoughts on Jesus."

Those words, from Hebrew 3:1—battered his soul.

And assaulted his mind.

"Fix your thoughts on Jesus."

"If something needs to be fixed, something is broken."

"Broken thoughts push Jesus from His exalted place in my thinking."

"Fix your thoughts on Jesus."

"Crap. That's so hard."

"Get crap out of your mind."

"Fix your thoughts on Jesus."

"At St. Amos Community Church, my thoughts were not fixed on

Jesus."

"At home, my thoughts are not fixed on Jesus."

"When I am alone, my thoughts are not fixed on Jesus."

"Fix your thoughts on Jesus."

"There is no hope for me."

"I am undone."

"Because I am a man of unclean lips."

"I live among a people whose words are sinful."

"And yet, with my own eyes, I have seen the King, the Lord Almighty."

Malachi sprawled to the ground.

He laid with his face in the dirt—crying.

All he could think about was Jesus.

He could see Jesus.

All he could see was Jesus—the King, the Lord Almighty.

He felt warmth on his lips.

It was hot!

Was it a voice?

He heard the Voice, "This has touched your lips. And now your guilt is gone. And your sins are forgiven."

Malachi cried even more.

And he heard the Voice again, "Whom shall I send? Who will go for Us?"

Malachi spoke up, "I'll go. Send me!"

Another Jesus Freak at Walmart

Chapter 36

Malachi felt like he had awakened from a dream.

Seeing his Suburban awaiting in the concrete Walmart parking lot edged against the holy-ground journey he had just emerged from left his brain reconciling the contrast.

"It was real. I'm positive…my eyes have seen the glory of the King."

Still, his feet marching across the hard surface tossed his thoughts to the place he would be in less than eight hours—flinging piles of stuff onto the shelves at his favorite Walmart.

Once he crawled into his tent, sleep engulfed him. It was good sleep. He awoke fully alert after five and a half hours of rest.

He did all the essentials. And then the idea, "Call Dad," resonated as imperative.

Malachi loved his Dad, but they lacked substance in their relationship. This superficial disposition was reflected in their phone conversations. There was zero spontaneity in the timing of the calls. Always—

birthdays, Father's Day, Christmas.

Malachi was envious when he noticed fathers and sons with significant relationships.

No animosity existed between Malachi and his dad. Just distance—relationally and geographically.

Of course, the meltdown between Annie and he was not something his father would have expected. And Annie had already recruited him to her camp. There was no way to look forward to fulfilling the obligated call.

"Dad. This is Malachi. How are you and Mom doing?"

"It's about time you called."

"Sorry. I've been really busy."

"Sounds like an excuse to me."

"You're right. You kind of know what's going on, so, ah..."

"Annie told me you left. And got fired. And you're causing all sorts of chaos in her life. So, what *exactly* is going on—Malachi?"

"It sounds like she has you convinced."

"You know I like Annie. I trust her judgment. And words."

"So, if I told you Annie was having an affair. The pastor at St. Amos Community Church was smoking and growing dope. And I had to leave or go crazy, you'd figure I was already crazy."

"What are you talking about?"

"Dad, I'm tired. Tired of pretending. It makes me want to cry when I think of how meaningless our father-son relationship is. The worst turmoil of my life, and I don't even want to talk to you. No reason to, except to give you a bad-news report. Here's a question—did you attempt to call me? I mean...this was the lowest point of my life...in my whole life...are you still there."

"I've been upset. Deep down inside, I sensed Annie was being.... ah...a...well I won't use that word. Let's say callous, heartless, harsh. I just didn't want to think about it. Or believe it. I didn't know what to do. So, I did nothing."

"I know what you mean."

"Malachi, I wish we were closer. If I would have done my part twenty years ago, our relationship would be better."

"I've failed to put any effort into honoring you as my father. And I'm sorry for that...are you there."

"I'm here."

"Dad, we can change. God's been changing me in so many ways lately. I see things differently. I see you differently. I love you, Dad. And appreciate you. We can change. We don't have to settle for living the rest of our lives missing something God wants us to have. I want to be your son. And I want you to be my father. Not in words. In heart…Dad are you there?"

"You're making me cry…Son."

"Why don't we start by calling each other once a month? Or more. You should come visit me. I'm living in Manistee. You need to come see your brother, Dale. And soon. What do you think about that?"

"You're so right, Son. I'm going to start calling you, and I'm going to come to Manistee this summer. I promise."

"That'll be great, Dad. I look forward to seeing you and Mom."

"Yeah…it'll be nice to see you."

"I love you, Dad."

"I love you, Son."

As Malachi drove to work that night, he mulled over, "Fix your thoughts on Jesus."

Over and over.

"What will that look like as I'm banging through my work tonight?"

He whispered a prayer before hopping out of the Suburban, "God don't let me do anything stupid."

"How's everybody doing tonight?" Sal asked. "A couple of things. First, everyone welcome Dean. He's our new ISS associate. He transferred in from Kalamazoo—store 5065."

"Let see what else I have…we have another associate coming on next week. With summer on us, we're starting to get hit hard with freight."

Sal glanced down at her paperwork. "Some good news. We don't have all the numbers in yet, but *Myshare* should be close to $400.00."

Even though Malachi wouldn't qualify for another six months for Walmart's quarterly bonus, he smiled when everybody got happy.

"Malachi, you're going to work in Sporting Goods with Martin. You two will be setting a new mod."

"Martin," she said, "this has to be done tonight. Got it?"

"We'll do our best."

"OK everyone," Sal said, "one, two, three—Walmart."

Malachi followed Martin over to Sporting Goods and ended up near the camping gear. It looked different. Someone had stripped all of the merchandise from both sides of the thirty-five-foot-long aisle.

"So, what's this *setting a mod?*" Malachi asked. "I've never heard the ·term *mod* here at Walmart.

"It's all about change," Martin said. "The layout of the shelves needs to be changed. I guess so they don't get boring. Sort of like us. If we don't change, we get in a rut. Life gets boring."

He went on to explain the procedure. *Mod* stands for model. The new layout is designed at the corporate office. Walmarts around the country would use this same shelving layout.

Another crew had already removed all the old merchandise. In addition, all the shelving, pegboards, and other display mechanisms had been reconfigured to conform to the new mod.

At eye level, sheets of paper hung at eight-foot intervals from the shelves. These papers mapped out the precise locations and quantities of the new mod merchandise.

Malachi and Martin had a huge task ahead of them. They needed to make shelf tags and price the new merchandise.

They retrieved prices, shelf tag formatting, and cleared up any confusion regarding merchandise placement with a hand-held barcode scanner, called a Telxon.

With a Telxon, a scanned barcode would produce the price, shelf tagging, merchandise location, and a vast amount of additional information linked to the scanned product. The Telxon displayed all of this on a palm-sized screen on top of the device.

Telxons are essentially hand held PC's connected to the store's computer system through a secure Wi-Fi system.

Walmart associates received varying degrees of access to Telxon functions. The more responsibility an associate had usually equaled more functions programmed into their *Telxon*. A shift manager's Telxon could access: the task everyone was on, the number of boxes of freight each department had for the night, the allotted time to complete the task. They could access inventory levels for any item, its storage location in the backroom, expected truck arrival times for the next day, vacation schedules, an associate's work schedule, planned mod changes, the day's picks, shelf capacities; they could order merchandise plus many more functions.

Malachi used his Telxon to determine the prices of merchandise and for configuring shelf tags. Once configured, Malachi printed them with a mini-printer the size of two pop cans held side by side. The Telxon prompted the printer through a wireless connection.

Martin, a productive, steady laborer, had been employed at the Manistee Walmart since it opened three years ago. He helped set up the store. Before that, he had worked at the Ludington Walmart. Twenty-six years old, most of his adult work-life had been with the company.

Malachi had heard Martin express his dislike for his job more than once. Even using the word *hate* to describe his discontentment.

Martin's routine facial expression reflected a depressed demeanor and outlook.

Still, Malachi was aware that Martin was a dependable, get-the-job-done type.

"So, what do you want to be when you grow up, Martin?"

"An ex-Walmart employee."

"Maybe you should aim a little higher."

"I just want to get out of here," Martin said. "I told you before; I've got too much going on to quit. I need the money. Two kids and all the other stuff."

"How long have you been married?"

"My girlfriend and I have been together for five years."

"You must have a dream larger than leaving Walmart alive."

"Music's my thing."

Instantly, the door to his big dream opened as he confided in Malachi.

Martin played the guitar, bass, keyboard, mandolin, and sax. Guitar was his first choice. His dedication to music was initially inspired by seeing U2 in concert when he was a sophomore in high school. He had devoured the guitar before branching out.

A member of several bands over the years, he had played in all the typical low-dough settings. A composer of dozens of songs, Martin had the majority of a CD recorded. The lack of time and money thwarted further progress.

"It's been a dry spot musically for me during the last year or so. My dream is shriveling...close to being dead...maybe forever."

"You need a wet spot, Martin," Malachi said. "It's like you're in the desert."

Martin looked around, "I'm definitely in a desert."

"Maybe you've never thought of it this way. You're wandering around the desert looking for your dream, and you can't find it or figure out how to achieve it. I bet you don't even know exactly what your dream is. You've asked yourself many times, 'What am I here for?'"

"Yeah. It's like you've been reading my mind."

"When a person is lost, they need a map. That's what the Bible is all about—it's a life-map. And we need Jesus to be our guide, to lead us to our wet spot—our promised land. When you start making these divine connections, you'll sense God's leading. And guiding. It's not always easy. And God will lead you through some rugged terrain, but when you get to where He's taking you, you'll look back and be amazed at His sovereign hand upon your journey. Am I making sense, Martin?"

"You sure are."

"One more thing and then we better get rolling on this new mod. God will lead you and give you ideas you never thought of. And cause miracles to happen. You know what, Martin? You would make an excellent high school music teacher. You could do your music on the weekends. And with three months off every summer, imagine what you could do."

"Wow, I never thought of that...but it's still impossible"

"With God, all things are possible, Martin—even getting this mod done by the end of the day."

Malachi felt lost as they turned to face the tuff reality of the night's assignment. Martin's years of experience rose to the challenge. He had the whole process visualized. He knew exactly where he wanted the freight stacked to aid in the efficient placement of the new merchandise.

"Malachi, you start over there with the tents and sleeping bags."

He pointed out, via the sheets of paper attached to the shelves, the general scheme of the layout.

"If you have any questions, let me know."

Throughout the rest of the night, Malachi asked Martin question after question. Each time, he responded with a clear, simple explanation and then turned Malachi loose until the next tutoring session.

Martin worked from the opposite corner of the work area, assembling a complex array of flashlights and accompanying accoutrements. And then moved to the next area. Malachi covered more ground with his larger merchandise, but lost speed when he had to work through the assortment of bug repellents and foggers and sunscreens and first aid kits and the like.

While constructing a new mod had many of the elements of stocking, a great deal more mental energy was required. They utilized the hanging sheets of paper or the Telxon to establish product location, pricing, and the correct shelf quantities.

Martin raced through the process.

Malachi felt deficient, even though he was working hard. Martin's output doubled his. As Malachi hesitated, Martin flowed instinctively through the process.

"Malachi, you start cleaning up. I'll fine tune things."

He killed off the two cardboard mountains that had grown at opposite ends of the aisle. And then they were done.

No one would understand the moment, unless they had hammered out the new mod themselves.

Martin and Malachi stood there looking over their work. The same way a new car owner eyes his purchase the first time he parks it in the driveway.

"It looks good," Martin said.

"It sure does."

Martin extended his hand. "It was good working with you."

"You know what, Martin? You're a good teacher."

"You think so?"

Malachi enjoyed the challenge of doing something different. He was hoping Sal would let him try something new again the next night.

He didn't exactly get his wish. Sal assigned him to work with the new guy—Dean. Chemicals got bombed, so Sal mercifully allowed the two of them to work it together.

He introduced himself to Dean as they rushed eight skids of freight to the floor.

The thought popped into Malachi's head, "I wonder what Stu said to Dean—about Jesus."

"So, you're from Kalamazoo."

"Just moved up."

"I've only been here a couple weeks, myself. How long did you work in Kalamazoo?"

"Year and a half."

"You met Stu last night?"

"What a bonehead."

"He's a good worker. The best."

"A bonehead. The dude ambushed me. He's blabbing about Jesus and going to Hell and acting like an idiot. I told him, 'Jesus is just another dude.' If you can't bring me some solid proof, leave me alone. Give me the evidence, Mr. Jesus Freak. He still wouldn't shut up. He's a bonehead."

"Well, just to let you know, I mean, I'm not fond of Stu's methods, but I'm a Jesus Freak too."

"What the...are you serious, dude?"

"To me and Stu, Jesus and His teachings are so real, we have our evidence."

"What?"

"It would be like if you and I were out in the parking lot looking at this building. And you said, 'I need some evidence Walmart exists.' I'd point and say, it's obvious to me."

"That doesn't make any sense."

"OK then. Give me one piece of evidence refuting Jesus and His teachings."

"Ah let's see...well I can't think of any. I mean...I'm not a theology major. I've never done any thorough investigation."

"So how much investigation have you done, Dean?"

"It's not like I've ah...well, I guess...nothing like investigating. I feel Jesus is just a person. A good man. But beyond that, it's opinion."

"See, Dean...you think Stu's a bonehead and now you probably think I'm one too. Yet, you have made only a miniscule effort to answer the most important question of all time. And we're the boneheads?"

"Well, I don't..."

"Think about this. I'll guarantee you that you've spent more time deciding which cell phone to buy than you have exploring a spiritual life. Am I right?"

"Well, probably...well yeah."

"Man, I'm concerned about you. If we didn't know Jesus was real, we wouldn't care about you. And your soul. Stu and I are on your side, Dean. I'll admit we sometimes act like boneheads. Who doesn't? That's why we need Jesus. There's a Bible verse, which, in essence, says, 'All have been boneheads and fallen short of the glory of God.' Or there's another one. It goes something like this, 'If we say we've never been boneheads we're a liar and the truth is not in us.'"

"I'm catching your drift."

"I'm sorry if I've talked too much. I just believe we need Jesus at Walmart."

"We're cool," Dean said.

Malachi eyed the barrage of skids patiently waiting for them. Then shifted toward Dean. "You ready to rock."

"I'm in. Let's roll."

With the two of them going at it, the skids melted away well before the end of the shift. It had been a long time since Chemicals had been deep zoned or received any extra cleaning. It was satisfying to see the aisles shine by the end of the shift.

"They trained you well in Kalamazoo. It's been good working with you, Dean. Hey, if you ever have any questions about God or Jesus or stuff like that, let me know."

"Sure. Thanks, Malachi."

It was Monday night—ten o'clock. The workweek had whirled by so fast—Malachi was amazed how quickly the *weekend* had arrived. He was back at his home away from home—Chemicals. Solo for the night. He could tell as he appraised his freight that he would be able to cruise through the night a couple notches below full velocity.

His mind drifted to his weekend plans. A cook out with Uncle Dale and Aunt Betty, church on Wednesday night, and he wanted to go to DT's.

But for now, he returned his focus to the three skids of merchandise that needed a home in Chemicals.

Soon, he heard JC, "Here are your picks, Malachi."

"Thanks. What time are you going to break?"

"I don't know. Why?"

"Can you come by when you're going?"

"Well, sure."

An hour and fifteen minutes later, he looked up from his boxes when he heard, "Hey, Malachi, I'm going to break."

"Can we go for a walk?" Malachi said.

"Where?"

He shrugged his shoulders. "Just around. Inside the store."

They strolled to the least congested part of the store.

"I really like working with you, JC. You're such a hard worker. And you're funny...well not exactly funny... ah, when you're...ah...this isn't going very good."

He stopped walking and turned to look directly at JC. "I don't want to hurt your feelings. I mean...oh maybe we should just talk another time."

"Malachi, just say it. OK."

"JC, I don't want our friendship to be about flirting. I could be misconstruing your behavior, and if I am, forgive me. I ah..."

"It's my fault. I flirt—it's like a bad habit." JC looked down at the floor. "And it gets me in trouble."

"JC, you're special in God's eyes. There's something missing in your life. You keep trying to fill it up with the wrong thing. You've never experienced pure love. You try to earn love. Deep inside, you don't think you're worthy of love. Lots of people feel the same way. That's what God is all about—God is love. Do you want to experience pure love—love you don't have to earn? Love that flows when you don't deserve it. Love that finds us when we deserve it the least."

JC looked up. "I must be feeling that love, right now."

"That's the love of Jesus. You need His love in your life."

Malachi glanced at his watch. "Do you want to talk at lunch?"

"I need to be alone—to sort some things out."

"I know what you mean. Take God with you. We can talk another time. Even after work...we can talk about God."

"Yeah...maybe we should."

Malachi worked the rest of the shift with his heart full of thanksgiving to God. When he walked out the door into his weekend, he raised his hands high above his head. "Praise God. Thank you, Jesus."

We're Family

By five in the evening, Malachi was heading back to Walmart. Not to work but to pick-up steaks and garlic bread for the cookout with Uncle Dale and Aunt Betty.

"Excuse me," Malachi said to an associate working in the Meat Department.

"How can I help you?"

"I'm trying to find the best steaks you have. I need three of them."

"So, you want Walmart's best? If you ask me, these Koviack Grain-Fed Angus T-bones are the best. It's hard to find a better steak any place than these babies."

"Thanks a lot. You've been very helpful."

Malachi stopped by the bakery to pick up a fresh loaf of garlic bread. And then he was on his way to Uncle Dale's.

It had been years since he'd been down Muskrat Road. He did have a fuzzy recollection of mushroom hunting out that way. "Was it over twenty years ago?" he asked himself.

When Malachi pulled into the driveway, he understood Uncle Dale's apprehension more clearly. Not that there was anything wrong with the house. A nice little place—a neat ranch-style house with white vinyl siding. Nine-hundred square feet with an attached single-car garage.

The contrast was beyond what Malachi had anticipated.

Uncle Dale's previous house had been a two-story. Four times as big. Brick and cedar siding on the exterior. Two and a half car garage. Deluxe—top to bottom.

"So what," Malachi thought. "What's really important in life? We're family. And we have steaks—good ones. We're going to eat like kings." More importantly, Malachi sensed a renewed and deeper love for Uncle Dale and Aunt Betty.

When Aunt Betty opened the door, Malachi said in a loud voice, "How's my favorite aunt?" He gave her hug.

And with the same loud voice, he said, "Where's my favorite uncle?"

The instant he stepped in, he saw Uncle Dale sitting in a well-worn green recliner. In a glance, Malachi also saw the living room, dining room, and kitchen. It flowed together as one modest-sized space.

"Thank you so much for having me over. You don't know how much it means to have you two as family. You two are the best," Malachi said—not quite as loud but with plenty of zest.

No one pretended Malachi wasn't acting a little over the top. All three recognized the undercurrent of what was happening.

"It's sure nice to see you," Aunt Betty chimed in.

"Do you have those steaks you promised?" Uncle Dale asked.

"Right here, Uncle Dale. We're going to eat like kings tonight."

"Good. That's what I was hoping," Uncle Dale said. "I've got the charcoal started."

"Perfect. Grilling on charcoal's the best," Malachi said.

Clouds were darkening the sky. But the grill was fired-up, and within thirty minutes, the steaks were done—sizzling and filling the house with an enticing aroma. And then, as they were placing the food on the table, rain pelted hard against the single pane windows.

"Good timing," Uncle Dale said

"Can I pray?" Malachi said.

"I thought you were through with God."

Malachi laughed. "We made up."

"Good for you. Go ahead and pray. I'm hungry."

"God, thank you for this food. Bless it to give us strength to honor and glorify You. Bless these good people with Your goodness. In the name of Jesus. Amen."

It was unanimous; the steaks were outstanding—fit for a king. And Malachi proclaimed Aunt Betty's potato salad was still the world's best.

"So, you guys have been going to church. Where?" Malachi said.

Uncle Dale looked at Aunt Betty and then back at Malachi. "What is the name of it...ah it's the one in Manistee with the tall white steeple."

Malachi thought, "There are about ten churches like that in Manistee." But he didn't say anything.

Then Uncle Dale said, "Well, we've only gone a few times."

"Ah...it's actually been once," Aunt Betty said.

Uncle Dale then nudged the conversation toward Malachi's work. Commented on the weather. And expressed his disappointment concerning the Detroit Red Wings' elimination from the Stanley Cup playoffs.

"They'd still be in it if it wasn't for the awful refing," he added.

"You've got that right," Malachi said. "But back to the church thing, Uncle Dale."

Malachi hesitated. And then said, "We're family. So, we need to talk about...ah...family things."

"Sure," Uncle Dale said.

"Uncle Dale, ah...you could die. Well, were all going to die. But I mean..."

"I know what you mean, Malachi."

"It's the age-old question," Malachi said. "If you died, do you know what would happen to you?"

"I've thought...we've talked about it," Uncle Dale said. "I've been reading the Bible. Struggling with faith."

He stopped for a few moments. His fingers brushed across his cheek. "Been asking myself, 'What does it all mean?'"

"What's your conclusion?"

"I really don't know. I'm not sure." Uncle Dale shifted his eyes toward the floor.

Malachi didn't say anything. He was praying silently, "God help me."

"Do you want to talk about it sometime...I mean...maybe now?" Malachi said.

"I'll clear the table," Aunt Betty said. "Go sit in the living room."

They got up, moved seven feet, and were in the living room.

Malachi said, "Do you guys have a Bible?"

"Yeah, I bought one," Betty said.

Malachi leafed through, reading verses.

"Romans 3:23 says, 'For all have sinned and fall short of the glory of God,'" Malachi said. "Everyone has sinned. Done something against God's rules."

"Romans 6:23 says, 'For the wages of sin is death but the gift of God is eternal life in Christ Jesus our Lord.' This is a bad-news/good-news verse. Sin in our lives equals death. Spiritual death. Eternal separation from God—that means a person's sins, without the remedy, adds up to eternity in hell. But there's good news. Jesus Christ died on the cross for our sins as a free gift, available for the asking."

"Everyone's heard this next verse—John 3:16," Malachi said. "'For God so loved the world that He gave His one and only Son that whoever believes in Him shall not perish but have eternal life.' Uncle Dale, this verse tells us that God's love sent Jesus to Earth to die on the cross, so us undeserving sinful humans can spend forever in Heaven with Him. Is that amazing?"

"That is amazing. Amazing grace," Uncle Dale said.

"Exactly."

"Acts 3:19 says, 'Repent then and turn to God, so that your sins may be wiped out that times of refreshing may come from the Lord.'" Malachi said. "*Repent* means we tell God we're sorry we've sinned. And beyond that, we turn away from our sins and stop doing the things we know God is opposed to. This doesn't mean we're perfect. However, we do aim to love what God loves and detest what God detests."

"Here's the last verse I have for you, Romans 10:9; 'That if you confess with your mouth, Jesus is Lord, and believe in your heart that God raised him from the dead you will be saved.'" Malachi explained, "There appears to be a lot in here. It's straightforward though. *Confess with our mouth*—from our mouth we speak what our heart believes. Lord means, we make Jesus the boss, the King of our lives—our God.

We must believe Jesus died and rose from the dead on the third day. And we must have faith that all these verses are true."

"I believe every one of them is true." Uncle Dale said, "I don't know how to explain it…I can feel it…inside—faith to believe. So now, what do I do?"

"You pray. Talk to God. Just talk to Him. Right now."

"I can act like Jesus is here in the room? And start talking? As if He was with us in the room," Uncle Dale said.

"Uncle Dale, Jesus is here. Can't you almost sense His presence?" Malachi said softly, "God is with us. He's right here."

For several seconds, no one said anything.

And then Uncle Dale, with eyes wide open, said, "Jesus, this is Dale. I guess you already know who I am. And what I've done. I've messed up a lot in my life."

He looked over at Betty and took a deep breath. "I know that's sin. And I know, just like when I do wrong against Betty, it screws up our relationship. You know I've been in the doghouse plenty. With You, the dog house lasts forever. And that's what Hell is all about. Except a lot worse. And I would deserve it. You created everything. God, You get to call the shots. Malachi has told me some good news. And that's what I want. I believe Jesus is Your Son. I know He's God too. I don't exactly know how that works. I know Jesus died on the cross to kill my sins. His death is the payment for my sins. It's a gift. But I've got to accept that gift, so You can take away my sins. And give me eternal life with You."

Uncle Dale held out his hand. "God, I'll take the gift of Jesus from You. Who wouldn't? I believe in Jesus. And I'm not going to be the same person. I'm sorry for all the stuff…the sin I've done. I'm going to quit. Please help me. Dear God, I think I'm through. Hope I didn't miss anything."

Uncle Dale stopped and glanced over at Malachi.

Malachi nodded.

Then Uncle Dale added, "God, I sure don't deserve this. Please clean me up from the inside out. Thank you for your mercy. Thank you for wiping out my bad record. Please keep in touch, God. You're the best. Amen."

Uncle Dale grinned at Malachi. They both had tears in their eyes.

Aunt Betty was weeping as she hugged Uncle Dale.

Then Malachi hugged Uncle Dale. "Now you're in another family—the family of God."

"Let's celebrate," Aunt Betty said. "I made a fruit tart."

"Fruit tart?" Malachi said. "I love your fruit tarts."

They talked about finding a church.

"Our neighbor, Seth Miller, invited us to his church—Pleasantview Christian Fellowship," Aunt Betty said. "It's only about two miles from here."

"We've been thinking about going," Uncle Dale said. "We'll go on Sunday."

"Promise me you'll go to church," Malachi said. "The Bible says, 'It's good to draw near to God.' Church is a good place to draw near to God. And to other Christians."

They both assured him they would go to church on Sunday.

"Malachi, do you remember what you told me the night we ate at DT's," Uncle Dale said.

"What do you mean?"

"You said to me. 'Things are going to work out better than you expected. And in a way you would have never imagined.' You told me you were sure of it. Malachi, tonight it happened just like you predicted."

"Praise God. Praise God," Malachi said.

The hugs were huge. And the love was large. The goodbyes were tender and teary.

And the rain on Malachi's face as he walked out to the Suburban felt like kisses from Jesus.

Malachi Becomes

Chapter 38

Anticipation greeted Malachi when he woke up on Wednesday. An eager enthusiasm built all day as he yearned to return to Become Ministries. With all that had transpired in just a week, going back to the place of his new-beginning was essential for Malachi.

He arrived at Walmart at 6:12 that evening. He spotted Carl sitting on the black steel bench outside the Walmart entrance.

Carl said, as he stepped into the Suburban, "How are you doing this evening, Malachi?"

No other questions needed asking. For twenty minutes, the air danced with Malachi's voice. He was talking so fast, Carl felt like he was being blustered by a wind off Lake Michigan—a warm one.

Malachi's retelling of Uncle Dale's story brought Carl to the edge of tears.

"Wow. It sounds like God has given you a remarkable week," Carl said as they pulled into a parking place at Become Ministries. "You ready to go in?"

Carl introduced Malachi to Pastor Jonathan.

Malachi's words were still running over the speed limit as he profusely thanked Pastor Jonathan for the previous week's service—adding the highlights of his own experience.

"Thank you for sharing what God's doing in your life," Pastor Jonathan said. "We always pray for God to change lives, here at Become. You've really encouraged me, Malachi." He then excused himself as he prepared for the service to start.

The music, like last week, communicated an awe of God into Malachi's spirit. His heart was straining with thankfulness to God. Tears came repeatedly to his eyes before the conclusion of the songs. And Pastor Jonathan's first words.

"Turn with me tonight in your Bible to Isaiah 6 and let me read what's probably the most familiar passage in all of Isaiah; we all know it. 'Whom shall I send and who will go for Us?' And we know, Isaiah responded, 'Here am I. Send me!'"

Pastor Jonathan stepped down from the platform and began moving back and forth, "Friends, a few verses earlier, Isaiah had the type of experience that we call around here, 'A mighty time in the Lord.' The kind of experience that will change your life forever. Though sometimes challenging. For us, the Presence of God during these experiences just feels so good. But now, God is sending Isaiah out to go tell the people. And in a parallel fashion, I hear God telling us—out, out, out, get out of the church."

Pastor Jonathan proclaimed the need for followers of Jesus to get outside of the church. "Friends, we need to send you. Imprint a big Holy Ghost stamp on you. Get the address of where God wants you to go inscribed on your heart. And out you all go as letters—proclaiming the good news of Jesus Christ. Friends, people need Jesus at school, people need Jesus at your workplace, people need Jesus at McDonalds, people need Jesus at Walmart..."

When Malachi heard, "People need Jesus at Walmart," he felt like jumping up and power punching the air, "Yes!"

Instead, he internalized his fervor as it fueled him with inspiration. Ideas spun around in his brain. Softly, he kept repeating, "People need Jesus at Walmart. People need Jesus at Walmart."

Pastor Jonathan continued to charge the gatherers with the task of seeking their place of serving God outside of the church. "Friends, who will go for God? The opportunities to serve God outside of these four walls are endless. Jesus said, 'The workers are few.' And may I add—the non-workers are plentiful. Friends, God has a place, a niche, an opportunity for you."

He pointed toward the door, "Go."

Pastor Jonathan then concluded his sermon with, "There will be people up front at the altar who can pray for you. Please come up if you need prayer."

Malachi was the first to the front.

He approached a couple who had a hint of resemblance to Uncle Dale and Aunt Betty. Early sixties. Gray hair. Pleasant countenance. Malachi sensed a warmth, a feeling of security as they placed their hands on his shoulder.

The man prayed fervently for God's direction and for Malachi's perseverance.

Next, the woman said, "I have a *word* for you."

Malachi bowed his head and closed his eyes.

"What did you come to see…a reed shaking in the wind? This was said of John the Baptist. And now, the Lord is saying it to you. You have been shaken like a reed blowing in the wind. You have not broken—except in your brokenness before Me, says the Lord. Now, you are strong. And yes, you will still experience shaking, but you will not break. And now, you will minister, you will serve people whose lives are shaking. Because you have offered your life to Me—in brokenness. And as you keep your thoughts fixed on Jesus, people will look past you and see Jesus."

Malachi opened his eyes and looked at the man. And then over at the woman. "Wow. Thank you so much. That was very meaningful to me."

His heart had been inscribed. It was as if God had put his life into a funnel—all his experiences, all his shaking, all his abilities, all his hopes, all his dreams, and now, his life was going to be poured out serving his co-workers at Walmart. He already sensed the step God was leading him to take next.

Malachi was just as wound up on the return trip to Walmart. "I'm going to start a Jesus-group at Walmart. A Bible study. More than a Bible study."

"People need Jesus at Walmart," Carl said. "I will be on my knees praying for you."

They talked the entire way back about the ideas God had placed in Malachi's heart. They agreed to pray, plan, ponder, and praise God together in this new God-venture.

Mandy
-Do You Want Some Good News?

Chapter 39

Mandy was on Malachi's mind. He couldn't help it.

He followed what had become a regular routine. Run on the trails. Start a fire. Play his guitar. Read the Bible. Pray. Eat breakfast. And then clean-up.

Malachi knew if he arrived at D.T's before the lunch crowd, he would have his best opportunity to talk with Mandy. So, he walked in the door right at eleven o'clock.

Mandy saw him, "You been doing OK?"

"I've been great. And how have you been?"

She gave Malachi a playful look. "I've missed you."

He smiled. Enjoying the tingle.

Malachi took his regular seat in the corner and opened his laptop. He had a few e-mails to answer, but he would rather talk to Mandy.

One e-mail jumped out at him. Subject: *Guitar sold.*

Hey Malachi,

Sold one of the Kerr Creek Guitars you put on consignment.

It was cool. A musician from a band that was in town—The Subdudes—awesome band—came in. He fell in love with the guitar's black Manchurian Ash face. Said he had never seen anything like it. He was amazed by the quality and sound and artistry for $188.00. And he was digging the Kerr Creek logo—the cross and all.

He came back later with an autographed copy of their CD Miracle Mule for you.

Thought I would pass on the good news. I'll get the money and CD to you.

Best,

Tommy L.

"Here's your coffee and water," Mandy said. "You sure look happy."

"One of my guitars sold."

"You sold a guitar? You play guitar?"

"It's a long story."

"I like long stories. You can tell me when we go out to celebrate your new job...like you promised."

Malachi laughed. "I did?"

"Excuse me," Mandy said. "Hold that thought. I've got a customer."

Malachi's heart was beating. Faster. And faster, when he saw Mandy returning to his table.

"Mandy, are you messing around with me. It's not quite making sense. I mean...ah...do you really want to go out?"

She lightly touched his arm with her long fingers. "You seem different, Malachi. In a good way. I bet we would have a lot of fun together. What do you think?"

"Ah...when?"

"Tonight. I have the night off. My mom could watch Alex."

"Alex?"

"My son, he's eleven. Do you like children?"

"I love children," Malachi said. "I work tonight. I have to be there by ten."

"That's OK. We'll have plenty of time."

They agreed upon seven o'clock. Mandy gave Malachi directions to her apartment and her cell phone number. Malachi folded up his laptop, preparing to leave.

"Aren't you going to order?"

"Ah, oh…I'm saving my appetite for tonight," he laughed.

Malachi spent the rest of the afternoon finishing his weekend to-do-list. But all he could think about was his upcoming evening with Mandy.

He easily found her apartment. On 12th St., about fifteen blocks north of downtown and less than half a mile from Walmart. In a tree-lined residential area, she lived in the upper unit of an old white two-story house converted into two apartments.

When she opened the door, Malachi stood gaping at her. She wasn't wearing her loose, oversized-style that he was accustomed to.

"What's wrong, Malachi?"

"You look…ah…different."

He stopped. Suddenly realizing how stupid he sounded.

"…I mean…you…ah…"

"I have curves."

Malachi had always found Mandy's appearance to be pleasing. But now, he was taken aback by her attractiveness. Rather stunning. And not at all in a seductive way.

"Yeah…you look…wow…really nice, Mandy. I just never saw you this way."

"Thank you, Malachi," she said. "If I dressed this way at DT's, what do you think would happen? I feel safe around you."

"So, where should we go to eat? You know Manistee better than I do."

"I thought you might ask me. Here's an idea. And if you don't like it, let me know. We could grab a couple of subs at Subway and go down by the beach. It would be kind of like a picnic. And it wouldn't be very expensive. But whatever you want to do."

"That's perfect."

"I know a nice spot," she said. "Really beautiful."

When she said that, Malachi gazed at her. And enjoyed what he was thinking.

They picked-up two subs at the Walmart Subway. Mandy directed Malachi to Merkey Rd.

"There's a nice little park at the end of the road."

"I've been there a couple of times," Malachi said.

There was only a hint of coolness in the air. The big lake rippled. Light danced on the water—silvers and grays—all the way out to where the sky touches the water. Blue curved overhead, accented with timely swirls and teacup-colored white puffs.

"Do you mind if I pray before we eat?"

"That would be nice."

"Father in Heaven, thank You for this food. Give us strength to honor You. Thank You for my friend. Bless her with Your goodness. In the name of Jesus. Amen."

Malachi looked at Mandy. For some reason, his nervousness had disappeared. She unwrapped her sandwich. He watched her perfect-guitar-playing fingers.

"Do you play guitar, Mandy?"

"I've picked up a guitar a few times and messed around—like a lot of people. I don't play, though. I know the first time you flirted with me, you used the beautiful-fingers line."

He laughed. "I guess it worked."

"I don't know. It seems like I asked you out."

"I'm shy."

Conversation flowed easily. As if they had been friends a long time. Except they had all of the we're-strangers questions to ask. From silly to serious. Awkwardness was never perceptible. And the unspoken, even indefinable boundaries of privacy and respect formed naturally. Neither one turned a shovel to find a body or a bone.

Mandy was divorced. They had both: "Been through a lot of junk." Moved to start over. Are lonely sometimes. Like children. Like coffee better than beer. And think smoking dope is for dopes. And wished they were closer to their dads.

Maybe it slipped out accidentally. "When I was growing up," Mandy said, "if my dad got mad at me, he would say, 'I wish you had never been born. Your mom should have had an abortion.'"

When Malachi heard those words, he felt an intense love for Mandy. He wanted to wrap her up in his arms and tell her how valuable she was. How much Jesus loved her. He wanted to kiss her with fatherly kisses. Malachi had never heard words like that in his life. He knew they existed. And now, Mandy's words would remain etched into his mind for the rest of his life.

"I hope you never believed those words."

"No. I don't think so," Mandy said.

Malachi then guided the conversation to a subject they hadn't talked about yet. "Do you ever go to church?"

"Not since I was a little girl."

She had attended church many times with her grandma. She would stay overnight, go to church, and then go to a restaurant for pancakes. This was their ritual. Going for pancakes was Mandy's favorite part.

"Did you learn about Jesus?"

"I was a kid. From what I remember, at church, they talked mostly about social issues."

"So, do you know who Jesus is? And what He's all about?"

"Not really. Alex tried to explain it to me once. He's been to church quite a few times with friends and neighbors and my cousin Nancy."

"Interesting."

"I believe in God…I just never got into it."

"So, when people, Christians, talk about the Good-News, do you know what they're talking about?"

She shook her head, "No."

"So, you don't know why Jesus came to Earth and died on a cross or any of that?"

She shook her head again.

"Are you OK with me talking about this stuff?"

"Sure. It's interesting."

"I can't stay much longer—with work tonight," Malachi said. "So, can we talk about this when we have more time? Could we do that?"

"That would be great, Malachi."

"Mandy, this is really nice. I hope we can do this again."

She smiled. "I haven't enjoyed myself like this in a long time…it's been a long time."

"We better get going."

Neither one said much on the way back to Mandy's apartment. They were both deep in thought.

Malachi parked in front of Mandy's house.

She touched his arm, "Can you come in…. please."

Malachi's emotions rocketed off the charts. He looked at Mandy. So beautiful. He nearly started to shake visibly.

He was resolute in honoring God in his relationship with her. He swallowed, took a breath.

He knew what he had to say...

Mandy interrupted, "I want you to meet my son, Alex. And my mom."

Malachi caught himself in the emotional freefall. "That...ah...sure. But only for a few minutes."

He followed her up the stairs. It was a quick round of introductions. Everyone was smiling. And with only a few words, Malachi decided he liked Mom and Alex.

Mandy walked Malachi to the door. He could feel his heart beating as she shifted towards him. They embraced.

So lightly.

So briefly.

Still, at that moment, Malachi knew he wanted to marry her. And he knew Mandy's thoughts toward him were the same.

Seconds later, as they said their goodbyes, feelings that deep remained properly concealed.

"Thanks for the great time, Mandy."

"Thank you, Malachi. See you soon."

Can Jesus Come to Walmart?

Chapter 40

"How's everybody doing tonight?" Sal asked. "We have two trucks tonight. It's going to be a big night. It's Memorial Day Weekend team. Erin, our second new associate, started last night. So, it's good to have some new guns on the floor. We have enough people to get all the freight up. I'll be out there on the floor, tonight. I need a topnotch effort from everyone. I'll be shifting people around at the end. So, when you're finished with your aisle, get with me right away. Any questions?"

"One, two, three. Walmart!"

"Sal, could I talk to you sometime soon?" Malachi asked.

"After the shift. Like I said in the meeting, I'll be working freight tonight. Is after work OK?"

"Sure. That's what I was hoping for—after work. Thanks, Sal."

Malachi worked with Dean in Chemicals.

His focus was off all night. Hashing through what to say to Sal occupied a sizeable slot of his thoughts. The busyness of the weekend, combined with how swiftly the *Bible Study* idea emerged, equaled minimal preparation. So, he kept reminding himself, "This is God's plan."

And the reruns of the Mandy and Malachi Show looped all night, further sidetracking his concentration.

Yet, even on autopilot, Malachi generated a respectable showing in his stocking efforts.

He spent lunchtime and both breaks in the Lawn and Garden Department. He set up office with his notepad and ink pen.

Nailing down a name for the Bible Study was Malachi's first priority. And then, he would add four or five bullet points defining the purpose. He struggled to come up with a name but jotted down the best he could come up with:

1. Biblical Principles for Better Walmart Employees
2. Exploring Principles of Faith Through the Ancient Scriptures
3. Teamwork, Conflict Resolution, and Jesus
4. Building Character Through Biblical Application

He reviewed the list as the last few minutes of his first break ticked away, thinking, "These all stink."

Walking back to his aisle, Malachi was intermingling prayer and pondering, "God, what do You want to call it?" And then he spotted Martin.

"Hey, Martin."

"What's up, Malachi?"

"You're creative. If you were going to have a get together here at Walmart—during lunchtime to talk about the Bible and Jesus and how all this ties into everyday life, what would be a good name?"

"Hmm? Let me see. You'll be talking about Jesus and the Bible and stuff...and life and working at Walmart...and how it all connects. Hmm? How about *Jesus at Walmart*?"

"I like it. I think God just gave us the perfect name. Would you come?"

"Maybe. Is there free food?"

"Spiritual food."

"Does it give you heartburn?"

"You're funny, Martin," Malachi said. "Thanks for your help. I knew you would have something."

Shortly after his last break, Chemicals was stocked and zoned. And

Malachi was ready for his next assignment.

"Sal, where do you want me next?"

"Go help Gary in Frozen."

"Gary in Frozen?"

"Yeah, go help Gary."

"OK. Sure."

Malachi had effectively steered clear of Gary since their run ins a couple of weeks ago. Gary seemed to be doing the same thing. As Malachi took the short walk to Frozen, he was devising a plan for avoiding Gary.

However, there seemed be a Preacher in his head, saying, "Apologize."

The Preacher wasn't too concerned that Gary had taken Malachi's pallet jack to launch the quarreling.

The Preacher said, "I can give you a bunch of Bible verses why you should apologize. And you know many of them. Can you give me one verse to uphold your actions?"

"Gary, I'm supposed to work with you," Malachi said. "First, I want to apologize. I was just being a knucklehead the other day. I'm really sorry."

Gary stared at Malachi. He didn't say anything, but his eyes said, "Hun?"

"I want to apologize," Malachi said.

"Accepted."

They shook hands.

"So, what do you need me to do?"

"Finish stocking this skid of ice cream. And then start zoning."

"You got it," Malachi said. "You ever go to church, Gary?"

"I used to. I need to start going again."

Gary headed to another aisle. And Malachi pulled out his Monarch 1131, whacking pricing stickers on a mini-mound of ice cream.

He prayed silently, "Thank you, Jesus."

The Overnight Stockers won again. A nail biter. Sal made a couple of well-executed manpower shifts to avoid extra innings. And she hit a round-tripper herself, coming off the bench to devour a sizeable quantity of freight in Aisle Three.

When Malachi arrived at Sal's office and saw her, he recognized the look. It was the blend of fatigue warring against adrenalin's last stand.

"Come in, Malachi."

"You doing OK, Sal."

"Wow, that was a lot of work," she said.

Malachi had nothing but respect for Sal. She would bark at you if she suspected you were slacking in the slightest. She had earned the right. The way Malachi saw it—she led by pure example. Her work ethic defined busting-your-behind.

Malachi didn't cherish the idea; it made his muscles sore the next day, but he was always willing to put it all on the line for Sal. He had never had a boss he respected more.

And Malachi knew—deep inside, she was soft as a marshmallow.

"Go ahead sit down," Sal said. "Malachi, you're aware that Walmart has an open-door policy. Anyone in management is available to talk to you about any concerns you have. If we don't resolve your issue, the door is open all the way to the regional and even to the corporate office."

"I don't have any complaints. I do want to thank you again for the job. It's an excellent place to work. I really appreciate the tight ship you run."

"Thank you, Malachi. You're fitting in well. You're coming along, but you still need to dial your speed up a couple of notches—you're getting there, though."

"Faster? Are you trying to kill me? Just throw my body in the baler when no one's looking."

"I think that's against Walmart policy." She laughed. "So, how can I help you?"

"What's Walmart's policy regarding holding a club-like meeting during work hours—at lunchtime?"

"I'll double check, but I'm almost certain that Walmart is thumbs up on any activity that aims to benefit employees. Building teamwork and camaraderie. Positive, life-enhancing type activities. Do you have a name or description of the group you're proposing?"

"Jesus at Walmart," Malachi said.

Sal slowly repeated, "Jesus...at...Walmart."

"It's exploring and applying Christian principles through Biblical studies," Malachi said.

"Why don't you call it that?"

Malachi rubbed his chin. Looked over her right shoulder. And then directly at her, "Which name strikes you as the best, *Sam Walton's Giant Store Which Sells Everything* for *Less* or *Walmart.*"

"I'm not making the connection."

"Here's my other reason; God gave me the name."

"That's good enough for me," Sal said. "Let me get the paperwork rolling and check on some details."

"Thanks, Sal. You're invited. Do you ever go to church?"

"Let's talk about that another time."

"Thanks again, Sal. I appreciate you."

Preparing for Jesus

Chapter 41

Malachi was so excited about Jesus at Walmart that he had to share with Carl what was happening.

Making his way toward Carl's cottage, he was praising God out loud as he traipsed down the two-track.

Carl had a big smile on his face when he opened the door. "Come on in, Malachi. Good to see you."

"Hope I'm not interrupting you," Malachi said.

"No," Carl said. "Do you have time for some coffee?"

"Sure."

"I just made some."

Malachi detailed his meeting with Sal. "God's so good," Malachi said. "Jesus at Walmart is going to be awesome. I know God's hand is upon it. Keep praying for me."

"You know I will."

"Carl, I would like to meet with Pastor Jonathan. I want to ask for his prayers and blessing as I launch out."

"That's doing things the right way, Malachi. I'll work on making the arrangements. Maybe Sunday after church?"

"Great. I appreciate your help, Carl."

Malachi had something else spinning in his brain, even while he talked further about Jesus at Walmart. "Should I tell Carl about Mandy," he thought. Since Carl had never been married, Malachi wondered if his exhilaration would stir up loneliness or longing in Carl.

"Carl's my friend. He would want to know. He must have trusted God many times in similar situations," Malachi concluded.

Still, he presented Carl with the toned-down version. Which was difficult for Malachi to do. It was like trying to detonate a firecracker halfway. Oddly, Carl's facial expression reflected to Malachi that he wasn't connecting with the magnitude of the experience.

So, Malachi let the dial spin up on his exuberance. This seemed to draw the opposite reaction from him.

Carl was listening intently. And Malachi kept thinking, "Come on—get happy!"

"I met her at DT's."

"I know the place," Carl said. "Malachi, you're still married—right."

"She knows it. All we did was get something to eat."

"Sounds like it's beyond simply eating a couple of sandwiches," Carl said. "Hear me out. Because of your wife's unfaithfulness, you can Biblically get a divorce and not be sinning. But you are *still* married. At this point, your relationship with Mandy would have an appearance of evil. And that's not good for anyone. Especially for someone who has ministry aspirations. Like you do."

"Mandy and I are just friends."

"You're racing swiftly into a meaningful relationship."

"You've never been married before and you're telling me..."

"I'm trying to tell you what the Bible says," Carl said. "Is she a follower of Jesus?"

"Probably not."

"So, what would you tell a teenager regarding this type of relationship—a Christian dating a non-Christian? I'm sure you know the Bible verse to cite on this one."

"I'm not a teenager."

"So, the Bible verse doesn't apply? What's the age limit?"

"Come on. You know there's no age limit."

"That's my point."

"Well…OK. I guess…I mean …you're right."

"Fix your thoughts on Jesus. Fix…your…thoughts…on…Jesus," Carl said.

Malachi rubbed the back of his neck with his right hand. Drawing a long slow breath, exhaling slowly. He shook his head, "This is going to be difficult. Really difficult."

"Malachi, where does your help come from?"

"My help comes from the Lord, the Maker of Heaven and Earth."

"It's not going to be easy. Or painless. But you have to keep trusting God. Let me pray for you before you leave." Carl placed his hand on Malachi's shoulder. "Finally, be strong in the Lord and in the strength of His might. Put on the full armor of God so that you will be able to stand firm. And God, I pray that Malachi will walk in the full measure of the Holy Spirit. And the full measure of your love. In the name of Jesus. Amen."

"Thanks, Carl."

As Malachi walked back to his Suburban, he thought:

"This is like a death march."

"How would you know?"

"You've never been on a death march."

"You're being a weenie head."

"What a cry baby."

"Last night, you wanted to marry her."

"And now, all you're thinking about is how hard this is on you."

"Me, me, me, me, me."

"How many times have you thought about Mandy's feelings?"

"A precious soul who doesn't know Jesus."

"Remember—the greatest of these is love."

"God forgive me. Help me to show your love to Mandy."

"God help me to honor You."

When he returned to the Suburban, he called Mandy—intentionally sounding upbeat.

"Hey Mandy, this is Malachi. How are you doing?"

"I was thinking of calling you," Mandy said. "I sure had a nice time last night."

"Me too, Mandy," Malachi said. "Do you have time for some coffee?"

"Ah...sure."

"I don't know a lot of places. Is McDonalds OK?"

"That's fine with me. What time?"

"I'm in town. I'll head over to McDonalds. Whatever time you get there will be fine."

"Is a half hour OK?"

"Sure. See you then."

The wait offered Malachi too much time to churn all the possible outcomes through his brain. He had resolved to trust God. And now, he was drawing on advice he had offered to others—mainly teenagers. He could hear his own words, "If she's the one God has for you today, she'll still be the one God has for you in five years."

And there was his other line, which he had often cited regarding relationships, "Go slow. Go slow."

He knew the words were true, but when he saw Mandy, his heart started racing.

She touched his arm when she sat down, "Good morning, Malachi."

He looked at her for a long moment. Captivated.

"I'll get you some coffee," Malachi said.

He returned with the coffee and sat down. "Mandy, last night was special. Really special. But I made a mistake."

"What do you mean, Malachi?"

He peered down at his coffee. And then at Mandy. "I'm married."

"You told me that. And you're getting divorced. Right?"

"That's right."

"So...what's the mistake?"

He shook his head. "This is so hard. I can't think of an easy way to tell you this."

"You're confusing me. I mean...you're telling me how wonderful a time we had. And at the same time...you're telling me you don't want to see me. Are you getting back with your wife?"

"No, that's not it at all."

"Are you telling me we're through?"

"No, Mandy. Here ah...let me see—as a Christian, God has a way He wants me to live. God doesn't force me. I choose to live the way God desires because I love Jesus…"

Mandy looked confused.

"Please hear me out. And because I love Jesus, I choose to live a certain way. To Honor Him. And going out with someone before you're officially divorced is something I can't do. I made a mistake."

Mandy relaxed, "So when your divorce is final, then we can see each other—date. But until then, you'll come by DT's? Right?"

"Coming by the restaurant is fine. I want to keep seeing you. I enjoy being with you, Mandy."

"But there's more," Malachi said.

"What?"

"Mandy."

"Just say it. I'm a big girl."

"Here's a good way to explain it. When I talk to teenagers considering dating, and not only me, but most Christian youth workers, we council teens who are Christians not to date those who are not Christians. And when…"

"I've had enough. I'm leaving."

"Mandy! Mandy please!"

Alone—he stared into nothingness as his coffee turned cold. And old feelings pounded on the door of his heart.

"No…No," he said to himself, "Malachi—fix your thoughts on Jesus."

He got up, walked to the Suburban, and drove out to his campsite.

He crawled into his tent. Sleep eluded him for nearly two hours.

When he woke up, he called Mandy. Her voice mail answered. "Mandy, this is Malachi; please call me. Please."

Malachi wanted to say, "I love you, Mandy." But he was afraid.

He strummed his guitar for a few minutes.

And put it away.

He paced, pondered, and prayed, "God help me."

And then he stood up and shouted, "No, no, no! I'm not going back!"

He paced back and forth some more. "I will press on. I will press on."

He prayed. Talking boldly into the sky, "God, you brought me back. You've given me people to serve. You've given me a new life. You've given me a purpose. You've given me friends. You saved Uncle Dale's soul. I praise You, God. I praise You, God, for how good You are. I dedicate my life to serving You. Dear Father, please draw Mandy to Jesus. Please let her experience Your love. Let it be this very day. Amen."

Yes to Jesus

Work awaited. During the drive to Walmart, Malachi's mind traveled a lot more miles than the Suburban. For the duration of the ride, he struggled to pry Mandy from his thoughts. It took the full twenty minutes. Still, he checked his cell phone once more before heading into the store—nothing.

Tonight, the intensity of work eased the mental bombardment barraging Malachi's soul.

Like jerking a steering wheel hard-left to avoid a collision, he forced his thoughts away from Mandy—and toward Jesus at Walmart.

The steering wheel tried to yank him back several times, but there was another Hand on the wheel helping him.

Early in the shift, he heard, "Malachi call 307. 307. Thank you."

It was the office. Sal's voice.

He picked up the nearest phone. Kitty-corner from Chemicals in the Infants Department

"This is Malachi."

"Sal here. I need you to put everything regarding your meeting in writing. Time. Purpose. Place. The basics. There's a form I pulled off the WIRE (Walmart Internet Resource E-source). You'll need to fill it out. Then, if everything checks out, you'll be good to go."

"Thanks, Sal. I'll get the paperwork during first break. I'll try to have it filled out by the end of the night."

"That'll be fine."

"Thanks for all your help, Sal."

"No problem. It's good to see an associate taking the initiative to improve the work environment here at Walmart."

As Malachi pondered all the aspects of Jesus at Walmart and its potential, he delighted in the thought, "God, this is the good work You prepared in advance for me to do. Just like the Bible says."

He picked up the papers from Sal and took them to the break room.

Stu was at his table. Alone. Malachi sat down and told Stu about Jesus at Walmart.

He asked plenty of Stu-like questions—which habitually carried a tang of negativity. Yet, it was obvious that he approved of the idea.

"Stu, I was hoping you would want to get involved with Jesus at Walmart."

"Well, sure, brother. Praise God. Whatever I can do to help."

After work, Malachi headed to the office, hoping to see Sal. She was there.

"Sal, you have a minute?"

"Sure. Come in."

He handed her the paperwork. She studied it for several minutes—taking her time.

"This looks good, Malachi. I double-checked the guidelines again during my lunch. I like what you're doing, Malachi. It looks like you meet all the Walmart guidelines. So, when are you thinking of launching Jesus at Walmart?"

"Next week."

"You're really going for it."

"It's the Walmart way. We give it our best."

A big smile painted across her face.

"One more thing," Malachi said. "Could I use the conference room?"

"I'll make it happen for you."

"Thanks, Sal. Don't forget you're invited."

When Malachi walked into Walmart the next night, the atmosphere was different. He was different. With Jesus at Walmart a *go*, Malachi felt God had promoted him to the best job in the place.

With that, Malachi further dedicated himself to being an even better employee. He thought, "Jesus at Walmart is my passion. Being the best Walmart worker possible is my obligation."

Outside of the store setting, Malachi had set another piece of Jesus at Walmart into motion. He believed in the concept of having spiritual authority in his life—Godly oversight. Even though he had experienced its abuse through Pastor Neil, Malachi had requested a meeting with Pastor Jonathan to discuss his Walmart ministry.

Carl and Malachi had already made plans to attend Become Ministries on Sunday, so Carl had arranged a meeting with Pastor Jonathan.

As they drove to church, the subject of Mandy moved quickly to the forefront. Malachi told Carl in detail how their conversation had unfolded.

"That must have been difficult," Carl said. "James 1 says, 'Consider it all joy my brethren when you encounter various trials, knowing that the testing of your faith produces endurance.'"

"I'm not doing very good on the all-joy part. I've forced the whole ordeal out of my mind. I'm putting my relationship with Mandy behind me. It's almost killing me. Only my relationship with Jesus is saving me. I'm going to press on."

"Still, it's tough. Just plain awful, I'm sure."

Malachi sighed, "Yeah, it is."

After church, Malachi, along with Carl, met with Pastor Jonathan. His careful, thorough questioning impressed Malachi. Thought provoking queries he would have never considered.

"You told me God's hand is upon Jesus at Walmart. So, if twenty people showed up, what would you do?" Pastor Jonathan said.

"That would be awesome. I would be praising God. That would be great."

"Let's say none of your associates showed up at the first meeting. Would you still say God's hand is upon Jesus at Walmart?"

"I never thought of that possibility. I know Stu will be there, and out of the thirty other workers, at least a few will come by."

"Malachi, I have no doubt you'll have a nice group on your first night. Here's the point. We trust God, not the results. We trust the results to Him. The first part of Hebrews 11:8 says, 'By faith Abraham, when he was called.' God called Abraham. The middle part of the verse says he obeyed God. Abraham obeyed God; we obey God. And then the last part of this scripture shows us the crux of what serving God is all about. 'He went out not knowing where he was going.'"

Pastor Jonathan put his hand on Malachi's shoulder. "Father in Heaven, Malachi has heard Your call. He's obeying You in faith. He's going out, even though he doesn't know where he's going. He thinks he knows where he's going on this faith journey called Jesus at Walmart. God, even though You know the end from the beginning, help Malachi to understand that Your leading is usually one faith-step at a time. Another one and then another one. God, increase his faith as he ventures into unknown territory. Increase his trust in You. I pray for much fruit for Your Kingdom through Jesus at Walmart. Bless Malachi's hands as he serves You. In the name of Jesus Christ our Savior. Amen."

"Thank you, Pastor Jonathan."

"I bless you in the name of the Father and the Son and the Holy Spirit," Pastor Jonathan said.

When Malachi arrived at work that night, with Pastor Jonathan's blessing on Jesus at Walmart, he was ready to start inviting people. Getting the word out.

He had been pondering different approaches. And was praying, "God, open some doors for me to talk to people."

He had only opened a few boxes of the night's freight when he heard over the intercom, "Malachi call 307. 307. Thank you."

When he called, Sal asked him to come down to the office—right away.

Both Sal and Burt, the store manager, were there when he arrived. Malachi had never seen Burt at the store this late.

"Sal, you can leave," Burt said.

"Go ahead and sit down, Malachi."

Malachi took a seat in the cramped office as Burt closed the door.

"We have an important matter to discuss. Someone you know,

Pastor Neil Renner, called me a couple of days ago. Our conversation revealed the fact that you falsified your job application. I also have reason to believe you may have threatened or coerced Sal."

"That's not true!" Malachi said.

"Are you going to let me finish, or do I need to call security?"

Malachi glared at Burt, "Go ahead."

"After the things Neil has told me," Burt said, "we have made the decision to terminate your employment here at Walmart. The action is going to take effect immediately. I have some paperwork we need to complete. After that, security will escort you to your locker, so you can pick up your possessions. And then they will escort you out of the store."

Burt then read Walmart's guidelines regarding falsified documents, concluding with, "Falsifying documents may result in immediate termination."

"What if Pastor Neil is lying? Because he is," Malachi said.

"He has e-mailed me everything. And we have talked a couple of times on the phone—I trust him. Plus, I have had three days to check out the information thoroughly. We have made our final decision. That is it—decision made."

Malachi started rubbing above his right eye with his right hand. His face became warm on his right side. Between his ear and eye—above his cheekbone.

"We will cut you a check tonight," Burt said.

Malachi continued his rubbing. "It sounds like the Walmart policy says *may terminate*, not *must terminate*."

"That is right. As the store manager, I have the final say. Corporate office does not micromanage us."

Malachi continued to rub above his eye as the warmth on his face intensified.

"Malachi, the verdict is final. You have brought an element here I do not like."

"You mean Jesus at Walmart," Malachi said. "And you're casting stones. As if you're without sin. Are you without sin?"

"What are you talking about? I am calling security."

"How about your affair with Carol Ann Siggs in August of 2007? And before that with Millie Reuben."

Burt hung up the phone. "What are you talking about? You are full of it."

"Is Sal next? Do you want me to continue, Burt? I have more."

They stared at each other. Like two gunfighters trying to anticipate the draw. It was six seconds; it seemed like three minutes.

Malachi drew first. Calmly. Slowly. He spoke, "You're not breaking any rules by letting me stay. Give me a *coaching*, a stern mark on my record. I'm a good worker. I've never missed a day, and I'm always on time. I give it my best every day. Ask Sal."

They both sat silently.

And then Burt measured out his words, "Even though you do not know what you are talking about, I do not know where you got that stuff...you are a good worker. Very good."

Malachi could almost hear Pastor Neil as Burt continued.

"Walmart needs people like you, Malachi, to fulfill our mission—to help people to save money, to live better. I do not think an official coaching is necessary. I think my warning to you tonight has hit the mark. Know this; Walmart maintains the highest level of integrity and honesty. We value the individual and the customer. We are all about excellence. And that is what I expect from you, Malachi. Excellence. I think we have come to an understanding. Is that right, Malachi?"

"Yes, we have."

"And we can trust each other to keep our conversation a private matter?"

"Absolutely."

Burt stood up, offering his hand to Malachi. "Keep up the good work."

"I will, sir."

Jesus at Walmart

Malachi set in motion his approach for getting the word out about Jesus at Walmart. He designed a simple one-sheet flyer, which he tacked on the four bulletin boards that were designated for associate oriented materials.

And then, he set a goal of talking to every overnight associate— offering them a flyer. Accompanied by a short verbal invitation. If they wanted to talk further, it would be their choice.

"This is about the love of Jesus. And trusting God," Malachi determined.

He prayed often about Jesus at Walmart. Stu said he would pray. He knew Carl and Jonathan were. Along with other members of Become Ministries.

At least half of the overnighters Malachi had never talked with before. He even returned to the store on his days off to catch up with a handful of people whose *weekends* were opposite of his.

There were two groups of associates Malachi worked with indirectly. The maintenance staff—Todd, Rick, and Mary. The cash register team—Suzy, Madeline, and Carla. Malachi especially cherished inviting the associates he had the closest relationships with.

"Hey, JC, I have something I want to invite you to. Maybe this is what you're looking for."

He handed her a Jesus at Walmart flyer.

"Maybe...I need to do something."

"How have you been doing?"

"Alright."

"Please...ah...please consider coming, JC."

"Thanks, Malachi."

"Gary, you said you needed to get back to church. Check this out. Church is coming to you."

"What's this? Hmm. I should go."

"Martin, look at what you inspired. You need to come check it out."

He perused the flyer. "Jesus at Walmart—cool."

Malachi received varying reactions. No one seemed put-off or offended.

Connecting with people's spiritual lives, no matter what level, made Malachi feel like a pastor again. He found, most who mentioned it said they knew God or believed in God. And to some degree, having a church experience was nearly unanimous.

Malachi was not sure what to think or how to respond as he encountered a significant percentage of associates who said they needed to re-connect with God; yet, they were unwilling to put forth any effort toward their desire.

Two people, Eddie and Todd, were faithful, dedicated followers of Jesus. But neither one worked on the night of the meeting—Thursdays.

Malachi initially approached the pre-meeting ad campaign with apprehension, but the task proved to be enjoyable.

As he entered the break room, he noticed the newest associate, Erin, sitting at a table with Gret—just the two of them. They were on his short list of people he hadn't spoken with about Jesus at Walmart. He had never spoken with Erin and only casually with Gret.

"Hi, I'm Malachi. Sorry I haven't introduced myself. Welcome to the team."

"Thanks."

"How are you doing tonight, Gret?"

"I'm good."

Malachi handed them both a flyer. And gave them a brief invitation, saying a few words about Jesus at Walmart.

They both studied the handout.

Erin looked at Malachi. And then at Gret for a few seconds.

Malachi could tell they were communicating something to each other. But he didn't know what.

"We're a couple," Gret said.

Malachi thought he knew what she meant. But...

"We're a gay couple," Erin said slowly.

Malachi didn't say anything. No one did for a long moment.

"You probably don't want us at your meeting," Erin said.

"Why's that?" Malachi said.

"We're gay."

"So?"

"You must think we're...sinners."

"I'm not going to pretend I agree with you...about what you're doing. Or understand what you're doing," Malachi said. "You know what...I can't even figure out why I do some of the stuff I do."

Malachi paused. He gazed at both of them. And heard words in his head, "Follow the way of love."

"Is it just me," Malachi said, "or is it hard to be a human, sometimes?"

Erin and Gret said, "Yeah," in perfect unison.

All three of them chuckled.

"Here's the deal," Malachi said. "Jesus at Walmart isn't about me figuring out all the stuff everybody's doing wrong. Jesus said, 'I came that they may have life and have it abundantly.' There's no dash, dash: except Erin and Gret at the end of that verse. And if you look on the flyer, you won't find a list of excluded people. I want you two to come."

"Thanks," Erin said. She glanced at Gret. "We just might drop by."

"Hope so. See you around."

Thursday arrived impossibly fast. Malachi was fully prepared. But shaky-nervous.

The response to the invitations was encouraging. He tried not to estimate how many people might attend. But he did. Besides himself, the number five repeatedly popped into his head.

He prayed intensely. And had a strong sense of knowing God's heart regarding the meeting's agenda. Not the way he would have proceeded, but Malachi could not escape the firmness of God's guidance he was encountering.

The chairs were set up in the corner—to the right of the door. In a room that could hold a couple hundred people, Malachi had placed eight chairs in a semi-circle facing away from the door.

Malachi's seat faced the semi-circle with a view to the door—the door leading to the store's foyer. His guitar rested in a stand behind his chair.

In addition, he had a table immediately inside the door. With Bibles and a handout for the night's meeting and the leftover Jesus at Walmart flyers. It was arranged self-serve style with the note: Please Take One.

He sat in his chair—half praying, half glancing at the door. One hundred percent nervous.

At 2:55, he noticed movement near the door. It was Burt—he passed by the door, heading into the store. This perplexed Malachi. "What's he doing here tonight...I hope he doesn't...no...God, I will trust You."

At 3:06, Malachi was the only one in the room. He began jostling with the mathematics in his head—if someone started their lunch at exactly three o'clock, it would take five minutes or so to get to the conference room. And then he heard a sound at the door.

It was Carl. And behind him—Mandy.

For several seconds, Malachi was unable to speak or move. As he recovered, he moved toward Mandy—acting as if Carl was invisible.

"It's ah...so good to see you, Mandy."

He wanted to grab her and hold her tight.

Instead, he stepped back half a step. "Why did you...ah ...ah...come in and sit down."

Carl found a seat.

Mandy and Malachi remained standing.

"Malachi. I've been thinking a lot."

She looked down.

All Malachi heard was the muted buzz of the fluorescent lights.

Mandy raised her head, gazing at Malachi.

"You're different, Malachi. In a good way. I decided...I mean, I started thinking how difficult it must have been for you to...to tell me you loved Jesus. So much that you had to change what you were doing. Malachi, that first night when you were leaving my apartment, I knew exactly how you felt toward me."

She looked down again, "And I feel the same way."

Malachi could see tears in her eyes as she lifted her head. "After I thought things through, I realized how hard it was for you to say what you did. If you're that much in love with Jesus, I want to learn more about Him."

Malachi hugged Mandy and whispered into her ear, "We can talk later."

Malachi turned around, only Carl was there.

"Why don't we sit down. Take a Bible and one of tonight's handouts. Let's get started."

He took a glimpse once more at the door.

"Let me pray," Malachi said. "The Bible says wherever two or more are gathered in the Name of Jesus, He will be in their midst. So, we thank you, Jesus, for Your presence. Please lead and guide this meeting. In Your Name Jesus. Amen."

Malachi leafed through his Bible. "Here it is. Let me read this, 'What did you go out into the desert to see...a reed swaying in the wind?' These words were written to people who were seeking God. Out in a dry place. Out in the desert. Walmart can be a dry place. By Lake Michigan can be a dry place...a spiritually dry place. We're here tonight because we don't want to live in the desert of spiritual dryness. Tonight, I feel like a reed swaying in the wind. You probably can see me shaking from nervousness. Recently, my whole life has been shaken to the core. Did you come to see me? Or to see who would show up? I'm a reed shaking in the wind. So, look past me. And look to Jesus."

Malachi glanced at his notes. "We're going to talk about healing relationships tonight. And... I sense that God wants me to play you a song first. It's about healing the most important relationship in our lives."

He picked up his guitar and played a few chords as he watched his hands. "I've played this song for children. It's really a children's song.

The Bible tells us to approach God, childlike—humble. Each one of us needs to know, needs to encounter, needs to embrace God as our Father. A Father who love each one of us—always. Tonight, let us draw near to Father God as children... children ready to receive."

Malachi then began to sing:

    Every good girl needs Jesus
    Every good boy needs Jesus too

    For all have sinned and fall short of the glory of God

    And every good girl needs Jesus
    Every good boy needs Jesus too

    If we say we have not sinned, we are a liar

    Every good girl needs Jesus
    Every good boy needs Jesus too

    For God so loved the world He sent his only Son

    Because every good girl needs Jesus
    Every good boy needs Jesus too

    Whoever believes in Him, shall not perish
    But have everlasting life

    Will have everlasting life

    And every good girl needs Jesus
    Every good boy needs Jesus too

    Jesus said I am the way, the truth, and the life
    And no one comes to My Father
    Except through Me

    Every good girl needs Jesus
    Every good boy needs Jesus too

Every good girl needs Jesus
And I need Jesus too

Malachi continued playing softly for a few more moments before returning the guitar to its stand.

Once back in his chair, he started rubbing above his right eye with his right hand. His face became warm on his right side. Between his ear and eye—above his cheekbone. He gazed at Mandy and smiled. "Mandy, thank you for coming. You too, Carl. Hey, welcome to Jesus at Walmart."

Smiling some more, Malachi fixed his eyes on Mandy. "God has something special for you, tonight, Mandy. Could you turn to page 655 in the Bible?"

She opened the Bible, shuffling back and forth until she found the page.

"Carl, could you help her find Psalm 37:4? It should be at the top of the second column."

"Sure," Carl said. After a few seconds, he touched his finger to the page. "Right here, Mandy."

Malachi's delight fluttered like a reed blowing in the wind as his eyes absorbed the pleasure of seeing her fingers cradling God's Word. So much so that he had to prod himself back to the moment. "Mandy, can you read Psalm 37:4. Father God has something He wants to tell you."

She bowed her head toward the Bible as she spoke the words, "Delight yourself in the LORD and He will give you the desires of your heart."

Author's Note

Dear Reader,

Every author must face his 3:06 moment.

In one of the final scenes from the book, Malachi sits alone with his churning thoughts. It's 3:06 a.m. His speculation intensifies because no one has showed up for his first Jesus at Walmart meeting.

As a writer, the essence of Malachi's thoughts also jostle through my brain, "Will anybody show up? Will anybody read the carefully placed words—written while attempting to sense the still small voice of God? Will anybody connect with the book's message? Will anybody...?"

Hey, thanks for showing up. Welcome. Thank you so much. Your participation, your involvement makes me smile.

And our journey will continues with two more books in the **Jesus at Walmart Trilogy**—*Jesus at Walmart...the cost* and *Jesus at Walmart... fire on the Earth*. You can visit: **rickleland.com** for updates, information, etc. And some surprises. There you will also find three more titles featured:

Preparing for Revival, which is a free e-Book.

Inspiration Point...living the God imprinted life. An inspiring, God-focused devotional.

An Amish Awakening...a tenderhearted sojourn to Heaven and back. This is a true Amish story like no other!

Some special thanks need to go out.

Thank you Tommy Malone of the subdudes. An amazing song writer/musician who allowed me to include *Known to Touch Me* in the book. Please visit all of the subdudes—Tommy Malone, John Magnie, Steve Amedée, Tim Cook, and Jimmy Messa at **subdudes.com.**

Thank you Dr. Stephen Swihart. The author of **Preparing for Revival.** And dozens of other books—high octane, God-loving, Jesus-focused, Holy Spirit infused works. Thank you for allowing me to use snippets from your book. For more visit: **masterplanministries.com.**

To all, thanks again for stopping by. It's always a great pleasure to hear from you. You can email me at **rickeland1@outlook.com**. And if you've enjoyed the book, please share a review on **Amazon**. It really helps others discover my works. Thank you so much!

Fix your thoughts on Jesus,

Rick Leland